A Killing Frost

A Killing Frost

Michael A. Black

Five Star • Waterville, Maine

This novel is a work of fiction. Names, characters, places, and incidents are either the product of the author's imagination, or, if real, used fictitiously.

Five Star First Edition Mystery Series.

Published in 2002 in conjunction with
Tekno-Books and Ed Gorman.

Set in 11 pt. Plantin by Myrna S. Raven.

Printed in the United States on permanent paper.

Library of Congress Cataloging-in-Publication Data

Black, Michael A., 1949–
A killing frost / Michael A. Black.
p. cm.—(Five Star first edition mystery series)
ISBN 0-7862-4309-0 (hc : alk. paper)
1. Private investigators—Illinois—Chicago—Fiction.
2. Chicago (Ill.)—Fiction. I. Title. II. Series.
PS3602.L325 K45 2002
813′.54—dc21 2002023179

For My Father and the Memory of My Mother

Acknowledgments

The publication of this novel represents the fulfillment of a dream for me, and, like any long journey, I was assisted along the way by many others. In no certain order I'd like to thank Wayne Dundee and Gary Lovisi, the former and current publishers of *Hardboiled* magazine, for giving me my start, and Janet Hutchings of *Ellery Queen Mystery Magazine*. Thanks also to Tom and Ginger Johnson (Fading Shadows Press) and Stefen Dziemianowicz for believing in my writing . . . to all the people at Five Star . . . to my former teachers, especially Len Jellema, Mary Sue Schriber, and Patricia Pinianski, and the entire faculty of the Fiction Writing Department of Columbia College . . . to the members of my writing group, including Earl Merkel, who read my stuff with his customary helpfulness, and Julie Hyzy, who helped me with the manuscript in more ways than I can count . . . To Cathy Green, who used to type my stories before I became a slave of my own keyboard, and who helped me immeasurably . . . to Mr. Andrew Vachss, who inspired and assisted me in countless ways . . . to my writing partner, J. Michael Major, who also gave me the critical suggestions that helped me make the novel the best it could be . . . to my best buddy, Ray Lovato, with whom I've shared many an adventure since we first climbed up that dirt hill many years ago . . . to Debbie Brod and Wendi Lee, who generously lent their expertise to my fledgling attempts at writing . . . to Ms. Sara Paretsky, who gave me the encouragement when I needed it the most . . . to Ms. Barbara D'Amato for always taking the time to offer assistance . . . to Paul Engelman, who read an earlier version of this book and helped me believe in myself . . . to Big Dave Case, Chicago PD, a talented writer and brother in blue for giving me the encouragement to go on . . . to all the guys and gals on the Matteson PD who stood next to me those countless times when our backs were against the wall . . . to Zak Mucha for his assistance and support . . . to Mike MacNamara, who used to remind me that I was no Ron Shade in the ring . . . to all my old army MP buddies who rode shotgun with me on the other side of the world as we patrolled those mean streets and meaner bars, and listened to my dreams of becoming a writer . . . and to my family, who never stopped believing in me.

There are many more people whom I'd like to thank, and if I've left you out, don't despair. I'll get to you in the next one.

Chapter 1

They say if you don't like the weather in Chicago, just wait a minute, and it'll change. I could relate to that as I grabbed a file from the stack and wedged it into the box. It was early October and the temperature was doing its usual bounce back and forth between winter and summer. Hot one day, cold the next. Sort of a reflection of how the whole year had gone for me. Highs and lows, ups and downs. More downs than ups, it seemed. My old, faithful Camaro had turned over on its second hundred thousand miles. So I'd put it out to pasture, and bought a brand new Z-28. It was sleek, and shiny-black, with spoked chrome wheels and a big 310-horsepower V-8. The first car that I'd ever special-ordered, right down to the color. It ran like a charm, too. Well, almost. I had noticed a slight rattle when I accelerated real fast that I wanted to get checked out. And there was a problem with the burglar alarm that coincided with the installation of my new CD player.

I placed another file in the cardboard box and pushed it up tight against the others. These files were the last things I had to pack. I'd borrowed my buddy George's pick-up truck for the furniture I had in my office that was worth salvaging. I'd already dropped that stuff off at the storage place and figured the files and filing cabinets would be an easy final trip. The cabinets were down in the back of the truck, and just two boxes of files remained. Then I could close the door for the last time.

I was going to miss this office. When I'd gotten bounced from the police department and started my own private investigations business, it had seemed important to me to have a downtown office in a place like the Ruskin Building to meet new clients in. I had visions of throngs of people struggling to get in the door. And, of course, I'd be inside talking with the gorgeous redhead about my fee for finding the Black Bird. But since I was getting most of my clientele through referrals rather than walk-ins, I'd slowly come to realize that the office was one expensive luxury that I couldn't afford.

Not that business was bad. Just a little tight. Ups and downs. I'd cracked the biggest case of my P.I. career last year and gotten a huge insurance-settlement recovery. Things were hot for a while, and I lent Chappie, my friend and trainer, enough to make a sizeable dent in the mortgage on his gym. Even after paying off all my debts, I still had a reasonable bank balance for a while. Well, maybe what I'd call reasonable. Most other people would call it a cut above the poverty level.

The title shot that I'd been hoping for with Elijah Day had fallen through, due to an injury I'd sustained on the big case. Day had subsequently lost the World Heavyweight Kick-Boxing Championship, and the current champ didn't seem too interested in fighting me. And then my main lady, Cathy Shawn, was offered a new, managerial position in Los Angeles.

We'd tried to talk it out, with her telling me it was a good opportunity to upgrade things for herself and her son, and me wanting to tell her to stay, but not being able to. The ending left us both crying as she drove off early one Sunday morning, headed half a continent away. We still talked on the phone. Regularly at first, then less and less. She spoke vaguely about coming back for a visit, but we both knew this new job in California was anything but temporary.

And in my heart I couldn't blame her, because we both knew, despite all the posturing, that the real reason she'd left was her frustration at not being able to gain a commitment from me. The old "C" word had driven a wedge between us. I was still too gun-shy from the breakup of my own marriage to think about something permanent. Plus, there was somebody else to consider. She had a son. And I couldn't blame her for wanting to do something that she felt was the best for both of them.

So it all came back to the same, familiar pattern: highs and lows, ups and downs. More downs than ups.

I took a look around at the faded green walls. Yeah, I was going to miss this office, but I had to start looking at things more realistically. I mean, when was the last time I had a walk-in customer? I couldn't remember.

A knock on the outer office door shook me from my ruminations. I rose somewhat stiffly, having forgotten how long I'd been squatting, and walked on prickly, still-asleep feet to the door. The knock persisted.

"Come on in," I called. "It's open."

The door swished inward and two dark and lovely women came in. One I recognized as Maria Castro, whom I'd known professionally for a few years. Maria worked for DCFS as a social worker. We'd first met back when I'd been a cop. Then, when I was struggling to get my P.I. business going, she'd steered whatever clients she could my way. It was mostly basic surveillance work, but it helped me pay the bills. Maria was dressed in an attractive brown skirt and a tan blouse, carrying the matching jacket over her arm. She canted her head and smiled, her black hair fanning over her shoulder like a raven's wing.

The other woman looked to be in her early twenties, slightly younger than Maria. She was dressed less elegantly and eyed me like a frightened bird. Maria placed a gentle, reassuring hand on the woman's shoulder and urged her forward, murmuring in Spanish.

"Hi, Ron," Maria said. "Busy?"

"Just vacating my office," I said. "I'm afraid I wasn't expecting visitors." I indicated my blue jeans and work shirt.

"Sorry for barging in on you," she said. "But your answering service said you'd be in your office today. We tried to call, but couldn't get through." She looked around with a questioning expression at the barren waiting room. "Is everything okay?"

I realized that I'd taken the phones on the first trip. I wasn't even wearing my beeper.

"Yeah," I said. "I'm moving out of here. Sorry if I was incommunicado. I broke the belt clip for my cell phone. I left it in my truck. What can I do for you?"

Maria smiled again. "Ron, this is my friend, Juanita. She wants to hire you to find somebody."

So much for never having any walk-in customers.

"Come in," I said, holding open the door to the inner office. Then I realized there wasn't any furniture left.

Chapter 2

"On second thought," I said, closing the inner door, "why don't we go get some coffee?"

"We took the bus over here," Maria said. "I took an early lunch from work, but I don't have a lot of time. I just came to help Juanita."

I scratched my head and, flashing a feeble smile, said, "Ah, you see, there's no furniture inside there either. I was moving out when you dropped in."

"You're not thinking of quitting, are you?" Maria asked.

"No," I said. "Just eliminating this office. Got a cell phone and a high-powered ad in the Yellow Pages."

Maria laughed and said something in rapid Spanish to Juanita, who laughed, too, but tentatively.

"My Spanish is a little rusty," I said.

"Oh, Ron, you've been keeping up with your practicing, haven't you?"

"Yeah, I have. But when you talk fast like that . . ." I shook my head.

"Sorry," she said. "I told Juanita what you said about having an ad and a cell phone, but no furniture." She smiled again. She had a very nice smile.

"Just the same, let me put these boxes down in the truck, and I'll buy you both a cup of coffee while we discuss Juanita's problem."

We took the elevator down to the first floor, and went through the brown mahogany door that led through the maintenance room to the loading dock. Even though it was zoned for commercial use only, I figured I qualified, more or less. As I hit the button to raise one of the overhead doors on the dock, I could hear the blaring of a truck horn in the alley. The noise continued as we stepped out onto the cement platform and walked toward the stairs. There was a two-and-a-half ton delivery truck sitting perpendicular to my buddy's pick-up. A big guy, with a face like a pit bull, sat behind the wheel smoking a cigar. He stared at me angrily as we descended the steps.

"That piece of shit yours?" he yelled out the window.

"Actually it belongs to a friend of mine," I said, trying to be cordial.

"Well don't you know that this's a loading zone?" he said. "You been holding me up. I got a delivery to make."

"Sorry," I said. "Be out of your way in a second." I set the boxes in the back of the pick-up.

The truck lurched forward, blocking me in.

"Nah, I don't think so," he said. "Maybe you should see how it feels to have to wait."

I helped Juanita and Maria into the pick-up as he spouted off.

"Ron," Maria said. "I have to get back to work."

I nodded.

"Look, bud," I said, trying to maintain my cordiality. "I was picking something up inside there. That's why I parked here. Now will you please move your truck so I can get out of your way?"

"Yeah," he sneered, staring at Maria and Juanita. "It looks like you picked something up in there, all right."

"I'd sure appreciate it if you'd move your truck," I said again.

"Tough shit. I had to wait. Now you gotta wait." He got out of the cab and stepped down to the alley.

"I've been trying to be reasonable."

"You shoulda thought about that instead of jacking around picking up a pair of spic hookers." Then, looking at the truck, "I ain't seen them working the Loop before."

I instinctively glanced back toward the pick-up. If Maria had heard, and I didn't see any way she wouldn't have, she didn't show it. I turned back to the truck driver. He had a stocky build with huge hands and arms. Probably about two-forty, considering the drooping gut that hung over his belt, which gave him the edge in weight. But I was at least three inches taller than he was. Plus I was in shape.

I followed him around the side of the truck to the back and told him he could either move his rig himself, or I would.

"You and what army, pretty boy?" He twisted the handle securing the door, and it rolled upward into the roof of the truck bed.

I heaved a sigh.

"I don't suppose it would do any good to tell you that I have a black belt and usually carry a gun," I said.

"Fuck you, asshole," he snarled. "Now get outta my way."

"Not till you give me the keys," I answered.

He made a half turn away from me, then tried a sucker punch. For a guy his size, it wasn't bad. But the punch was too slow and looping to give me any real problem. I backpedaled away and raised my hands to a ready position.

"This the way it's gonna be?" I asked.

He grunted and came after me, balling his hands into huge fists. I fired a couple of quick jabs at his face to throw him off, then slammed a right into his belly. It was like hitting a pillow. He grunted and stopped. I sent a pair of body punches to each side, the left hook catching him in the liver. Coughing and hacking, he sagged to his knees. I resisted the temptation to give him a good shot to the head.

No sense taking the chance on injuring my hand. Besides, he didn't look to be much of a problem anymore.

"Keys," I said.

He reached in his pants pocket and pulled them out. I snatched them from his hand and walked around to the driver's door. The big engine kicked over on the first try. I jammed it into first gear and moved the truck down the alley about thirty feet. When I got out and jogged back to the pick-up he was still on his knees.

"Keys are in the ashtray," I yelled out the window as we pulled by him.

Maria twisted around to look out the back window as we proceeded down the alley.

"What a jerk," she said. "What was his problem, anyway?"

"He thought he was trying out for *The Jerry Springer Show*," I said.

"Aren't you worried he'll get your license number, Ron?" she asked.

"Nah," I answered with a smile. "This is my buddy George's truck, and he's a Chicago cop."

I couldn't take the pick-up on Lake Shore Drive so I cut over to Clark and went north till we got to a restaurant in the North Loop area. Not one of my usual haunts, but it had an empty parking spot. The place had big windows and I figured I could keep an eye on the filing cabinets and boxes in the back. Just to be on the safe side, I threw a tarp over them and tied it down.

Inside, I bought three coffees and we sat in a booth. Juanita spoke almost no English so Maria translated.

"Juanita's fiancé, Carlos, has disappeared," she told me.

I nodded. "How long?"

"Three days. He didn't come home from his job Friday night."

"They live together?"

Maria shook her head. "Juanita lives with her parents. Carlos lives in Lincoln Estates with some friends."

"You reported him missing to the police?" I asked.

"We can't," she said. "He's an illegal."

"I see. Where did he work?"

"At this warehouse in Lincoln Estates. It's like a big storage facility." She handed me a card: TWO THOUSAND AND ONE—SPACE ODDITIES. "It's the only job he could find, but he's very intelligent. He fled here from El Salvador."

"Estudio en la Universidad de San Salvadore," Juanita said.

"He has a degree from the University of San Salvador," Maria translated. "In chemical engineering."

"And the only job he could find here was in a factory?"

"As I said, he's an illegal. He was marked by the death squads so he had to leave El Salvador. I've been trying to work on the political asylum angle, but will you look into it?"

"Well, I can give it a shot," I said. "You know my rates. Can she afford me?"

"We've already discussed that," Maria said. "She works as a seamstress and I will help out too, if need be."

"Fine," I said. "I'll dig one of my standard contracts out of the truck. In the meantime, write down some basic information about Carlos for me like his name, date of birth, and all that."

"Already done," she said.

I grinned. "You were pretty sure I'd take the case then?"

"Let's just say," she smiled, "that I was sure I could convince you, one way or another."

Chapter 3

After dropping Maria off at the DCFS office on Western Avenue, I took Juanita back to a small tailor shop on the South Side. She gave me a Polaroid of her and Carlos. The picture wasn't real good, but it would do. I got back on the Dan Ryan and shot down to 95th Street. From there I headed west till I got to Chappie's gym.

It was a big brick structure that had once been three separate buildings. Chappie started out in the one on the corner. Then slowly, and mostly with money that I'd loaned him, he bought out the others and expanded his business into one of the largest karate-boxing-weight lifting gyms in the city. Certainly the largest on the South Side. We called it the Beverly Gym.

There were body builders, aerobics classes, amateur and professional boxers and kick-boxers, a steam room, a ring, and just about everything else you could think of. Plus, there was Chappie Oliver, one of the finest trainers for boxing in the city. Hell, in the country.

I'd known Chappie for ten years. He'd been a middleweight contender in the sixties, coming close to the championship a couple of times, but never quite getting there. That was back when there was only one champion per division. He kept his head shaved, as he had during his fighting days, and despite being three decades past his prime, he still occasionally got mistaken for Marvelous Marvin Hagler.

He'd been my trainer ever since I'd come home from the service. Having grown up in the Beverly section of Chicago,

I'd worked out at his gym back when it was only some mats, a heavy bag, and a few weights. Chappie's son, James Junior, and I had been good friends. After the army, and the little excursions that Uncle Sam sent us to in the Gulf and Somalia, James was the favorite to win the Olympic trials. But two weeks before he was set to go, he was killed in a drive-by shooting.

Chappie's other son, Leon, was serving time in Stateville, having been involved with the same gang violence that had taken his brother. Chappie'd disowned him. All he had left now, he'd always say, was his daughter, Darlene, and me.

I'd been lucky enough to win a full-contact karate title right after I got out of the army. One of my tours was in the Far East where I'd been able to augment my karate knowledge with some Thai kick-boxing. I got on the police department and dropped out of competition. Then when I lost my job, I'd started fighting again. It kept me in shape and gave me some extra money, though not nearly enough. Most of all it gave me an incentive. I wanted to win back the title that I'd regarded so cavalierly before. Perhaps I saw it as a way to restore some of the order into my life. Or maybe to show those people who'd taken my police career away that I could still cut it. Anyway, it felt good to be able to work at recovering some little part of the past that I'd lost.

It was nearing three o'clock and the gym was pretty empty. I nodded to John, one of the bodybuilders who was standing guard at the front entrance. I asked where Chappie was.

"He's in the ring," John said.

"Julio been in yet?"

"I ain't seen him," he answered, and went back to

reading his muscle magazine.

I went inside and through the first section that doubled as karate dojo and aerobics room. The tiled pathway led to a door that opened into what had been the next building. Now this middle section was a boxing gym. There were heavy bags, speed bags, double-ended bags, a full-sized, twenty-foot ring, and an automatic timer that rang in proper round sequence. Chappie had also installed a vertical row of light bulbs that let you know how much time remained on the clock. I glanced at it. The yellow light meant that they were in the last minute.

Up in the ring Chappie danced around popping jabs, hooks, and crosses at an imaginary opponent.

"Twist that jab as you hit," I said, mimicking his voice. "Now double jab, straight right, left hook."

Chappie gave a quick glance at the ring timer and finished with a flurry. He looked down at me. "You come to work out, or just to mess with me?"

"I'll be in later," I said. "I'm working on a case."

"You better get your butt in here," he said with a grin. "Saul called me this morning. The fight's set for two months."

"Anthony Berger?"

"You got it," he said. The bell sounded, ending the minute's rest and he resumed his workout.

My mind raced ahead to the fight with Berger. I'd been in top shape when I was set to fight Elijah Day for the championship. Then I'd gotten hurt and it fell through. Day had apparently taken me too lightly and skipped on his training. Berger, a last minute substitute, used my game plan to stick and move and outpointed Day over the twelve rounds.

Day and I fought an elimination match two months later

and I'd beaten him. Now the new champ, Berger, seemed to be ducking me. Or so I thought. But he was good. Fast too. Could I get into tip-top shape again? The thought of all the countless hours of training, the roadwork every morning, the dieting, the sparring. I suddenly felt tired.

But I was exhilarated at the same time. If I could win, it would mean endorsements from a lot of the martial arts magazines, and a lot more publicity for the gym. We could put up a big sign in the window: Ron Shade, Full Contact Karate Heavyweight Champion, Trains Here.

But first I'd have to win, and to do that, I'd need to fight the fight of my life.

Somebody tapped me on the shoulder and I whirled. It was Julio, a Mexican kid who worked out religiously. He had a job at a factory and usually was at the gym in the mornings.

"Ron, John said you was looking for me."

"Julio, yeah. I need some help." I looked down at his street clothes. "I figured you'd be finishing up about now."

"My day off," he said. "I just got here. What you need?"

"How about coming along to talk to some Hispanics with me? Shouldn't take too long, and I'll drive you back 'cause I gotta work out too."

"What's the matter? Your Spanish getting rusty?" he asked with a grin.

"This is a special case," I said. "Some of these guys may be illegals and I don't think they'd open up to me."

"Sure," he said. "Just let me put my stuff in my trunk."

We drove to my house where Julio helped me unload the filing cabinets and files. Then I drove over to George's and left his pick-up in the driveway. My new Z-28 sat gleaming by the curb. Julio was impressed.

"This your new car?" he asked, running a finger over the

black sheen of the fender.

"That's it. Ain't she sweet?"

I told George's wife that I'd settle up about the truck when I saw him. I'd been in such a rush that I'd neglected to fill it up, and knew I'd hear about that later.

We headed over to I-57 and went south. Lincoln Estates was one of the far southern suburbs, and that was where Carlos worked and lived. Strange that he'd been able to develop a relationship with Juanita, who lived on the south side near Maria. I guess true love can conquer long distances. Except distances like between Los Angeles and Chicago. I glanced at the changing leaves on the trees and wondered what Cathy was doing.

Chapter 4

Two Thousand and One—Space Oddities, was located in what had formerly been a large automobile parts factory. When the American auto industry fell on hard times, the former company went belly-up. The ad in the phone book listed Space Oddities as "a capacious answer to your business storage problems." Capacious. I liked that word. And the building was immense all right. Space Oddities occupied only the southern portion of it, next to the railroad tracks. The sign in the northern-most section of the parking lot stated that there were 50,000 square feet still available for rent.

A fancy brick office section sat in front, attached to a massive, windowless two-story structure immediately behind it. We pulled in the parking area, which seemed to extend completely around the plant, broken only by the presence of a heavy, seven-foot cyclone fence that was topped with barbed-wire. There were maybe a half-dozen cars in the lot.

A security guard sat in a glass cubicle just inside the building entrance. He looked up from a newspaper and asked if he could help us. I told him I needed to see the plant supervisor.

"That'd be Mr. Jordan," he said. "What's the name of your business, sir?"

"Ronald Shade Enterprises," I said. Julio looked at me with suspicion.

The guard called somebody on the radio, and another uniformed guy appeared and took us into an office area adjacent to the foyer. It had several doors, a small coffee table covered with some magazines and an ashtray, and some plastic chairs. The walls were painted a dull green. A stacked blond secretary sat behind a glass partition, typing on a computer keyboard. She told us that Mr. Jordan was in a conference and would be with us shortly.

"In the meantime," she said. "If you'd fill out this form."

I took the form and sat in one of the plastic chairs. The form asked general business questions like company name, address, what type of material I wished to store in 2001, and for what duration.

"Ain't you afraid you'll get in trouble?" asked Julio quietly.

I shook my head. "This'll cut out the middlemen."

Maria had said the plant had been uncooperative about Carlos when she'd called, saying only that he was no longer employed there. We sat and waited a good ten minutes before the door opened and three people came out. Two were middle-aged men in suits. One guy, who looked to be the older and smaller of the two, had his arm around a young girl of about eighteen. He was at least fifty. She was a pretty, fresh-faced kid with the kind of reddish hair that was almost blond. Strawberry blond. The other guy was heavier, with a big, fleshy face and a mustache. He turned to me and said he'd be with me in moment.

"Tom, Kelly," he said to them. "I think this'll be the start of something big."

They all laughed. The heavy guy shook hands with both of them, and the man and the girl turned to leave. They didn't hold hands or touch as they passed us and their body language suggested that maybe they weren't the May–December couple I'd first thought.

The smaller guy stopped suddenly and said to her, "Honey, could you wait for me in the car. I forgot something in Uncle Harold's office."

"Sure, Daddy," she answered.

As she walked past us I admired her muscular legs. The two men went back inside the office and shut the door. They stayed in there for a minute, then came out again. When they exited this time, the smaller guy seemed less ebullient. He nodded curtly to the heavy guy, Harold, and left.

"Sorry to keep you waiting," he said, moving toward us with his hand extended. "I'm Mr. Jordan, the plant supervisor."

I stood and shook his hand. As he shook hands with Julio, I gave him one of my cards. His brow furrowed when he looked at it.

"We don't get many calls from private detectives, Mr. Shade. What can I do for you?"

I showed him the Polaroid of Carlos and Juanita. "Know this man?"

He studied it for a moment.

"Should I?"

"His name is Carlos Sanchez," I said. "He works here. He's been missing and I've been hired to look for him."

Jordan's mouth twisted quizzically. "You say he works here?"

"That's what I've been told."

Jordan handed the picture back to me and told me to have a seat. He went back into his office and closed the door again. The secretary, who'd obviously heard our conversation, eyed me with a mixture of curiosity and resentment. After about three minutes Jordan came out again, with a stupid smile stretched across his face.

"It took me a minute to check it out, but it's just as I suspected," he said. "The man did work here, but he was fired three days ago."

"Fired? Can I ask why?"

"The foreman's on his way over," Jordan said. "We just bought this place a year ago and we're trying to get it started. We've got a lot of Mexicans working here who don't speak English too good, so they just kinda fade in and out, if you know what I mean." He looked at Julio and added, "No offense."

Before Julio could reply, two guys came in. They were both dressed in blue work clothes and black safety shoes. The Hispanic one was short, with glasses and a mustache. He looked about forty. The other guy was enormous. At least six-five and close to three hundred pounds, with a chest like a barrel.

"Mr. Shade," Jordan said. "This is Frank Bristol, our plant foreman."

The big guy extended his hand. I did the same, but instead of shaking hands like a normal person he grabbed my fingers and squeezed them together as we shook.

"You can call me Big Frank. This is Enrique Torres," he said, still grinding my fingers. "You got some questions about Carlos?"

"Yeah," I said, finally managing to extricate my hand from his. "He no longer works here?"

"That's right."

"What happened?"

Big Frank cast an oblique glance at Enrique, who began squawking like a trained parrot.

"Look, mister. I'm a Latino too, but when somebody's wrong, they're wrong."

"Translation?" I asked.

"You want to know why we fired him, correct?" Big Frank said impatiently.

I nodded.

"It's simple," he said. "He showed up here tanked to the gills. We operate a lot of equipment in here. Forklifts, carts, and stuff like that. One thing I don't tolerate is somebody being drunk on the job."

"I see. When's the last time you saw Carlos?"

"Friday afternoon, when he came in. I fired him on the spot."

"Seen him since then?" I asked.

"Huh-un," he grunted. "How 'bout you, Rico?"

Enrique shook his head.

"Know anywhere he might have gone?" I asked.

"No. Why?"

"He's missing," I said. "I'm trying to locate him."

Frank's face cracked into a smile. "Oh, is that what this is all about? I thought you was accusing us of being prejudiced, or something."

"Why?" I said. "Are you?"

Frank blinked before he answered. "Not hardly."

"Where'd Carlos live?" I asked.

"I can give you that," Jordan said. He went into his office and opened a file cabinet. Sorting through some files, he pulled one out, opened it, and read off an address. It was the same one that Juanita and Maria had given me. "It's here in town," he added.

"How'd he take getting fired?"

Frank shrugged. "He knew the rules. He didn't say much. Just left, that's all."

"Know where he went?"

"I seen him going toward that bar down the road," Frank said. "He wanted to use the phone to have somebody come pick him up, on account of it was raining. Wanted to use the phone in the office, but I wouldn't let him."

"Were there any incidents when he left?" I asked. "Was he despondent, argumentative, or anything?"

Frank twisted half his mouth up in a smile. "Nah," he said. "People usually don't get too argumentative with me."

Chapter 5

The bar that Big Frank had mentioned was a couple of blocks north of Space Oddities on the same highway. A pair of drainage ditches separated it from the road. Behind the bar, a long, brick, L-shaped motel sat in a state of disrepair. *No Occupancy* stickers were on most of the doors, and a large sign in the office window said: *Closed for Remodeling—Regular Residents Only*. I pulled over one of the gravel driveways that spanned the drainage ditch, and parked near the entrance. The rest of the lot was filled with Harley Davidson motorcycles.

As far as I could tell, the place didn't have a name. The outside was red cedar, and the white trim was peeling badly. One section of the easement along the side looked about ready to invite the raccoons in. A neon *Old Style* sign hung above the door with another in the front window which faced the road. All the other windows had been covered with the same dirty white plywood as the trim. To accommodate the balmy October weather, somebody had propped open the side door.

The interior of the place was a typical tavern, only slightly more dingy. Immediately inside the door was a room with a large pool table. Three men were playing a round. Two looked like bikers: Levi jackets with the sleeves cut off, long hair, and plenty of grease. The other guy was a skinny fellow with straggly blond hair that curled around his collar. He had a nose like a hatchet. A chest-high wall separated this section from the rest of the bar. Julio and I walked around it and approached the bartender. She was a prune-faced gal whose hair had been rinsed blond one too many times. Several more bikers eyed us from the other end.

"What'll it be, gents?" she asked.

"How about some information?" I said, trying my best to be charming.

From the look she gave me I could tell it hadn't worked. I took out the Polaroid of Carlos and Juanita.

"I'm looking for this guy," I said. "Recognize him?"

She shook her head after barely a glance and moved back to the middle of the bar. There was a jukebox behind us playing some country and western song accompanied by the loud pinging of a pair of pinball machines.

"Are you sure? He worked down the street at Space Oddities."

She acted like she hadn't heard, but some old alkie came stumbling over from one of the pinball machines holding a bottle.

"Space Oddities?" he said. He snorted out a heavy breath and asked to see the picture.

"Recognize him?" I asked.

He stared at it blinking several times. "Looks like a Mexican."

I nodded. "I was told that he might have been in here last Friday."

"Don't remember him," he said. "But maybe old Needle Dick'll know him."

"Needle Dick?" I repeated.

He nodded with a smirk. "Nick," he said thickly. "We call him Needle Dick." He laughed as if we were sharing a mutual joke.

"He around here?" I asked.

He held up his bottle to the light and shook it, a drunken

grin spreading over his face.

I ordered another one for him. Pruneface opened it and sat it on the bar. I paid her and pocketed the change.

The old guy took a long swig from the bottle, then winked me a thanks.

"He's over there playin' pool," he said after a long belch. "Come on, I'll introduce you."

He stepped gingerly around the partition and over to the pool room. "Hey, Nick. Got somebody here wants to meet you."

"Get outta here, Al," the blond guy said. "Before I knock the shit outta you." He leaned over and smacked the cue ball with his stick, but scratched. "Goddammit!"

Al turned away from him and staggered back to the bar.

"You work at Space Oddities?" I asked.

"Maybe," he said. "Why?"

I showed him the photo. "Know this guy?"

He ignored me. One of the other guys missed a shot and Nick yelled, "All right." He leaned forward to make another shot, but he missed that one too. When he straightened up I repeated the question.

"Why don't you get outta my face, mister," he said. "You're messing up my game."

"I just asked you if you knew him," I said. "He's missing, and I've been hired to look for him."

"You heard Nick, didn't you?" one of the long-haired biker guys said, leaning on his pool cue.

"Yeah," I said. "I hope he shoots pool better than he carries on a conversation."

Nick whirled and looked at me. "What's your game, man? Who the fuck are you?"

"Just a guy looking for some answers," I said.

"Well I don't know nothin' about no fucking spic," he

said. “I don’t hang around with ’em, and we don’t allow ’em in here.”

I felt Julio stiffening beside me.

“What did you say?” he said.

“Julio,” I cautioned. “Take it easy.”

Nick smacked the heavy end of his pool cue into his left hand and grinned. He had bad teeth.

“Wanna make something of it, spic?” he taunted.

The other two guys straightened up at the prospect of a fight. One laid his stick down on the table and grabbed a beer bottle by the neck. “We got us a couple of tough guys, Nickie?”

Behind me I heard some feet shuffling and pulled Julio around the table. Three other bikers from the bar area moved across the room, cutting us off from the door. Nick moved forward still smacking the pool cue into his palm.

“Hey, guys,” I said. “I understand completely. You don’t like Hispanics, right? Well, how do you feel about Italians?”

“Why?” one of the bikers said. “You a wop?”

“No,” I said, reaching inside my jacket and pulling out my pistol. “But I’d like to introduce you to a friend of mine. Meet Pietro Beretta.”

When Nick saw the gun he stopped and began to back up.

“You think you’re the only one with a piece?” one of the bikers sneered.

I leveled it at him.

“No, but I’m sure I can blow the fucking heads off at least three of you. Now, get away from the door.”

They started to shuffle back toward the bar area, grumbling and eyeing me warily. Suddenly the front door slammed open and Big Frank Bristol sauntered in. He stopped and surveyed the scene with raised eyebrows, then walked over and stood between us and the rest of the group.

"Thought I'd better come down here and check on you after I got to thinking," he said. "Kind of a rough place for newcomers. You see, lots of people in this area are out of work since the plant closed down. Makes 'em unsociable."

He turned to Nick. "I thought you were sick?"

"I was," Nick answered.

"Well, where's your manners?" Frank said. "You tell this man what he wanted to know?"

Nick looked at him and swallowed nervously.

"Did you tell him that we fired Carlos last Friday for showing up drunk?" Frank said harshly.

Nick shook his head.

"Well, now ain't that right, Nickie?" Frank continued.

"Yeah, that's right, Frank."

I was ready to see Bristol put Nickie on his lap like a ventriloquist with an oversized dummy.

"I told Mr. Shade that the Mexican might have come down here," Bristol said. "To use the pay phone for someone to come pick him up. You remember him using the phone last Friday, Maggie?"

"I dunno," Old Pruneface said. "He might have. We get too many people in here for me to keep track of."

"Anybody else know anything at all?" Big Frank asked loudly.

Silence. He turned back to us. "There you have it, Mr. Shade. I told you nobody argues with me."

"I appreciate it, Mr. Bristol." I lowered the gun, but kept it by my side. "Let's go," I said to Julio.

"If I hear anything I'll give you a call, Mr. Shade," Big Frank said. "I still got your card."

I thanked him and left. Outside Julio was still fuming.

"Why didn't you let me knock the shit out of that son of a bitch?" he said.

I twisted the keys to start the Z-28, backed out of the parking place then peeled out, spewing a lot of loose gravel.

"Sometimes it's better to do your fighting in the gym," I said.

The address that Juanita'd given me for Carlos was about two miles from the plant. We found it with a little help from a gas station attendant. It was on a block of somewhat shabby-looking apartment buildings. They were all brick three-and four-story jobs. The city had made an attempt to beautify the street by planting trees along the parkway. A rag-tag group of little kids romped over gray patches of dirt scattered among the weed-infested grass. Even with the saplings, the scene looked dismally artificial.

Carlos's building was toward the end of the block. We parked in front and went up to the door. There were no names by the doorbells, but Juanita had told me it was apartment 3N/W. The security door wasn't locked so we went right on up. I knocked hard on the door until a voice called out in Spanish from behind it. Julio answered.

The guy who opened the door was short and dressed in a T-shirt and blue jeans. He looked to be in his mid-twenties. Inside, I could see several other Hispanics sitting around a table eating. They all eyed me uneasily so I let Julio do all the talking. None of them had seen Carlos since he left for work on Friday. But since he usually took the train into the city to stay with Juanita and her family on the weekends, they didn't think anything of it at first. Until Juanita called on Sunday wondering where Carlos was. One of the roommates, Paco, was working at a new restaurant in Joliet where he was staying. He'd worked at Space Oddities with

Carlos, but they'd fired him on Monday.

"When will he be back?" I asked. "I'd like to talk to him."

Julio repeated the question.

The guy who'd answered the door counted on his fingers, then answered, "*Jueves.*"

"Thursday," Julio translated.

I thanked the guy, gave him one of my cards, and told him I'd be back on Thursday to talk to Paco.

Chapter 6

We stopped at a Mexican restaurant located on the highway in front of a strip mall. I figured I owed Julio a late lunch for tagging along and helping me out. We both were hungry and ate heartily. On the way back I began to regret it. I still had a workout ahead of me tonight, and had enough gas to fly to Kansas City. By the time we got back to Chicago I was really regretting my gluttony. Nonetheless, I dropped Julio off at the gym, and told him I'd be back as soon as I got my gear.

At my house I checked my electronic timers that turned on the lights. The cats sauntered out from their hiding places. Up until last year I only had one animal, a big tan tom cat named Georgio, after my cop buddy, George. Then, on the way home from the gym one night last winter I spied a little white and black kitten shivering in the snow. I hadn't been that far from the animal welfare office, but it fit so easily in the palm of my hand, crying with pathetic mews. I decided to see how Georgio would react to some feminine company, and named her Shasha. They became fast friends.

Both cats cried to let me know that they hadn't eaten all day. After dishing up their food, I packed my workout clothes in my bag, grabbed the rest of my gear, and was off. By the time I got to the gym, Julio was already working on the bags, and Chappie was standing at the door tapping his foot.

"Maybe you didn't hear me this morning," he said. "I did tell you that you got a title-fight coming up in two months, didn't I?"

"Yeah," I said. "I had to get my stuff. Besides, me and Julio ate some Mexican food before we came so I needed some time to let it digest a little."

"That why he been farting so much?" Chappie chuckled. "Oh well, get changed and we'll do some work. You need to do some sparring."

"Whatever you say, boss."

"I got to talk to you 'bout something, too," he said. "But get changed first."

I wondered what he meant by that, but went straight down the tiled section of floor that led to the locker room. Chappie'd put both the men's and women's locker rooms side by side at the rear of the first building in back of the karate/aerobics room. This way people using the equipment had to walk by the ring in the middle section before they could get back into the locker room. It cut down on pilferage. It never ceased to amaze me how many guys would try to sneak out with dumbbells and weight plates. But God help them if Chappie caught them.

I stripped down and tossed my stuff in an empty locker. Then I stepped on the scale. Two-twenty-five. That meant about twelve pounds had to go before the fight. Chappie'd insist that I come in at two-twelve, but it didn't seem like an awful lot to take off.

"How much, Ron?" Phil Brice, one of the bodybuilders who pumped iron regularly at the gym, asked me.

I told him.

"No, I mean how much you got to lose?"

"Oh, probably ten to twelve pounds," I said.

"I don't know, you look pretty good. You ought to try bulking up. You got a real classic build. Could probably compete in bodybuilding."

I grinned, and told him that kickboxing was about all I

could handle. After slipping on the rest of my sweats, I raced out the door to the boxing gym. Julio was pounding some hooks into the heavy bag. I tapped him on the back as I passed.

"Too many tacos," I said.

"Burritos," he replied with a wolfish grin.

Chappie was standing at the ring and slipped on the focus pads. He slapped them together, grinned, and then led me around the ring working on different punch combinations. The next round he made me work kicks and punches, then a round of just kicks. In regulation kickboxing, the rounds are only two minutes in duration. He always made me work the standard, three-minute boxing rounds.

At the end I was panting like a dog on a hot summer day.

"Pretty bad for a man who wants to take on the champ," Chappie said. "You got a lot of work to do."

"It's all that Mexican food I ate today," I said. "Look at Julio. He's not working hard either."

"He ain't fixing to go up for no title, neither," Chappie countered. "Are you?"

"I will be."

"That's what I wanted to talk to you about," he said.

I stared at him.

"How much you want it?" he asked.

"What? You don't think I can do it?"

"I didn't say that. But if your head's not on right for this one . . ." He looked up at me. "We can't afford another problem like the last time."

"Hey, that wasn't my fault, Chappie."

"I know that. But it don't have to be. You could have won that damn title. But you had to run off playing *Magnum PI* and get yourself all fucked up."

"What are you saying? I shouldn't work?"

"I'm saying that maybe you shouldn't fight if you ain't got it in you anymore."

"You don't want to train me?"

He put his hand on my shoulder. "You like a son to me. I'll always be willing to train you. You and Raul are the closest things I gots to World Class Fighters. Even though it's this kickboxing shit. But you the one gonna be up here, taking the hits. You taking the chance on getting hurt." He sighed. "That last fight with Elijah Day was something. I never saw a man with so much heart as you had. But if you ain't got the fire in your belly no more, then let's call it quits."

"How can you even think that?"

"Okay, I kind of figured that's what you'd say. Now comes the bad news. The purse is only two thousand."

"For a championship fight?" I said. "That's ridiculous."

"I always told you, there ain't no money in this damn kickboxing. And I got a feeling Berger's people are keeping it low hoping that you won't take it."

"Let's make sure we don't offer him a rematch," I said.

He grinned and slapped my shoulder. "Just wanted to be sure that's how you saw it," he said. "Now, let's get to work."

The rest of my workout went pretty well. I worked on the bags, throwing punches and kicks, then jumped rope for a couple of rounds. By the time my sweatshirt was wet all the way through, Chappie told me to hit the steam room.

"And don't forget to run in the morning. Five miles," he called out after me.

I went through the doorway and saw that Darlene, Chappie's daughter, was leading an aerobics class. Smiling, she waved for me to join them, never missing a beat of the music.

"Not the way I smell," I called out. There were a couple of new girls who looked pretty good in Spandex, though.

Chapter 7

After the workout I'd just had, sweating in the steam room seemed anti-climactic. I was already dehydrated and didn't feel like being parboiled. Five minutes inside was all I could stand. Naked as a jaybird, I stepped on the scale and saw I'd lost ten pounds, but acquired a powerful thirst. I wondered how much of it I'd gain back once I started to drink. Outside, the beat of Darlene's aerobic class was still going strong. Maybe I should go out and join them now, I thought. Probably make a definite impression on some of the females. But instead I headed for the showers. I'd known Darlene since she was a little kid and didn't want to shock her. Besides, one of the best things about working out was when it was over. I felt dead dragging myself under the shower nozzle, but by the end I was feeling great again. When I was drying off Chappie came in.

"You feeling better now?" he asked.

"If I say yes you'll work me harder next time?"

"Damn straight. And remember, don't you be forgetting about the road work," he said as he turned to leave. "Five miles. No cutting corners."

"Heaven forbid," I said. "See you tomorrow."

I stopped at the twenty-four-hour Jewel on the way home and bought a gallon of low-calorie cranberry-apple juice. By the time I was walking in the door I was so thirsty that I regretted I hadn't bought two of them. The cats came running to see who was coming in. Georgio stood in my way whining and Shasha took a quick look and pranced into the other room.

"Yeah, yeah," I said to him. "I know it's time for supper."

Actually it was close to ten. I'd been at the gym for two hours, but it hadn't seemed that long. Georgio seemed to disagree, looking up at me and making a few abbreviated mewing sounds. I opened a new can of cat food and split it between the two dishes. Shasha came strolling back when she smelled that, and they both began feasting. Scooping some ice into my glass, I poured the juice over the cubes and downed it in one long drink. Then, pouring another one, I went in to catch the *Ten O'clock News.*

Stacks of old newspapers littered the floor. I had to scoop the old mail from my TV tray to find a spot for the glass. Tomorrow was garbage day, so I'd have to clean the cat pans and stick all the papers, cans, and glass in the recycling bin tonight. A familiar face on the screen snapped my attention. I turned up the volume.

"And at the Dirkson Building today reputed mobster Sergio DeKooning appeared before a federal grand jury," the announcer said. "Here's more from Laurel Ann Dean."

The film of DeKooning, flanked by several bodyguards, appeared on the screen as Laurel Ann did the voice-over. DeKooning's face looked grim, head down, as he walked toward the elevators.

"Reputed mob boss Sergio DeKooning was subpoenaed to appear before a federal grand jury probing corruption in the south suburbs. DeKooning, shown here with his lawyer, Lawrence C. Peck, is purported to be a major figure in organized crime in the south suburban area. Federal prosecutors declined comment on what specific allegations are being probed at this time, but it is believed to be connected with DeKooning's business dealings with numerous South Side businesses. DeKooning was rushed away by bodyguards and declined comment, preferring instead to be heard through his attorney." The voice over faded and a picture of Lawrence Peck, looking dapper in his dark suit, came on.

"This is another attempt by the government to harass my client merely because he has achieved a pinnacle of success as a legitimate businessman," Peck said. He then displayed for the camera the slyest hint of a smile.

"Mr. Peck," some off-camera reporter asked. "Do you deny the allegations that your client has connections to organized crime?"

"As I said, Mr. DeKooning is a legitimate businessman," Peck repeated. "Any efforts to paint him as anything but that are pure fantasy. And, I might add, spurious allegations."

Spurious allegations, I thought. Peck, you've outdone yourself.

"It is unknown if DeKooning invoked his Fifth Amendment rights during this session as he has done on previous occasions," Laurel Ann Dean concluded.

I sipped the juice and considered this as the news shifted to the next topic. It was common knowledge that DeKooning was the big boy on the block out south. His territory was rumored to cover all the way from the Southwest Side to the Indiana state line. He'd risen to power because of his shrewd ruthlessness and keen business sense. Not the least of which was retaining Lawrence C. Peck to represent him.

Peck and I had tangled before. He was as sharp as they came, having graduated from the University of Chicago. He was gregarious and witty in his expensive, hand-tailored suits. I wondered if he'd ever been just an idealistic law student at one time, intent on serving justice. Or maybe he saw it all clearly from the beginning: The road to heaven's paved with Rolex watches. Why bother with idealism when there's tons of money to be made? Of course, if I would've had him as my attorney when the PD fired me, I probably would have been reinstated instead of enduring an endless series of appeals that would never be decided.

When the commercial came on I drained the glass and went for a refill. On the way I picked up the papers and dropped them in the plastic recycling box. By the time the weatherman came on I had a semblance of order restored to the living room. Too bad I'd already expended so much energy at the gym. It would have been a workout in itself to clean up the other rooms. I decided that would be a good task for another time and got ready for bed.

Chapter 8

As I ran down the grassy incline that went under the railroad viaduct my feet slogged through uncollected stacks of sheared grass. The county had been by with their extension mowers again, leveling the three-foot-high shrubbery alongside the road. We'd had a rainy summer and the plant life had responded accordingly. I hadn't minded it. My daily running had worn a path that was delightfully populated with several varieties of wild flowers. I'd looked forward to seeing them every day.

But now it was October. Early autumn. Most of the wild flowers were gone, except a few of the hearty blue ones and the late-blooming sunflowers that had escaped the mower. Their presence still reminded me of the vestiges of summer even though winter was looming on the horizon. There was a chill in the air this morning, and I could see a vapor cloud with each breath. Soon I'd have another birthday behind me. I was already pushing thirty. How much longer would I be able to fight? To seriously pursue my dream of winning the world title?

A languid grasshopper leaped feebly in front of me, bouncing off my leg. Soon he'd be gone too. After the first heavy frost. Hopefully I wasn't at that stage quite yet.

I rounded the last corner and came to the third and, thankfully, final hill of my five-mile course. I'd been running the same one, with a couple of variations, for the past seven years since my days when I'd been a hot-shot cop on the SWAT team. Each of the three hills had a name: Agony One, Agony Two, and Miss Agony. The last one was the steepest as well as the longest. Once I cleared her, it was a straight nine-tenths of a mile to my house.

I tried to give it that final sprint at the end, but I just plain didn't have it today. I hadn't slept well. Intermittently at best, and I'd awoken in the middle of the night from my old, familiar nightmare: the SWAT operation where the wrong person had walked into my field of fire at precisely the wrong time. I lay in bed trying to fall back into a restful slumber. But all I could do was recall the feeling of a faceless dread that flirted on the edge of my consciousness like some powerful, invisible foe.

After my shower I toasted a bagel and poured the water into the top of my coffee maker. I wanted to catch the traffic report before I headed downtown to see George. Flipping on the radio, I caught the end of a newscast about a big fish kill in Lake Calumet. What surprised me was that there were any fish in the lake to begin with.

The toaster buzzed and I had the bagel smeared with cream cheese just as the coffee was ready. I hoped my perfect timing would hold up for the rest of the day. When I turned back to the table after putting milk in my coffee, I saw Shasha licking the cream cheese off the bagel. So much for my perfect timing.

After eating breakfast, feeding the cats, and taking out the garbage and recyclables, I opened the garage and got into the Z-28. She roared to life at the turn of the key, and I shot down the alley, using the remote to close the garage door.

I still hadn't heard the traffic report, but it didn't look too bad when I got on the expressway. With only the slightest pressure on the accelerator she shot forward, easily outdistancing the other northbound cars. The noise that I'd noticed before was no more than a whisper today. The express lanes were crowded, but I stuck to the locals and got off at 51st. Area One sat right on the corner. I parked in the circular driveway in front.

Inside I got behind a group who'd come in to report a domestic dispute.

"He hit me when I told him he couldn't take my car," a heavyset woman was saying.

"Man, I told her, I just got to get to work, or I'm gonna lose this job," the man standing beside her groaned. He was dressed in a blue, gas station-type shirt with "Gus" stitched above the left pocket.

"Take a seat," the desk sergeant said implacably.

"You don't understand," the woman said. "He hit me and I want him arrested."

"I understand just fine," the sergeant answered. "Now, take a seat." To underscore his meaning he gestured toward the metal bench that ran along the huge glass windows. He turned to me. "Can I help you?"

"Yeah, I'm here to see Detective Grieves," I said. "He around?"

"I'll see." He glanced at a female officer who was seated behind the counter. Without being asked she dialed the phone, spoke softly into the receiver, then turned back to me.

"What's your name, sir?" she asked.

"Ron Shade."

She spoke again, then smiled. Turning back to me, she said, "He says you know the way back there."

"What else did he say?"

"It's better you don't know," she answered, still smiling.

I smiled back and headed down to George's office. I saw him standing in the middle of the room by the big, battle-scarred wooden desk. The sleeves of his shirt were rolled up over his forearms. His tie was hanging slackly from his neck. He put a hand on each hip and greeted me with his usual friendliness: "Where's my fucking gas money?"

His partner, Doug Percy, was on the phone. He nodded to me.

"Is that any way to greet a buddy?"

"A buddy doesn't borrow somebody's truck and return it on empty," he said.

"A minor oversight," I replied, handing him a twenty. "I didn't have time to top it off. Didn't Ellen tell you?"

He looked at the twenty and smirked. "Top it off? This wouldn't even bring it to half. And it was riding on fumes when you brought it back."

"Well, the sucker was only a quarter full when you gave it to me."

He grinned and shoved the twenty into his pocket. "You must be on a case."

"How'd you know that?"

"What other reason would you have for coming by? I know it wouldn't be to pay me twenty bucks."

"Talk about a cynical cop," I said.

"I suppose you want a cup, too."

"It's the least you could do."

He turned back to Doug and said, "I'll be downstairs, Pers."

George was the only person that could get away with calling Doug by his dreaded nickname to his face. Doug was about the size of defensive lineman, however, George and I both knew he was a gentle giant.

We walked down the hall to the stairs. George pressed the button for the elevator, but I grabbed his arm and pulled him toward the stairway.

"Come on. It's only one floor. And I'm in training." I

told him I'd be fighting Berger for the championship.

"That's great," he answered. "But I ain't walking back up."

The break room consisted of a couple of vending machines, a public telephone, and several porcelain tables. A lone uniformed copper sat at one of the tables reading the *Sun-Times*. George dropped some coins into the coffee machine and told me to pick my poison. I hit the coffee with cream and then the extra light buttons. The cup dropped down and the liquid poured into it. After George had his, we sat at one of the far tables next to the phone.

"So what you need, Ron?"

"What makes you think I need something? Can't I just come over to see my old friend?"

"Come on. I got a lot of shit to do."

"Well," I said, taking a sip from the cup. "I do need a favor."

He rolled his eyes and drank some of his coffee.

"I'm working on a missing person case," I said. "Here's the photo."

He looked at the Polaroid.

"He in the computer?" George asked.

I shook my head. "He's an illegal. No report was made. Can you check the morgue for me? And any type-threes from NCIC?"

"Yeah," he said. "I guess so. For a price."

I saw the sly grin on his face.

"What?" I asked.

"Tickets for me and Doug to your next fight."

"Sure. No problem." I didn't tell him that the fight was set for West Palm Beach, Florida, where Anthony Berger was from. It was another tactic of theirs to discourage me from accepting the match.

"I was watching the tape of the Day fight last night," George said. He shook his head. "That was one of the greatest battles I ever seen."

"I hope I do as well against Berger."

"Shit, Ron, quit being modest. You knocked Day out. It was all Berger could do to out-point him."

"Yeah," I said slowly. "But now he's the champ. That usually adds a lot to a fighter."

George hit my shoulder. "You'll do great," he said. "Just like the old days in the neighborhood."

George had watched me grow up on the South Side. He was a lot older than I was, and had been in the Marines in Vietnam with my older brother, Tom. Years later, when I'd gotten into some minor trouble right after high school, he'd convinced me to enlist, and then to join the police department after I got out of the Army.

"Well," I said, getting to my feet, "I'd better get outta here before I run into Lieutenant Bielmaster."

George grinned. "Good idea."

"I got to make a call," I said. "My cell phone's in the car." I reached into my pocket and took out some change.

George put his hand on my shoulder. "You can use the one upstairs, if you want. The guys just use this phone to call their squeezes."

We went back upstairs in the elevator. Far be it from me to turn down a free phone call at the expense of fitness. Inside the office Doug was typing a report. I called DCFS and asked to speak with Maria, but she was busy. I told the secretary I'd call back later. As we began walking back toward the front doors, I heard someone bellow George's name.

Chapter 9

"Grieves," the bellow continued. I didn't have to turn around to know who it was, but I did anyway. His face was flushed, nostrils flaring under the weight of the thick glasses. I nodded courteously and smiled.

"Lieutenant Bielmaster," I said. "How you doing?"

He ignored me and turned to George. "What the hell is this?"

"Ah . . ." George was struggling. "Shade just dropped by with some information about a case, Lieu."

Bielmaster snorted. "In other words, he's here soliciting unauthorized departmental assistance for one of *his* cases." He gave George a hard stare. "Grieves, we've discussed this matter before."

George exhaled loudly through his nose, but said nothing. Bielmaster turned his attention to me. "Shade, I believe that I've been explicitly clear on how I feel about you hanging around here undermining the legitimate efforts of the police department."

Since I was a civilian I could tell Bielmaster to go to hell and he couldn't do squat to me. But I knew that he'd take it out on George if I did. So I bit my tongue.

"Lieutenant," I said. "Like Detective Grieves said, I ran across some information that I thought might be of use to—"

"Don't give me that bullshit." He turned so that his considerable bulk faced me. His sharp chin jutted out from a dollop of blubber. "Every time you come around here it's trouble."

"Well," I said. "I was just leaving."

"Lieu," George cut in. But Bielmaster wouldn't even listen.

"Ain't you got work to do?"

"Yes, sir," George said.

"Then do it." He shot a harsh look at each of us. "I'll see you in my office in five minutes, Grieves." On that note he turned and left.

We watched him waddle down the hall.

"Sorry, brother," I said.

"No problem," he said. "He's had a hair up his ass lately. Come on, I'll walk you out."

George told me he'd make some calls and give me a beep later. We shook hands and I thanked him.

"Take it easy in the hot wheels," he called out after me.

In the Z-28 I called Maria again, but she was still busy with a case.

"Tell her to keep lunch open for me," I said. "I'll be there at twelve sharp."

The girl on the phone said she'd give Maria the message. I checked with my answering service as I got back on the Ryan and cut over effortlessly to the express lanes. Luckily there were no troopers running radar along the shoulder. I'd have to watch it in this car, I thought. It responded to my slightest touch.

My answering service said there'd been a call from some Mexican guy who could barely speak English. He did leave a number. It was a Lincoln Estates exchange. I thanked her and pulled out my notebook. The number matched with the one Juanita had given me for Carlos's apartment. Rather than calling and wasting airtime trying my pidgin Spanish on his roommates, I decided to wait and let Maria talk to them.

When I pulled up in front of the Department of Children

and Family Services I wasn't sure if Maria had gotten my message. But after parking and venturing inside I found her standing by the hallway, coat on and purse in hand. She glanced at me and smiled. The raven-black hair fell to the shoulders of her brown coat. Underneath she was wearing a white sweater and dark skirt. I admired the sleek, nylon-textured look of her calves.

"If I don't get out of there now I might never get another chance," she laughed.

"Rough day?"

"You don't want to know."

From the experiences I'd had on the police department with those type of problems I figured she was right. When we got out to the parking lot Maria stopped to admire the Z-28, walking around it slowly and running her finger over the sleek blackness of the fender.

"Here's my baby," I said.

"Oh, Ron, it's so beautiful. How long have you had it?"

"Three weeks."

I opened the door for her and she slid inside. After I got in I asked her where she wanted to eat.

"There's a nice place down a few blocks," she said.

I followed her directions to a medium-sized restaurant called the Red Wheel. A huge, perpendicular wagon-type wheel, with neon spokes, stuck out above the entrance.

Maria kept marveling at the design of the Z's dashboard and its black leather interior. The parking lot was pretty full, but I found a space in back. As we walked toward the entrance a beater Chevy with three Latino punks in it pulled in. They eyed us as we passed. A good-looking Hispanic girl with a white guy in this neighborhood must not have been a common sight. I mentioned this to Maria.

"Oh, don't be silly," she said, smiling. "They probably check out all the girls."

I considered this. "Or maybe they recognized me from ESPN."

"You're still doing that?" Maria asked.

I gave her a brief run-down of the latest developments in my kickboxing career. The waitress seated us in a booth near the rear. After she poured our coffee and took the order I got serious.

"Has Juanita heard from Carlos?" I asked.

Maria shook her head.

"I've checked out the place where he worked."

"I hope they were more cooperative with you than they were with me," she said, loading some sugar and cream into her coffee. She was Cuban and really loved the sugar. "What did they tell you?"

"That Carlos was fired last Friday for showing up drunk."

She'd been sipping her coffee as I said it. Her reaction was startling.

"That's crazy," she said, setting the cup down with such force that some of the amber liquid splashed out.

I looked at her dark eyes for a moment. "Maria, I've got to know some things about Carlos in order to have a chance of finding him. Sometimes people try to hide unfavorable aspects of a person, and it works against my ability to look in the right places."

She nodded.

"Does he have a drinking problem?"

"No." She shook her head emphatically. "I mean, he might have a beer or two at a party, but that's it. I can't ever remember seeing him falling-down drunk."

"Is it possible you just don't know him that well?"

She answered slowly. "I think Juanita would have told me about it. She confides in me about everything. She's like my little sister."

I nodded. "Well, ask her for me, would you? I need to know if it might be a factor."

"Okay, but I really doubt it."

"Time for another tough question," I said. "Is it possible that he has another girlfriend somewhere?"

This time Maria smiled.

"I don't think that sounds like Carlos either," she said. "He's really a nice boy."

"How about him being deported? Or maybe just going back home?"

She shook her head again. "INS was the first place I checked. I'm not without my contacts there. And he couldn't go back to El Salvador. He was marked by the death squads."

The waitress came with our food. As we ate Maria told me how Carlos had met Juanita. Juanita's parents wanted her to learn the language of their new country. He'd been referred to them as an English tutor by a priest they knew. Carlos began taking the train into the city from Lincoln Estates every weekend. Soon he and Juanita had fallen in love.

"Just the same," I said, "maybe you'd better start preparing Juanita that there might not be a storybook ending to this one."

She looked at me, a crease forming between her artfully shaped brows. "Meaning what, Ron?"

"Meaning that I've dealt with cases like this before. When somebody's gone for this long there's got to be a reason. Not always a good reason."

She dropped her gaze to the table.

"Find out what you can from Juanita," I said, squeezing

her hand. "Maybe you can figure out a gentle way to ask her. In any case, with this kind of time frame, she should also be prepared for the worst-case scenario."

"You think he's dead?" she asked, her eyes widening.

"It's possible," I said. She looked down and I touched her hand. "Say, can you make a phone call for me? Carlos's roommate called my answering service and I wanted a native speaker to talk to him."

"Don't tell me you've lost your Spanish," she chided. "It was one of the things that attracted me to you."

That floored me. I hadn't realized that Maria felt attracted to me. So many girls these days had non-sexual relationships with men. She smiled at me, and as I stared at her I saw the hint of a crimson blush start to spread upward along her neck. She grabbed the check and stood up.

"Come on," she said. "I have to get back to work. We can make the call from the office."

"My cell phone's in the car. But let me get the check. I invited you, remember?"

"Won't this count as part of the expenses?" she asked.

"I'll bill you," I said with a grin, snatching the check.

When we went outside I took a moment to appreciate how the sunlight made the highlights of her hair look almost brown. She gave me a soft smile, full of promise. I'd better dig out my Spanish tape, I thought as we walked toward the back of the parking lot. Suddenly a nervous panic swept over me.

No Z-28.

"Wasn't your car over there?"

"Yeah," I said slowly. I looked around one more time. It was gone. We turned around and headed for the front entrance again. I trotted out to the street and gave a futile glance each way. Then we went back inside and I called the police.

It took the blue and white about twenty minutes to arrive, and by that time it was considered too long for a city-wide informational dispatch. Even after I dropped George's name, as well as Lieutenant Bielmaster's, the copper said he still couldn't broadcast it.

"It'll go on the hot sheet," he said. "Usually, if they just took it for a joy ride, it'll be recovered in forty-eight hours. So if you don't hear nothing after that, consider it stripped and chopped."

Stripped and chopped. I thought about the carload of punks that pulled in the lot after we did. I'd assumed they'd been eyeing Maria and me because she was beautiful and Hispanic. But they must have been checking to see if the sap driving a flashy car was going to be tied up for a while. Probably took them all of a minute to get in and peel the column. At least I'd remembered to set the lock code on my cell phone, so nobody'd be able to use that. If only I'd gotten that damn burglar alarm fixed sooner.

Maria put a hand on my arm. "I'm so sorry about your nice car," she said. "And after only three weeks."

"Ups and downs," I said, rubbing my fingers over my temples. "That's the way this whole year's been going for me."

More downs than ups.

Chapter 10

After a quick taxi ride back to DCFS Maria immediately took me to an empty office with a phone and told me to make as many calls as I needed. The first one I made was to Midwestern Olympia Insurance. I'd been dealing with them both as an employer and client for a couple of years. After getting put on hold and transferred twice, I finally got an adjuster named Ms. Davis. She had one of those voices that sounded as if she was always holding her nose.

"Do you know the policy number, sir?" she asked.

I read it off my insurance card. I could hear some typing on a computer keyboard, followed by, "Just a moment please."

I sat and waited, still devastated about my brand new car. Then Ms. Davis came back on the line.

"Mr. Shade?"

"Yes."

"I'm afraid I have some bad news. Your policy was canceled last week."

"Canceled?" I said. "That can't be."

"I'm afraid it is," she continued. "My record shows that your policy was dropped on September twenty-eighth."

My mind raced back over the last month. Had I forgotten to pay it? No, I was sure I had. But with moving out of the office and all, I hadn't been particularly vigilant about opening my mail. It might have been a little late. "Are you sure? I bought a new car and thought the policy would automatically be extended."

More clattering on computer keys. "Yes, sir. My record

shows that your renewal was mailed out in July, and no payment was subsequently received."

"That can't be right. I'm sure I spoke to someone just a couple of weeks ago when I bought the new car. They told me that a premium adjustment would be mailed to me."

"Did you speak to someone in sales or accounting, sir?"

"I don't remember. Look, isn't there something we can do about this? I need my car for work and—"

"I'm sorry, sir," she said, cutting me off. "Our policy is very strict regarding non-payment of premiums."

"But I did pay it, dammit!"

"Sir, I will not put up with verbal abuse."

"Dammit is not verbal abuse. Listen, I can give you some real verbal abuse if you want."

"Mr. Shade," she continued in her whiny voice, "I've adequately explained the situation to the best of my ability. For any further inquiries I'll have to refer you to my supervisor."

I took the name and number of her supervisor and hung up. As I sat there, dazed, trying to figure out how the hell something as basic and necessary as an insurance payment got so goofed up, Maria came in with a cup of coffee in a paper cup.

"Here. Thought you could use this." She looked at me. "Are you all right?"

I took a swallow of the coffee. "Not really. I just found out my insurance policy was canceled."

"On your new car?"

I nodded.

"Oh, Ron. That's terrible. What will you do?"

I wasn't sure. Cathy always took care of my insurance problems when she worked for Midwestern Olympia.

"Not to change the subject, but I thought I could make

that call for you," Maria said gently, touching my hand. "I've only got a few minutes."

I dug the number out of my notebook and listened, trying to pick up some of the conversation as she spoke in rapid Spanish. She paused, placing a hand over the receiver, and looked at me. "He says that Paco's back from Joliet, and that you asked them to call."

I blew out a slow breath. "I need to talk to him. When will he be available?"

Maria made the inquiry and turned back to me.

"He'll be there tonight at about six."

I considered this. I'd have to see if I could get a hold of Julio to accompany me again. And I'd have to get wheels. I told this to Maria, and she offered to drive me out there and translate.

"Are you sure?" I asked. "I hate to bother you."

"It's no bother. I'll tell them we'll be out there tonight."

"Ask if they've heard from Carlos."

"I already did," she said. "They haven't."

She left me by the phone and I contemplated my car situation some more. My first priority had to be getting this insurance problem straightened out. Otherwise I'd be making hefty monthly payments on a Z-28 that would either be re-tagged or chopped up. I stared at the supervisor's name and number that Ms. Davis had given me. The only other person I knew on a professional basis at Midwestern Olympia was Cathy's old boss, Dick MacKenzie. He was one of the honchos in the company, and had even hired me for some investigations a few times in the past. Shade's Law: When you can bypass the middleman and go straight for the top, do it.

The only problem was Dick himself. Cathy had always described him as an original, unadulterated asshole hiding behind whatever obscure policy clause he could to screw somebody, and never taking responsibility for his own mistakes. The dealings that I'd had with him convinced me that she'd been too kind. As far as I was concerned, he was about two hundred and fifty pounds of blubbering bullshit, capped by a bald head. I still knew the number by heart, because it was Cathy's old work number, but it seemed strange when an unfamiliar girl answered.

"Mr. MacKenzie's office." This voice had none of Cathy's musical charm.

I asked for Dick, and told her who I was. A moment later he came on the line.

"Ron-baby, how the hell you doing?"

"I've been better, Dick. How about you?"

We exchanged the usual formalities, and then I got down to brass tacks.

"Dick, I need a favor. My car was stolen, and there seems to be a slight problem with my policy."

"Oh yeah?" he said. "Give me the number."

I did and he put me on hold. A couple of minutes later he came back on the line.

"Hah," he grunted. "Slight problem. Hah. I love the way you always downplay everything, Shade."

So we'd gone from Ron-baby to just Shade. I had a sinking feeling in my gut that this was going to cost me big time.

"I just checked things out and found that you failed to renew your policy."

"That's a mistake. I'll admit that my payment might have been a little late, but—"

"No buts about it, Ron-boy," he boomed. "The question is, what can be done about it, right?"

I sighed. "Yeah."

"Well, I must say, I find this pretty damn ironic. The big time P.I. who stiffed me more times than I can count, is now asking me for help."

"Stiffed you? What are you talking about?"

"How about that overnight trip to Cape Giradeau, for example."

"I was on a case."

"Yeah, right," he said derisively. "I have it on good authority that you didn't go down there alone, either."

Actually, I had taken Cathy with me, but there was no need to confirm this for Dick.

"What about all the money I saved the company by cracking that case?" I said.

"Hell, accounting nearly shit when they saw the expense sheet. Couldn't you've stayed at Motel Six instead of the Holiday Inn?" His voice had taken on a patronizing whine. "And renting two cars. One of 'em a Cadillac."

"Okay, I get the picture. Where do I stand as far as my car?"

"I can look into it," he said slowly. "But let's get one thing straight from the beginning, buddy. If I can get this thing straightened out, and that's a very big *if,* you're really going to owe me."

I said nothing, letting him gloat.

"All right, Ron," he said finally. "Here's what we can do. I'll need you to bring over the full premium amount to my office this afternoon. In cash. Let's see. Better bring an extra two hundred, too. Ah, a late payment fee."

He did some calculations and came up with a figure.

"So that'll take care of it?" I asked.

"Yeah, it should. I can predate a receipt for you and push it through like it was a mistake. But like I said . . ."

"I know. I'm going to owe you. Thanks, Dick. I'll

be there this afternoon."

I had enough money in my bank account to cover it. I hated to dip into my savings like this, but what choice did I have? There was no doubt in my mind that Dick could get it straightened out for me. There was also no doubt in my mind that he would pocket the extra two yards, too. Late payment fee, my ass.

In the meantime, I needed a car, but didn't know if I could swing it without totally maxing out my credit cards. As much as I hated to, when Maria came back I asked her if Juanita would be able to give me an advance so I could afford to pay for a rental car, figuring it was a legitimate expense. Sort of. She said she'd ask, but from her expression I already knew what the answer was likely to be.

I told her to disregard and called George. He wasn't in, so I left a message for him to beep me. Then I said good-bye to Maria and told her I'd be back about four o'clock for our trip to Lincoln Estates.

"What about your car?" she asked.

"I'm going to get that taken care of now. Which way's the El?"

She gave me directions on which bus to take to get to the El. It wasn't really that far, but I was in a hurry so I ended up taking a taxi. It'd been years since I'd ridden the El, or any other form of public transportation for that matter. I trotted up the stairs and bought a ticket downtown.

On the platform a group of young blacks with a blaring boom box playing rap kept me entertained. They eyed me warily, speaking loudly and using extravagant gestures. Maybe they thought I was one of those plainclothes Chicago policemen who rode the CTA as bait for muggers. Why else would a big white guy dressed in blue jeans and a dark jacket be riding the El in this neighborhood?

I strode around the platform trying to exude confidence. But I still found comfort and solace in the reassuring weight of the Beretta on my hip. On one of the shelters a poster for some hair product displayed four female faces. Two black and two white. Somebody'd taken a blade and slashed the two white ones.

When the train pulled up I worked my way to a spot by the door and stood with my back to the wall all the way downtown.

Chapter 11

I stopped at a cash station in the Loop and got enough money to pay off Dick MacKenzie, hoping the damage to my meager savings would be offset by the security deposit from my old office. As long as that payment didn't get lost, too. With the cash in hand, I headed back to Midwestern Olympia. It was a typical fall day in the Loop. The sun was bright on Michigan Avenue as I emerged from the shadows of some skyscrapers. People walked by, appreciating the sudden warm-up, knowing that it wouldn't last long. I cut down Monroe to Wabash. The sun only peeped intermittently between the high concrete caverns as I walked along Jeweler's Row.

While Michigan Avenue, the Magnificent Mile, was more aesthetic, Wabash was pure Chicago. Lots of small shops crammed into the lower sections of the tall buildings. Huge, metallic beams springing from the street to support the tracks of the loudly clacking El. Across the street a young black man played a mellow tune on a saxophone, his hat spread on the sidewalk in front of him. The way things were going I figured I might be out there next to him with a tambourine before too much longer.

The moody tune floated down the street toward me. I thought back to the days when, as a small child with my parents, the Loop was full of people playing all kinds of instruments on every corner and train station downtown. But they were practically extinct now, replaced by the ubiquitous homeless legions selling *StreetWise.* I didn't know whether to blame the city, society, or just hard times in general.

"Hard times," I said as I went by. He nodded, and kept on with his blues tune. It suited my mood to a T.

Midwestern Olympia Insurance was located in the Pittsfield Building on Washington. I went inside to the express elevators and rode up to the nineteenth floor.

I found my way easily down the long marble corridor to the familiar office where I'd been so many times before. But this time, as I pulled open the glass door, I felt deflated. Not only was I going here to grovel in front of the original asshole, but there was no Cathy to brighten the task.

MacKenzie's new secretary was a dour-looking redhead who took my name without even a trace of a smile. After speaking on the phone, she told me to have a seat. I bit my lip and went to the row of chairs in the waiting area. The only recent reading material near the chairs was a financial report on Midwestern Olympia, which attributed the healthy profit margin to the company's greatest asset: its people. After dropping it back on the table, I used the rest of my time to study the surroundings.

The redhead at the desk had nice legs, and she happened to look up at just the right time and saw me checking them out. That brought a reproachful stare. I averted my gaze and looked around at the big office, full of metal desks pushed together and people busily talking on telephones and pounding computer keyboards. I wondered which one was Ms. Davis.

Finally, after keeping me waiting what he must have considered an appropriate length of time, Dick came out with one of his patented, salesman smiles. I stood and shook his hand.

Inside his office he indicated the seat in front of his desk. As soon as I sat down he went around the desk and settled his bulk into an extra-large swivel chair. Then, with a cocky smile, he leaned forward and asked, "You got it?"

I took out the envelope with the money and set it on the desk, resisting the temptation to toss it at him. After all, he was doing me a favor, in a sneaky, half-assed sort of way.

He slit the envelope with a letter opener and counted the money.

"Okay, Ron, here's what we'll do. I'll give you a receipt for the premium dated for September twentieth. Then I'll get your policy reinstated, saying it was an error."

The way he said it made me lose my cool.

"What about the extra two yards?" I asked.

"Huh?"

"The extra two-hundred?"

"Oh, that." He made a dismissive gesture with his hands. "I'll hold on to it just in case I run into some problems. You know, this is against company policy. I could really get my tit in the ringer doing this. But since we're buddies, I'll help you out."

"Haven't you forgotten about the part where I'm gonna owe you?" I said it with a disarming smile.

Dick smiled back.

"That goes without saying."

"I don't suppose the policy included a rental clause, in case my car was stolen?"

"Jesus Christ, Ron. What do you want? I'm going out on a limb as it is."

I nodded, barely controlling my anger. I knew I had to get out of there soon. Luckily, my beeper went off. It was George's work number. I patted my pocket, then remembered I'd left my cell phone in the car.

"You got that receipt?" I asked. "I have to make a call."

"If it's local you can use my office phone," he said generously.

"That's okay."

He nodded ponderously and wrote out a receipt.

"I should be able to get this straightened out by tomorrow," he said. "I'll give you a call."

"Sounds good. Thanks."

I stood to leave, then paused at the door.

"You're sure there won't be any problems?" I asked.

"Ron, baby," he said with a big grin. "Just leave it to your old friend Dick."

He was a dick, all right. But as I went through the office on the way out I took stock in the fact that I'd just been with one of Midwestern Olympia's biggest assets.

Downstairs in the lobby I went to the little tobacco shop and got change for a dollar. I dropped the change into the slot of the pay phone and called George.

"Hey, buddy," he said. "How's it going?"

"Not worth a shit. How about you?"

"Is this the same cheerful young P.I. that I talked to this morning?"

"Yeah, minus my new car."

"What? You have an accident?"

"Stolen." I filled him in.

"Aw, shit, Ron. I'm really sorry. Anything I can do?"

"Well, I was going to ask you if I could borrow the pickup. There's a problem with my insurance, and I really need a car."

"No can do. I got to take it in to get some work done on it." He paused. "You know, Doug's got an old car that he might be able to loan you. Just a second."

He put me on hold. After about a minute he came back on.

"Doug says it'll be no problem. As long as you remember about that promise to get us tickets to your next fight."

"For a favor like this, I'll get you tickets to all of 'em."

"Come by my place tonight, and I'll drive you over there," he said. "Oh, by the way, the reason I called in the first place was to tell you that I checked the morgue. No unidentified male Hispanics at this time."

"Thanks for checking, brother. I'll see you tonight."

It was still relatively early in the afternoon. As much as I dreaded it, I walked back to the El. By the time I got back over to DCFS, Maria would probably be just about ready to get off.

Chapter 12

When I called Maria from the El stop she told me to stay where I was. She'd already made plans to get off early and would come by and pick me up. That way we'd be close to the expressway and it'd be a straight shot out to Lincoln Estates. As I waited, I watched the people getting off the El. They looked back at me suspiciously, recognizing that I wasn't a regular and didn't belong in that neighborhood. Stranger in a strange land. All in all, I didn't regret not having to traverse the hostile, unfamiliar territory between the El and DCFS.

Maria pulled up about ten minutes later in her tan Honda. Her face looked grim, and I asked her if she'd had a particularly rough day.

"Every day is rough at that place," she said, then smiled. "But at least my car didn't get stolen."

I laughed.

"Did you get your insurance problem straightened out?"

"Yeah, more or less. But it cost me."

We passed the rest of the trip without mentioning my car again. The conversation gradually drifted to my kick-boxing activities, and Maria said she'd like to come to the championship match.

"It's gonna be in West Palm Beach, Florida," I said. "Still interested?"

"Hmm," she said with a sly grin. "I'll have to let you know on that one."

I pondered the possibilities of her answer in silence. Was she hinting that she was interested in me? She was a knockout, that was for sure. Then she asked me about Carlos.

"This conversation we're going to have with Paco should be enlightening," I said. "He was working at the same place until they fired him."

We called the apartment from a little restaurant just off the expressway. I didn't want to surprise them by knocking at the door and having them worry it was *la migra.* Paco was in and we went right over.

He was a small man with a sparse-looking mustache. I let Maria do the talking because he looked at me and smiled, *"No ingles."*

I listened to their fluent Spanish, trying to pick up as much of the conversation as I could. I got the basic gist of it.

"Ask him if Carlos and he went to work together last Friday," I said.

Maria asked him, and he replied that they had.

"Was Carlos drunk?" I said. *"Barracho?"*

Paco looked surprised and pointed a finger toward himself.

"Me?" he asked.

Maria laughed and corrected the question. Then translated his reply.

"He said that Carlos wasn't drunk that night. He hadn't been drinking at all."

"What time did they go in?"

"I already asked that," she said. "Two o'clock. They usually worked till ten. Sometimes later."

"Exactly what kind of stuff do they do over there?"

After a brief conversation she turned back to me.

"He says it's a big warehouse. They store things there. Sometimes they load items into trucks. Sometimes they unload the trucks."

"Did he say what time Carlos left?"

More conversation. Maria's brow furrowed as she listened.

"Paco says they both worked their regular shift. They wanted Carlos to stay longer because they had some special work to do and Carlos spoke English." Her dark eyes flashed for a moment. "Didn't you tell me they said they fired him for showing up drunk?"

"Yeah," I said. "Is Paco here an illegal?"

"I'm afraid so," she said.

I blew out a slow breath. "What type of work were they doing that day?"

He told us that they were moving metal barrels from a special section in the warehouse. It was a job everybody dreaded because the barrels smelled very bad.

"How often did they do this?"

"About once or twice a month."

"Is there anything else that he remembers about that day?" I asked. "When was the last time he saw Carlos?"

Maria asked and then translated his answer: "Paco says that Enrique, that's the Mexican they have there as one of the foremen, told him that Carlos was going to stay later. Work overtime." She turned and spoke to him again. "Carlos didn't tell him that himself. But the plant's so big that he didn't think anything of it. He just went home."

"And that was the last time he saw him?"

She nodded. "There is one other thing. He says Carlos and a man named Frank had an argument shortly before it was time to go home."

"An argument? What about?"

"He doesn't know," she said.

"Ask him if he remembers anything at all about it," I said. "This could be important."

"No entendia mucho," Paco replied. He didn't understand much of it. Maria pressed him and his lips compressed inward as he concentrated. Finally, he said that he did recall Carlos and Big Frank arguing over some sort of *simbolo,* but wasn't sure what it was about.

"Simbolo?" I asked. "What does that mean in English?"

"Symbol," she said. "It's a cognate."

"Ask him what type of symbol they were arguing about."

Maria spoke to him but Paco only shook his head slowly. Then he snapped his fingers and got up suddenly. We watched as he went to the kitchen area and paged through the newspaper that had been sitting on the counter. Apparently not finding what he was looking for he called to one of the other guys who was in the back room. There was a muffled response, and Paco went to the garbage can. He removed several items, then found a wrinkled copy of the *Chicago Sun-Times.* He paged through it licking his finger every few pages. Then he stopped, tore a page loose, and brought it over to Maria and me.

He pointed eagerly to an article on the Field Museum using magnetic fields to date fossils. I glanced quizzically at Maria.

"What's this mean?" I asked.

"He says the symbol looked something like this picture," she said, pointing to the illustration. It showed a bar graph and a directional compass. Paco traced his stubby finger around the open lid of the compass. Its circular face was enclosed in an octagonal frame.

I gave him my pen and he drew a crude circle inside of a hexagon.

"That mean anything to you?" I asked Maria.

She shook her head. I folded the article and the drawing and slipped them into my pocket.

We thanked Paco for his help and started back toward the city. I took about ten minutes to write up a summary of our conversation in my notebook. Then I asked Maria what she thought.

"It seems strange," she said. "The differences in the stories between him and the employers."

"Sure does. Obviously, there was some kind of trouble that they're trying to cover up at Space Oddities."

"What do you think that means, Ron?"

"I'm not sure, but it gives me something else to work on. Say, are you hungry? I'd like to take you to dinner for helping me."

She glanced at me briefly and smiled. I watched her sleek hand manipulate the gearshift lever up to fifth gear as we entered the expressway.

"I appreciate the offer," she said. "I really do. But I don't think it would be a good idea tonight. I have to work tomorrow, and still have a hectic drive after I drop you off. And I'm sure Juanita will want to know what's been going on."

"Have you talked to her?"

"If you mean have I told her how grave the situation appears, the answer is no. Not yet."

"That might be a mistake," I said.

"I know, but I can't bring myself to shatter her dreams unless I really have to."

I told her that I could understand her point of view.

"Can you drop me off at my buddy George's house?" I said. "It's on the way."

"Is he the one who's going to lend you the car?"

"Yeah."

"It must be nice to have such good friends." She smiled.

Yeah, I thought. It sure was.

Chapter 13

It was close to six when Maria dropped me off at George's. I thanked her again for helping me, and she said she'd take a rain check on the dinner. George was just sitting down to supper and Ellen insisted that I join them. Never one to turn down a home-cooked meal, I readily accepted. Midway through the dessert I began to regret it, however, because I remembered that I still had Chappie's workout ahead of me tonight. And asking Chappie to take it easy because I'd had a rough day was like asking the Pope if it was all right to skip midnight mass on Christmas Eve.

After explaining most of the details of my upcoming fight to George, Ellen, and their three kids, I discreetly asked George about the car.

"Oh yeah," he said. "I'll go give Pers a call."

A minute later he came back.

"All set," he said. "Let's go pick it up."

Doug Percy lived a few blocks away from George in Mount Greenwood. We pulled up in front of the house, a tan brick structure with a well-kept lawn and several big evergreen bushes planted in a row below the picture window. Doug was sitting on the steps smoking a cigarette. He nodded a hello.

"Here for the Beater?" he asked.

The Beater? I suddenly wondered about this arrangement.

Doug stood up and we walked across the lawn to the sidewalk that led back to the garage. There was an audible hum of a motor as we got closer.

"I got the battery charger on it, Ron," he said. "I haven't driven it in awhile so the battery went dead."

I grinned. You never look a gift horse in the mouth. Doug opened the side door and we stepped inside the garage. Next to his Olds Cutlass sat a big, cream-colored Pontiac Catalina. The long hood was up and the battery charger sputtered loudly on the floor in front of it. I could see why Doug had called it the Beater.

At one time it had probably been a nice car. But that was a couple of decades ago, and it had managed to survive every Chicago winter in between. But just barely. The rear fender sections were about gone from rust, and the front ones had enough holes to pass for an Afghan taxi. It had one of those half-landau roofs, except the landau had long since departed. And it was about twice as long as any car I'd driven in the last fifteen years. But the price was right. And with all the Fraternal Order of Police and Illinois Police Association stickers on the windshield I wouldn't have to worry about parking tickets.

"She runs good, Ron," Doug said. "Even though she doesn't look like much."

"She looks pretty good to me, Doug. I really appreciate this."

Doug disconnected the battery charger and lowered the hood. I got in and twisted the key in the ignition. The Beater started with a groan, then the engine began to hum powerfully. The interior was so enormous I felt like I was driving a tank. It took me three times before I was able to negotiate out of Doug's garage, due to the presence of a telephone pole across the alley.

"Someday I gotta get the city to condemn that pole," Doug laughed.

I thanked him again.

"No sweat," he said with a grin. "Don't forget about the fight tickets."

"I won't," I assured him, feeling a little bit guilty about not telling them that the fight was in Florida. But maybe I could get the promoter to spring for a couple of extra corner men.

"I'm going to work out. Either of you two want to come along?"

"Are you kidding?" George said. "After a meal like that?"

I said good-bye and drove down the alley. At the street I braked and switched on the radio. The in-dash was an AM only, but there was an FM converter mounted underneath. After a few minutes of heavy static, I found a decent light rock FM station that would lock in. But by the time I got to my house, the static had taken over again.

The cats came running when I opened the door. Something they probably wouldn't have even considered if they weren't hungry. Shasha rubbed up against my leg coquettishly while Georgio canted his head and gave a bewildered cry. I opened a can for them and plunked half of it down in their respective dishes. After checking my mail and making sure that the timers on my lights were operating, I grabbed my gear and headed for the gym.

Chapter 14

The next morning was chilly, so I dug out an additional sweatshirt to wear during my run. The hooded shirt had the pungent odor of my dried sweat. I made a mental note to toss the clothes in the washer while I showered. To protect my hands from the wind I wore my bag gloves. As I started out I felt tired and stiff. My breath was a wispy vapor in front of my face.

I threw some more punches as I came up to my first hill. Agony One. It seemed steeper than usual so I looked down at the ground in front of me and just kept putting one foot in front of the other. The grass was covered with a hint of frost.

By the time I cleared Miss Agony I was starting to feel renewed. A good run usually does that for me. For the last quarter mile my thoughts turned to the title fight, and I kept imagining Anthony Berger staggering away from me, bloodied and dazed, as I moved in for the knockout. The last hundred yards I even managed a sprint.

After showering, feeding the cats, and grabbing a bagel with cream cheese, I sat down and decided to plan out my day. I listed my run and workout first, then drew a line through the run with a great sense of satisfaction. I'd already accomplished something. I wrote: insurance, Maria, and 2001. I had to call Dick MacKenzie to check on that policy problem, touch bases with Maria, and I figured I'd pay a visit to Space Oddities to see how Big Frank Bristol could explain the discrepancies between his and Paco's accounts of Carlos's last day.

Since I didn't have my cell phone anymore, I decided to call Dick right away. It was almost nine and I figured he'd be in. The secretary said that he wasn't, but if I wanted to leave a number she expected him in a few minutes. I wondered if it was the same redhead that I'd seen there yesterday. I didn't want to wait on Dick to phone, so I told her I'd call back.

After loading the Beretta and slipping it in the pancake holster on my right side, I put on a necktie and got out a black leather jacket. It would look dressy and still be warm enough with the sudden temperature drop. I went out to the garage and hit the switch for the automatic door opener. I'd managed to fit the Beater inside, but there was only about an inch of clearance on each end.

When I twisted the key nothing happened. I tried again with the same result. After popping the hood and fiddling with the battery cables, I switched on the lights to see if the battery might be dead again. No lights. Since I'd spent my youth working out in gyms instead of working on cars, I knew next to nothing about them. I closed the door and went back in the house to call the neighborhood gas station for a jump.

While I was waiting for the tow truck I called Dick again. Miraculously, he was in this time.

"This is Dick MacKenzie," he boomed into the phone. "May I help you?"

"You sound a lot politer today," I said.

"What? Who is this? Shade?"

"Good guess. What's the situation on my policy?"

"Oh, I should be able to get to it sometime today," he said matter-of-factly.

"Sometime today? I thought you'd have it taken care of by now."

"Look, Ron. These things take time. Besides," he paused, "I've been kind of busy lately."

I figured that he was stalling because he wanted something. Probably more money. I said nothing.

"Look," he said finally. "Give me a call back this afternoon, I should know something by then."

I thanked him and said I would. After I hung up I felt mad enough to dance around the living room throwing combinations at an imaginary opponent. But this time, instead of Anthony Berger, it was Dick MacKenzie.

Bob Matulik put the cables on the battery terminals and adjusted the rev of the charger. Over the sputtering roar he said, "Try it."

I did. Still nothing.

"Shit," he said. "She's really dead, ain't she? We'll leave the charger on for a few more minutes."

Finally, it did kick over. Bob cut off the charger and removed the cables.

"Why don't you follow me to the station, Ron, and we'll check her out," he said as he lowered the hood.

I figured that would be wise. Rather than paying for jumps all day.

"What do you think it is?" I asked.

"Could be the alternator," Bob said. "Or something shorting out, draining the battery. Then again, the battery looks pretty old. Maybe she just don't hold a charge no more."

When we got to the garage, things were so backed up that they told me it would take at least an hour to get it diagnosed, removed, and replaced. Since I was running short on time, and patience has never been one of my strong points, I decided to go with a new battery. Well, not exactly a new one. Bob had some recharged trade-ins. I told them to put in something that would last a year. Anything else, for that jalopy, would have been flattery.

Despite Bob's guarantee that the battery would perform like a champ, and the twenty-minute expressway drive to Lincoln Estates, I took an extra few minutes to locate the nearest full-service gas station to Space Oddities. In case the Beater decided to act up again, I wanted to know how far I'd have to walk. And since the advent of self-serve gas pumps, full-service stations have become almost as rare as dinosaurs.

The parking lot at Two Thousand and One had maybe twenty cars in it. There was a big maroon Lincoln Towncar parked near the front doors. I remembered the car from the last time. It took me about ten minutes to jot down all the plates in the lot, with a description of each car. Then I went inside and asked to speak to Big Frank. The security guard behind the glass cubicle radioed to somebody and presently another uniformed guard appeared.

I recognized this guy. His stringy blond hair was slicked back and there were heavy bags under his eyes. As he pointed the hatchet-like nose at me I could tell he recognized me too. I smiled and looked at his nametag. It was brushed silver and had N. Coral printed across it.

"You here to see Big Frank?" he asked.

I nodded.

"Well, come this way then," he said, motioning for me to follow. We stepped around the cubicle and over to a hallway. It led past a room with a time clock, a lunchroom, and opened out into a huge expanse. From the outside, the building looked two stories high, but inside there was no second floor. Just a very big room with a fifty-foot ceiling. What had at one time been a factory filled with auto part machines, now was just stack after stack of various pallets, sacks, boxes, and whatever. Space oddities, I guessed.

The factory wasn't what you'd call brightly lit. High-pressure sodium vapor lights hung suspended from the corrugated metal ceiling. They gave off a faint humming sound. Although the lighting was adequate, the towering stacks, which extended thirty feet or more in some places, created large shadowy areas. Security-Nick led me to a spot by the entrance. There was a solid yellow line painted on the floor. It extended around the perimeter of the interior.

"What did this place used to be?" I asked, trying to get some conversation out of Nick.

He shrugged.

"Well, what kinds of stuff do you store in it now?"

"You name it," was all he said. He picked up a phone and dialed a quick number.

I looked around some more and saw a large, elevated structure in the middle of the floor. It appeared to be a group of offices, or perhaps a supervisor's section, set on pilings that allowed an overview of the entire facility. A stairway descended from one side, but the rest of my view was blocked by a section of stacked boxes. Suddenly I saw movement, and Big Frank shot around one of the stacks in some sort of small, motorized vehicle that looked something like a golf cart. He pulled up in front of me and shut it off.

"Mr. Shade," he said, sliding off the seat and grinning with the assurance of a big man. "What can I do for you?"

"Mr. Bristol, I wanted to thank you for your help at the bar the other day." I glanced at Security-Nick.

Bristol nodded. His lower lip was drawn up tight, giving him sort of a smug look.

"I wanted to go over the details of Carlos's last day if I could," I said.

"Still ain't found him, huh?"

"No. Can you tell me again about that last time you saw him?"

He raised his finger and scratched his temple, pushing back the yellow hard hat he was wearing.

"Not much to tell you really. He showed up crocked so I fired him. We got too many ways a guy can get hurt around here if he's not careful." He gestured at the cart. "Got lots of equipment. Forklifts too. Can't have no drunks around that kind of stuff."

"Did he work at all that day?" I asked.

"He might've punched in, but as soon as I saw what kind of condition he was in, I bounced him."

"How did he take it?"

"What do you mean?"

"Was he argumentative?" I asked. Then quickly added, "Carlos could speak English, couldn't he?"

"Yeah, he could speak English," Big Frank said. "And I told you, people usually don't argue with me."

"Do you have his time card?"

The protruding lower lip tucked inside his mouth for a second.

"I suppose. Why?"

"I was wondering if I could take a look at it."

Big Frank's mouth gaped slightly and his head rocked back and forth.

"Why you want to see it?"

"Just to see what time he punched out."

"He didn't. I signed him out. Now, what are you driving at?"

"Well, Mr. Bristol," I said. "Without breaking tradition and being argumentative, I did obtain a slightly different version of the events of that day. I wanted to try and—"

"From that other beaner Paco, I'll bet," he interjected.

I looked up at him, but said nothing.

"Well, that little fucker got fired too. He was just as bad as the other one when it came to showing up drunk." Bristol looked agitated.

"Don't you want to hear what he told me?" I asked.

"Listen, Shade," he said. "I don't give a shit what he said. What *I* said's the truth. That son-of-a-bitch probably wants to try and be paid for the whole day's work. Well, he ain't. Not even close."

"Mr. Bristol," I said. "I'm impressed. You figured out what Paco told me without my even telling you."

Big Frank snorted. "You know," he said slowly, "if it's one thing I can't stand it's a smart ass."

"Me too," I said.

He looked at me for a moment. Like he was sizing me up. I automatically adjusted my position so that I could step out of his range and, at the same time, give Security-Nick a good swift kick if I had to. But Bristol just told Nick to call Enrique.

"Shade," he said. "I'm gonna tell you this one more time. Then I hope I don't see you any more, for your sake. When Carlos showed up for work he was drunk and I fired him."

"Did you two have an argument?"

"He wasn't happy, if that's what you mean. I wouldn't really call it an argument."

"Where was Paco during this time?"

"I don't know where that lazy bastard was hiding. What'd he tell you?"

"He told me that he and Carlos worked the entire shift and were asked to hold over."

"She-it," Big Frank said.

Enrique pulled up on another one of those golf carts and parked his next to Bristol's. He sauntered up to the big man.

"Yeah, Frank," he said.

"Rico, I want you to tell Mr. Shade here that Carlos was fired when he showed up drunk for work that day."

"That's right," Enrique said, his dark face impassive.

"Can't get much plainer than that," I said.

"And if that wetback's claiming him and Carlos worked the whole day it's probably cause he's trying to squeeze a full day's pay for not working. Well, it ain't gonna work." Big Frank used a pointed finger to punctuate the sentence.

I looked at his buddy Enrique.

"A wetback?" I asked.

"Hey," he said with a smirk, "I was born here, man."

Chapter 15

Since my conversation with Big Frank and Enrique had gone so well, I figured I'd used up my bad luck quota for the day. But I was wrong. When I turned the key in the Beater all it did was make a funny sound and not start. I popped the hood and jiggled the battery cables. The terminals looked tight and clean, except for a layer of grease that Bob had put on them. I was trying to wipe the grease off my fingers when I heard a feminine voice behind me.

"Having trouble?" the voice asked.

It was the strawberry blond girl I'd seen on my first trip out here. I smiled as charmingly as I could.

"Yeah, I guess so. My battery seems to be dead."

She returned my smile.

"Didn't I see you out here on Tuesday?" she asked.

"Yeah. Ron Shade's the name." I started to extend a hand for her to shake, then stopped after noticing the grease.

"Kelly Lipton," she laughed. "Sorry, I didn't mean to laugh. I can give you a jump if you want."

I raised my eyebrows and told her that would be great, thinking to myself that one without cables and batteries would be preferable. She walked to her car, the maroon Lincoln, and pulled it over in front of the Beater. After popping the hood, she went into the trunk and took out a set of jumper cables.

I lifted her hood and connected them. Kelly came up as I was hooking them on and scrutinized my work. Satisfied that I'd put the proper cable to each terminal she looked at me and asked if I knew what the problem was.

"I really don't," I said. "My car was stolen and I just borrowed this one from a friend. Put a new battery in this morning, too."

"Probably a short then," she said knowingly.

I was biting my lip at being reminded, for the second time today, that I knew next to nothing about cars. This time by a young girl.

"Why don't you get in and try to start it?" she said.

I did and it started right up. Kelly disconnected the cables and threw them in her trunk. I got out to thank her.

"That's okay," she said. "Maybe you can help me out someday."

"Well, at least let me buy you lunch." It was getting near noon.

She glanced at her watch, then looked up.

"Okay," she said. "Where do you want to go?"

"You pick it. My treat," I said, hoping that I'd remembered to put my American Express card in my wallet.

We went to a Greek restaurant near the expressway. A dark-haired hostess seated us in a comfortable booth in the non-smoking section. I ordered a salad and Kelly had a chicken sandwich. It was the kind of lunch that I could eat and not feel guilty when thinking about the weight that Chappie'd been leaning on me to lose.

"I'm surprised you remembered me from Tuesday," I said.

"Well, actually I didn't," she said. "I'd seen you before that."

I looked at her quizzically. She giggled.

"At your fight last summer against Elijah Day in Rosemont."

"Oh?"

"My *sensei* took a group of us to see it," she said. "I've been studying Tae Kwon Do for five years."

"I see," I said, recalling the muscularity of her legs.

"I've got my black belt," she added. "I've competed in a few tournaments. The traditional kind. But I've always been fascinated by full-contact. I even thought about trying it."

"I wouldn't recommend it," I said.

"Why? Because I'm a woman?"

I stared at her for a moment, thinking that at her tender age I wasn't sure if I'd call her a woman.

"Not at all. It's just that there's no money in it. Compared to regular boxing, that is. So it becomes a question of taking a chance on losing your looks and possibly your brains for a small price tag."

She looked at me for half a beat, then said, "Your looks don't appear to have suffered too badly."

I took that for an overt bit of flirting, but I decided I'd better ignore it.

"Yeah, but I've been lucky. Most full contact fighters end up with a whole lot of injuries and not much money. Anyway, don't get me started on that. How did you get interested in the arts?"

"It was after my father took off," she said. "Tom, that's my stepfather, enrolled me in a class for self-defense. I liked it and stayed."

"Was that who you were with the other day?"

"Yeah," she said. "Tom and my father were partners. Did you ever hear of L and M Trucking?"

I shook my head.

"The L stands for Lipton. That's my fath—, my stepfather's name. My dad was Wayne McKay. He disappeared ten years ago."

"I'm sorry."

She nodded.

"Well, like I said, Tom and my father were business partners. After my real dad skipped, Tom took over the company and turned things completely around. It was practically bankrupt when my dad took off. Some money disappeared about the same time, but Tom never made an issue of it. He even kept the name L and M and continued to split the profits with my mother. After a few years my mom filed for divorce and married Tom. He's been a great father to me."

"Sounds like he's a real special guy."

"Oh, he is," she said emphatically. "You've never heard of him? He's a member of the Will County Board. Running for the President's spot this time."

"I don't follow too many political races outside of Cook County," I said.

"Oh, you Chicago people are all alike," she said with a smile.

"Well, for what it's worth, I hope your father wins. What's his connection to Space Oddities? Lincoln Estates is in Cook County."

"Harold Jordan's the plant supervisor there," she said. "He's been a friend of ours for the longest time. Sort of an honorary uncle, he's so close to us."

"How's business going for Uncle?" I asked.

"Pretty well, I guess. They've been talking of expanding."

Suddenly my beeper went off. It was Maria's work number. I excused myself and got some change from the hostess. There were some pay phones in the glass foyer by the front doors. I dialed the number and managed to drop in half the change, waiting while on hold. Finally Maria came on the line.

"Hi, Ron," she said. "Sorry to keep you waiting so long, but I was tied up."

"That's okay. What's up?"

"I was wondering if you've made any progress on finding Carlos?"

"Not much," I said. "Why?"

"I know this church in Pilsen," she said slowly. "The priest specializes in helping illegals. I thought we could go talk to him. There's sort of a network out there of illegals. Maybe somebody heard something."

"It's worth a try. But I might need some help. Can you go with me?"

"Sure. Could you come by my place at about six, or so?"

"I'll be there," I said. If the Beater is willing, I thought.

I went back inside and told Kelly I had to leave. I thanked her again for the jump. She thanked me for the lunch and insisted on giving me her number, in case I needed her help on this case. I gave her one of my cards with my answering service and beeper numbers on it. I figured the kid had a crush on me when I saw her waiting in her car until I got The Beater started. If she were only a few years older.

On the way back to the city I pondered the lack of any significant developments in the case. Besides the obvious fact that Big Frank, for whatever reason, was lying to me about Carlos's last day, I still didn't know much more than when I started. The Space Oddities connection bothered me though. There was something there, all right. Like a water moccasin hiding under a log in murky water.

When I pulled into Bob's gas station he was leaning inside the hood of a Ford Bronco. I told him about the problem I'd had earlier in Lincoln Estates.

"Aw, shit, Ron," he said. "I'm sorry. Guess it is a short after all."

"How long will that take to fix?"

He looked at his watch, then shook his head.

"Could be an all day affair," he said. "We'll have to go through the loom till we find it."

I glanced at my watch. It was one o'clock.

"If I leave it here could you get to it today?"

"Sure," he said. "We finished up all the business from this morning. I can put Todd on it. He's pretty good at finding shorts."

"Especially if there's a nice looking pair of female legs sticking out of 'em," Todd said from the other side of the Bronco.

I grinned and thanked them. Todd gave me a ride to my house and I called Maria back and told her about my car problem.

"You want me to drive then?" she asked.

"Let me get back to you," I said. "I've got to squeeze a quick workout in and then get back to the garage to find out what's up."

"Okay," she said wearily. "I could use some time to relax myself. I'll wait for you at my place."

"Great," I said.

After hanging up I quickly sorted out my gear. Luckily I didn't live too far from Western Avenue and the buses ran pretty regularly. I could take the bus down to 99th Street just like I used to do when I was a kid.

I pulled a stocking cap out of my bag and slipped it on. The warm weather of the earlier part of the day was fading fast. I saw the bus accelerating from mid-block. I frantically ran for it waving my arms. The driver gave me an abbreviated nod as he sped past me down the street. He waited for me at the next corner and I climbed aboard. Maybe, I thought as I handed him the fare, my luck was beginning to change.

Chapter 16

The workout didn't rate with one of my best, but at least Chappie was absent. Brice told me that Chappie had left about noon and said he'd be back later. I told Brice to tell him that I might not make it in for a workout tonight. Hopefully, for Brice's sake, Chappie wouldn't kill the messenger.

Going through the paces of one of my toned-down sessions is usually enjoyable. Although I worked up a good sweat, I knew that I wasn't pushing myself as hard as Chappie would. I remembered Elijah Day's mistake of underestimating Berger and vowed not to make the same one. But then again, Day had been training for a fight with me originally and Berger was selected as a replacement.

If that was significant, it escaped me as I pounded out a final rhythm on the speed bag. Hopefully Chappie would not be too upset at me missing tonight. But hell, I had to give my job first priority. That's what paid the bills.

By the time I was riding back on my return trip it was almost four. Everything was related to the loss of my new car, I decided. Then I remembered that I was supposed to call Dick and check on the insurance mess. But he'd be long gone by the time I got to a phone. The bus dropped me off across the street from Bob's garage. The Beater was parked by the curb at the rear of the station. Inside Bob greeted me with a big grin.

"Hey, Ron, your luck must be working overtime today," he said. "Todd found that short in about ten minutes."

"It was in the connection for that FM converter," Todd

said. “I had a hunch that it might be there, so I checked that first.”

“Hopefully that’ll be it now,” Bob said. “By the way, what happened to the Z-28?”

“Got stolen yesterday.”

“Aww, shit, no,” he said.

“Aww, shit, yes,” I answered. “How much I owe you for the Beater?”

“The Beater,” he said with a laugh. “I like that. Sure fits too.”

“I dunno,” said Todd. “It ain’t so bad engine-wise. Got a big 350.”

“Yeah,” I said, taking out my wallet. “That reminds me, let me add a fill-up to the bill.”

Filling it up I found that the Beater also had a huge, twenty-five gallon tank. I used Bob’s phone to call Maria’s house. There was no answer, but I left a message on her machine telling her I was on my way. After paying Bob, I had to stop at the bank again to visit the cash station machine. At the rate I was going, I would have to get some money from either Maria or Juanita soon if I were going to continue with the case. Because of my friendship with Maria, I hadn’t even asked for a retainer. I mentally added that to my long list of mistakes for the past couple of days.

Maria’s apartment building was on 24th and Troy. Figuring the expressway would be too mobbed with rush hour traffic, I took Western north. It took me about twenty-five minutes to make the drive, and another fifteen looking for a parking space. Finally, remembering the police stickers on the windshield, I pulled into an alley and walked to Maria’s building.

The name beside the buzzer for three-north said

M. Castro. I punched it and listened. Maria's voice inquired who it was and I told her. The apartment security door buzzed, and I pushed it open. I trotted up the three flights and met her on the landing. She'd changed into a pair of dressy-looking blue jeans and was sipping from a cup.

"Come on in, Ron," she said. "Do you want some coffee?"

I declined as I followed her in, realizing that, in all the time I'd known her, this was the first time that I'd ever been inside her apartment. There was a small hallway that led into a larger living room. Two bedrooms were off to the side. Everything looked neat and clean in the bedroom. The only sign of disorder in the living room were a *Chicago Tribune* spread out on the coffee table and a *TV Guide* perched atop a nineteen-inch portable. The walls were a light beige color and above the sofa was a huge painting of a city silhouette. On the opposite wall was a crucifix.

"I guess you want to leave right away," she said, slipping on a black leather, waist-length jacket.

"Probably be a good idea," I said. "Is Juanita going to come with us?"

"She wanted to," Maria said, smiling. "Is that okay?"

"Sure," I said, thinking maybe I could hit her up for some expense money.

After picking up Juanita we got under way. She lived in a three-flat a couple of houses down. Her father, a stern-looking man with a gray mustache, eyed me warily. I decided not to try to impress him with any of my fledgling Spanish. If it hadn't been for Maria's presence I doubted that he would have let Juanita go with me. But considering the heavy, dark coat, stocking cap, and faded blue jeans that I had on I couldn't blame him. If I had a daughter, I wouldn't let her go with me, either.

We took Western again. The church was about a block away from Humboldt Park. It was one of those hugely ornate structures that had been built in the twenties with two smaller steeples on either side of a larger one. The building itself was fancy gray brick, and the cement finishers had taken particular care to place a flourish design on the blocks at each corner. It extended in back to another building, which I assumed was a school. I pulled the Beater into an empty spot near the mouth of the alley.

Inside, the place was pretty empty. A lone nun seemed to know Juanita and spoke to her in Spanish. Juanita introduced Maria and me, and the nun left us in the chapel. The pews were solid oak and well varnished, with lots of hand-carved decorations. The ceiling was high and vaulted, the windows brilliant combinations of blues, reds, and golds. Above each stained-glass window was a different station of Christ. I looked down toward the altar, which showed more of the same craftsmanship, and thought how long it'd been since I'd been in church. Not in recent memory, that's for sure.

"Juanita, como estas?" I heard someone say. Turning, I saw a small, dark man with salt and pepper hair and a Roman collar. He moved forward and took both Juanita's hands in his own. After going through the introductions again, he smiled and shook my hand. His grip was strong. Maria introduced him as Father Felipe.

"May I see your driver's license and identification, Mr. Shade?" he said. "I'm sorry, but I cannot afford to be too trusting."

I took out my wallet and handed him my driver's license and the photostat of my private investigator's license.

"I'm listed in the book under shady P.I.s," I said with a grin.

As he scrutinized the two items, both Juanita and Maria opened up on him in rapid-fire Spanish. The priest glanced at me, nodding his head, as he listened. They spoke so quickly I was only able to pick up a few words here and there. He nodded again and handed my IDs back.

"My apologies if I seemed to doubt you, Mr. Shade," he said. "But, as I said, I cannot afford to be too trusting. Both of these young ladies speak very highly of you. They say you are a man of integrity."

"No apologies necessary," I said, pocketing my wallet.

"Come," Father Felipe said, bowing slightly and gesturing toward an office area to the right. "We can go in my office and Sister Helena will make us some coffee."

The room was well furnished with a heavy oak desk and some comfortable chairs. I let the women sit and remained standing.

"You know why we're here, Father?" I asked.

"I have heard," he said.

I removed the Polaroid of Carlos and handed it to him. He took it and blew a slow breath from his pursed lips.

"Ah, yes. Carlos," he said. "There is great trouble in his country now. He was marked for death by *los escuadadrones de muerte* because of his belief in freedom and justice. He is a courageous man."

"So he's not the type to disappear unexpectedly?" I asked. "The people at his job said he showed up drunk."

"Carlos?" Father Felipe shook his head. "I doubt that very much. Despite him working here for minimum wage, he was not . . ." He let his voice trail off. "Did you know that he has a degree in chemical engineering?"

"I'd heard that he was quite educated."

"And a very nice person, *tambien.*" He handed the picture back. "But I'm afraid I have not seen him recently."

"When was the last time?"

He stroked his chin pensively.

"I would have to say it has been about a month. He and Juanita came here to discuss, with me, getting married." A slight smile traced over his lips. "I recommended him to Juanita's father when he sought a teacher of English. You see, Carlos was one of the many that we brought here through our special channels."

"Can you think of any reason that he would have for leaving?" I asked.

He shook his head slowly.

"How about any place he might run to if he were in trouble?"

"He had nowhere else to go," Father Felipe said. "As I said, he was marked for death in El Salvador."

"Could they have found him here?" I said.

The priest shook his head.

"I do not think so. The men who threatened him are ruthless, but they have no power outside of their own little arena."

I felt that the interview was shaping up to be another dead end, but at least I was getting further confirmation on one of the two very different portraits I had of Carlos. I asked a few more questions about his personal habits. The priest was courteous, but not really helpful. Sister Helena came in with a silver coffee pot and several cups. We each took one and she poured. The coffee was a rich South American blend. So strong that I had to put lots of extra cream in it.

"I was told by one man that Carlos had a heated argument with his boss the day he was fired. Was he argumentative?"

"I cannot really say," the priest answered, setting his cup

down. "People do not often argue with me." He smiled to show me that his statement was intended to be on the humorous side.

"Funny, that's exactly what his boss told me."

My beeper went off. I checked the number and saw that it was George's work number. I asked Father Felipe if I could use his phone. He took me into an adjacent room which must have been a secondary office. On top of the desk was an old rotary phone. I thanked him and he left.

George came on the line after a few rings.

"Grieves," he said.

"Is that any way for a dedicated public servant to answer the phone? Suppose it was the mayor calling?"

"I figured it was you," he said. "If you aren't working out, or getting laid, you usually answer my pages right away."

"Ha ha," I said. "Did you find my car yet?"

"Haven't been looking," he retorted. "How's the Beater running?"

"Just fine."

"Well, look, Ron. Do me a favor, okay? When you're going to return it, at least fill it up, will ya? I went out on a limb asking Pers to lend it to you."

I closed my eyes and blew out a slow breath.

"Is that why you beeped me? To tell me that?"

"No," he said. "I was looking over the type-threes and found an entry about an unidentified male Hispanic. Fits the age and general description of the one you asked me to look out for."

"Where'd they find him?"

"Floating in the Cal Sag," George answered. "Been in the water at least a couple of days. Maybe a week. DCI entered it."

"Thanks, George," I said. "I appreciate it."

I hung up the phone and leaned back to stare at the ceiling. Juanita's voice was audible through the closed door. I was glad Maria and Father Felipe were with her.

Chapter 17

I took Western down to Cermak then cut over to California to get to Harrison. The morgue is not the most cheerful place to visit. Luckily, the priest and Maria had elected to accompany us. It was not something that I wanted to do at all with Juanita, much less alone with her. After explaining who we were, and why we were there, they took us down a carpeted corridor and into a long room with a wall of several very large windows.

The pervasive smell of bleach and disinfectant was overpowering. The attendant who led us into the cold room was a young guy with a perpetual smirk on his face. He had an irritating habit of constantly brushing back his hair from his forehead. Off to our right I glanced through the window and saw the swollen corpse of an obese black man on a cart. The belly was partially cut away, displaying roll upon roll of waxy-looking yellow fat. Another attendant quickly threw a sheet over the corpse and smiled benignly as we continued down the hallway.

The attendant paused at the door and spoke to me softly. "Who's the fiancée?" he asked.

"The girl in the tan coat," I said. "Why?"

"She speak English?"

I shook my head.

"We do," Maria said, indicating Father Felipe and herself.

The attendant nodded. "Then let me warn you, so you can tell her. If this is her loved one, he's been in the water for a while. That does a lot to a body. If she can give us some information as far as any scars or tattoos, so I can check first, it might be easier."

Maria spoke to Juanita.

"Si," she said. *"Tiene una cicatriz de apendicitis."*

"He has an appendicitis scar," Maria said.

After discussing the exact location and size of the scar, the attendant went in alone to check the body. I'd given him the Polaroid, too. There was no sense in us viewing the remains unless it checked out. When he came back he looked grim. He motioned us to move farther down next to one of the large windows. On the other side of the glass another attendant rolled a gurney up from the freezer area. He began unzipping the black body bag.

"He was in the water. Under the water actually, for at least a couple of days," the guy with us said. "Thankfully it was pretty cold and the fish weren't biting. He's not that bad." He tapped on the window and pointed. The man on the other side pulled the bag away from the corpse's side, showing the scar to Juanita. At the sight of the bloated, livid flesh she recoiled, then seemed to stare at the scar for a long time. Her hand reached out tentatively, her fingers brushing the glass.

"Mira frio," she said. He looks cold.

She looked at me. I tried to nod reassuringly.

Maria asked her something that I couldn't understand.

"Tengo que mirar su cara," Juanita said.

"She must see his face," Maria said.

"That might not be such a good idea," I said.

It wasn't. The other attendant lifted back the zippered edge and Juanita took one look. Her eyes rolled back and she collapsed.

"Aw shit," the attendant next to me said. "I had a feeling this was gonna happen. Bring her over there." He pointed toward a small couch against the rear wall. I stepped around and picked her up. She couldn't have weighed more than a hundred pounds. In my arms she felt small and fragile. After they helped us get her conscious the crying began. Father Felipe went in and removed his stole from his pocket, kissed it, crossed himself, and looped it around his neck. He bent slightly and began praying over the body. I had to hand it to him. I knew from personal experience that the smell in that room was a killer. When he finished I gave the attendant one of my cards and told him I'd call back in the morning.

On the return trip, Maria held Juanita in the back seat. Father Felipe sat next to me in front, although he spent most of the trip curled around chatting with them in Spanish, assuring Juanita that Carlos would have a proper mass and burial. I thought she had herself composed until we got back to her house. Then the wailing started again.

I dropped them off in front and went looking for a parking place. That took me a good ten minutes. Finally I found a spot near an alley. The Beater would be all right there if no one made too sharp a turn.

Juanita's father met me at the door. His brow was creased and he stared at me without recognition momentarily, then gave a slight nod and opened the door. I sat in a chair in the living room. The TV blared with some old cowboy movie that had been badly dubbed in Spanish. In the next room, a big dining area of sorts, everybody huddled together and spoke too quickly for me to even attempt to understand.

Juanita seemed to have gained a little more control over herself. She was able to talk without continually breaking down into tears. The slow, comforting voice of Father Felipe drifted like a thread through all of the conversation. I tried to watch the television, but couldn't concentrate enough to pick up much from it either. All in all, as W. C. Fields once said, I would have rather been in Philadelphia. Finally Maria came in and sat next to me. She always wore a lot of eye make-up and her mascara had left dark streaks down her face.

"Are you all right?" I asked, gently reaching over and touching her hand.

She nodded.

"It's just so hard when I see her so *triste.* So sad."

"It's rough," I agreed.

She looked up and gave a weak smile. "I must look a mess. Could you drive me home?"

"Sure. You want to leave now?"

She stood.

"Yes. Father Felipe is going to stay awhile, then Señor Valdez will take him back to the church. There's nothing more we can do here."

Maria went into the washroom and I stood, awkwardly waiting. I wanted to say something to Juanita, but didn't know what would be appropriate. The door of the washroom opened and Maria came out. She'd washed her face and I thought how different she looked without the make-up. I wanted to tell her that she looked better. Less flashy. But I kept that to myself and went in with her to say good night to Juanita and her family.

When I started up the car I glanced at my watch. It was close to nine and I hadn't eaten since lunch. I was starved, but didn't know if I should ask Maria if she wanted to grab something. The temperature had really dropped and I switched on the heater. We rode to her apartment in silence. When I pulled up in front I decided, what the hell, it wouldn't hurt to ask. "Look, I know it's been a rough night, but would you like to get something to eat?"

She looked at me for a moment, her smooth cheeks illuminated by the light from a nearby streetlight.

"I really don't feel like going to a restaurant," she said.

I nodded.

"Why don't you come up for a while, okay?" she said. "I'll fix us something. I don't feel like being alone just now either."

Chapter 18

I dropped her off in front and began to search for a parking place. Again. After circling the block three times I got lucky and found a spot that somebody recently vacated. The Beater was big and hard to maneuver, but at least it had power steering and after a couple unsuccessful tries, I was in. I walked briskly up to Maria's building wondering what the rest of the night would bring. For the second time that day I rang her buzzer. She'd gone up first to get some food ready.

"Who is it?" the speaker asked.

"Your favorite private eye," I said.

The security door buzzed and I pushed it open. The stairway was carpeted in that green indoor-outdoor stuff that crunched under my feet. This would probably be my only contribution to physical training tonight, I thought as I went up to the third floor. The door to her apartment was standing open. I thought about teasing her for not buzzing me in right away, but I didn't. It was better to be safe than sorry if you lived in the city, and I didn't want to chide her for following strict safety measures. They were probably ingrained as a way of life.

She'd taken off the jacket and rolled up the sleeves of her light green blouse. "I hope you don't mind sandwiches. It was all that I could come up with on such short notice."

"Sounds great." I slipped off my jacket and hat and Maria took them from me. The next thing I did was visit the washroom. It really was getting cold out. After making sure my hair was combed and my hands washed, I went into the living room.

"I think there's a leak in your car," she said. "The leg of my jeans was all wet."

"Sorry. I've had more trouble with that damn thing."

"How's the insurance problem with the other one?"

I remembered that I hadn't called Dick.

"Hopefully I should find out something tomorrow," I said.

"I hope everything goes well," she said, motioning me into the kitchen.

It was a medium-sized room with a porcelain sink set right into the wall. Opposite was a refrigerator and stove. A microwave sat on a cabinet and inside I could see two cups full of something heating up.

"Is that coffee?" I asked.

"Hot chocolate," she said. "I thought it was too late for coffee."

"Oh, that's right. You have to get up for work in the morning, don't you?"

"No, I'm taking a sick day. I already called in. Juanita's parents both work and she'll need someone with her to make the funeral arrangements."

"She's lucky to have a friend like you," I said.

The microwave pinged. Maria set the steaming cup of cocoa in front of me along with a toasted cheese sandwich, and I sat down.

"I hope you like it," she said. "I really don't have too much on hand. Saturday is my usual shopping day."

"It's fine."

"I can make you some eggs if you want."

"No, really. It's fine. Honest."

She smiled and sat down across from me. Picking up her cup with both hands she brought it to her lips, her eyes watching me over the rim.

"Aren't you going to eat?" I asked.

"I already ate. Earlier, before you picked me up."

"That was hours ago."

"Yes, but I don't need as much food as you do. Besides," she said, setting down her cup, "I like to watch my figure."

"Me too," I said, grinning.

A moment later she smiled back.

It started as a hug when, after a long conversation about everything that happened that day, I headed for the door. A gentle, commiserating hug that was meant to convey the shared emotion we'd both expended that night. She gave me a brief kiss on the lips, and lingered close. Our eyes met, and then our mouths again. Only this time it was longer, deeper. Her hands traced over my face as my arms encircled her, drawing her closer.

"Oh, Ron, we've been friends for so long," she said.

I kissed her again, but this time she seemed more tentative.

"What's wrong?" I asked softly.

"It's just that," she looked away from me, "we're going so fast all of a sudden. And I don't want things to change because you've always been one of the few people I felt I could trust."

I traced my finger gently over her cheek, admiring the healthy glow of her skin. The symmetry of her face. The sleek line of her neck. And the sweeping cascade of her raven-black hair.

"You're right," I said. "We have been friends for a long time."

Our eyes locked and we kissed again.

"After this evening . . . I'm not sure I could stand being

alone," she said. "But what'll happen if you stay?"

"We'll be better friends," I said. "If you want, I'll just stay and hold you for awhile."

She didn't reply. I was about to speak again, when her fingers grazed my lips. Without a word she pulled off my jacket and dropped it on the chair by the door. Then, after kissing me again, we moved toward the bedroom. Sitting on the edge of the bed, our mouths explored each other with eager tenderness. I felt her fingers unbuttoning my shirt. My hands went to her breasts.

Slowly we undressed each other and Maria pulled down the covers of her big bed. The sheets felt clean and soft against my skin. And Maria's warm, taut body pressed close to mine.

We drifted in ecstasy for a long time, each relishing the joy of exploring and pleasing the other, until the climactic rush of sexual excitement swept over us with the inevitability of an incoming tide. Finally, after we both were totally spent, we settled into each other's arms.

I was on my back and Maria lay on her side, half of her resting on me. She told me I was a gentle lover.

"I never realized how sweet you are, Ron," she said, shifting so that her chin was on my chest. She looked at me, then turned her head away. I reached down and stroked her dark hair.

"What's wrong?" I asked.

"It's just been a long time since I made love," she said.

I suddenly wondered who she'd been thinking about when she'd said that. But I knew better than to ask, not wanting to tell her that I'd been remembering my last time, too. With Cathy.

"I can't help thinking of poor Juanita," she said.

"Should I take that as a commentary on my technique?"

"Oh, no," she said, raising her head. "I just meant, it's so sad. She really loved Carlos. And now . . ."

I kissed her gently.

"You don't have to feel guilty because you're alive," I said. "She'll get through it all right. And so will you."

"What do you mean by that?" Her tone changed slightly.

"Just that you've been through a rough time yourself. You've tried to help a friend, seen someone you knew dead, and consoled your friend. Psychologically it takes its toll on you." I gently brushed away some of her long, black hair from her face. "And you don't have to feel guilty about wanting to be with me tonight."

"Oh," she said with a trace of indignation.

I could feel her starting to tense up. I knew I'd better say something fast to clarify what I meant.

"Listen, making love with you was beautiful," I said. "Special. It feels good to be alive. Sometimes, in times of crisis, we reach out to others. Those special people we know we can trust, when we need to reaffirm our own humanity." I felt her body soften.

"I never realized that you were so deep," she said.

"In other words, you thought I was just this big, handsome stud," I said with a self-effacing grin.

She laughed, but then the serious look came back and her eyes narrowed slightly. She shifted so that her breasts rested on my chest.

"Ron, I know you haven't been paid yet, and you're such a gentleman you haven't even asked."

"I'm not worried about it."

"No," she said. "I'll make sure you get paid by the end of the week."

"We can settle up after the funeral. I'm not hurting."

She kissed me again. "You're so sweet. But what I'm trying to ask you is, will you stay on the case?"

That kind of floored me.

"Well, Carlos has been found," I said slowly. "That's what I was hired to do, wasn't it?"

"And what happens now?"

"Now it's a police matter."

"How hard will they investigate? I mean for a dead illegal?"

"I don't know." Her eyes were big and dark in the twilight of the room. "Hey, they've got a lot more resources than I do."

"But answer my question. How much effort will they put into it?"

"I'm not sure. Shade's rule number 165 is that you don't get involved in an active police investigation."

"So you're saying you really think they'll make an effort?"

I sighed and said nothing.

"Do you?"

"Probably not a strenuous one," I said.

"Well, how about you? Will you stay on the case? I'll pay for your services."

I gave her a long sideways glance.

"For this type of service, I usually charge quite a bit more," I said with a sly grin, stroking her bare shoulder. She shrugged my hand away.

"I'm serious. And I want it to remain in a professional context. Please, Ron. It's important to me."

She looked at me imploringly with those obsidian eyes. They seemed to bore into my soul. Cradling her head in my hands, I kissed her softly.

"Okay," I said. "If it's important to you."

Chapter 19

Mornings after the first night can be difficult, even for old friends. I awoke early at quarter to five, like I usually do when I'm in training. But I didn't feel rested. I hadn't slept well. I figured it had something to do with not being in my own bed. Even the times when I used to stay overnight at Cathy's it had felt the same. Plus I wasn't used to sleeping with anyone. Maria, on the other hand, must have been exhausted. She didn't even wake up when I got out of bed to go to the bathroom and came back in to get dressed.

She'd left a soft night-light on while we made love. I switched it on again and tore a page out of my notebook to write her a note. I tried to make it as romantic as possible: how I'd love to stay and make her breakfast but wanted to leave to save her any unnecessary explanations to nosy neighbors. It sounded stilted and terrible. I tore it up and began writing another one. I didn't want to just leave, but I knew I'd feel guilty if I missed my roadwork this morning. And I needed to sort things out on this case, if I was going to stay on it.

She stirred awake as I was working on the second draft.

"What time is it?" she asked sleepily. Then, after blinking a few times, the space between her eyebrows creased. "Why are you dressed?"

I put the notebook in my pocket and bent down to kiss her.

"I was going to try to make you breakfast," I said. My attempt at a note had been a failure, so why try to verbalize it?

"Oh, you're so sweet," she said, raising up and putting her arms around my neck. "But you're my guest, and I'll make you breakfast. Just let me freshen up."

She kissed my cheek and pulled herself out of the bed. Naked, she walked across the bedroom floor and grabbed a white terry cloth robe that hung on a hook behind the door. As she turned slightly to slip into it, I saw the dark curls of her pubic hair against the white material. She pulled her hair out of the collar as she went out of the room.

Seeing her, I suddenly recalled last night's pleasures and a sense of renewed passion swept through me. I sat down on the bed and lay back, my feet still on the floor. Missing the roadwork didn't seem so significant anymore. I could always get it in later. Maybe.

I stared at the ceiling. It was one of those high plaster ones that they used to put in houses. Now everything was plasterboard. The toilet flushed. I heard running water. After stretching, I took off my shoes. When Maria came back, I saw that she'd re-done her make-up.

Smiling, she climbed on top of me. Her breath had that just-brushed freshness as she drew her tongue over my neck and up to my mouth.

"You need a shave," she said. "So what do you want to do?"

"You really have to ask?" I said with a sly smile. Yeah, the roadwork could definitely wait.

It was about ten when I got home. After we'd finished making love we'd held each other, talking for a while. Then, to my surprise, Maria practically hustled me out of bed and began whipping up a big breakfast of eggs, toast, coffee and juice. I usually don't eat much in the mornings because it's not a good idea to run on a full stomach. But this morning I figured I'd make an exception. She apologized for the rush, but said she'd better get ready to help Juanita today. I told her I understood and left.

The cats met me as soon as I opened the door. They let me know in no uncertain terms that they expected to be fed before I did anything else. After seeing to their needs I went in and looked for some clean sweats in the dresser. Three drawers later it dawned on me that there weren't any clean ones. Cleanliness is next to godliness, I thought as I went to the hamper for yesterday's pair. The weather had really taken a downturn and it felt almost cold enough to snow. I was still feeling the chill from the ride home. The Beater seemed to be blowing cold air out of the vents instead of heat.

I slipped on my musty-smelling hooded sweatshirt and made another mental note to remember the mental note from yesterday to throw my sweats in the washer when I got back. With my bag gloves on my hands acting as mittens, I was ready to take on the world.

I started out slow, just kind of easing into the run. After a couple of blocks I expected to begin to warm up. But this morning each step was torture.

Chappie had always harped to me about the virtues of abstinence in the weeks leading up to a fight. I remembered the time we were over at his house watching *Rocky* on television. When Burgess Meredith began berating Sylvester Stallone about women weakening legs I'd laughed. That brought a stern lecture from Chappie on how true it was. He even told me a story, after making sure his daughter was out of the room, about how, when he first started fighting, an unscrupulous promoter had lined him up with a prostitute on the night before a fight.

"Did you lose the fight?" I'd asked him.

"Hell, no. I whupped that sucker," he'd said. "But I took ten rounds of punishment doin' it, and the fight ended in a draw. Point is, I coulda knocked him out if I'd had my mind on fightin' instead of fuckin'."

His words always seemed to hang in my mind whenever I deviated from this unwritten rule during training for a big fight. But last night had been so spontaneous, and so beautiful. I knew if I had to do it all over again, I wouldn't hesitate.

I pushed aside my aches and pains and forced myself to think about the case at hand. As I'd figured, Carlos had turned up dead. Now the questions were finding out who was responsible and why? The who could possibly be somebody connected to Space Oddities. Big Frank had lied about the circumstances of Carlos's departure. But for what reason? To hide something? Maybe he'd beaten the hell out of Carlos and accidentally killed him. An ironic end for a guy with a college education who came to *el norte,* the land of the free, to escape the ruthless killers in his own country. One thing was certain, illegal or not, the guy deserved better.

But what could I prove? I'd have to wait for the autopsy to find out the cause of death. In the mean time, I could do some discreet checking on Big Frank and the Space Oddities crew in general. I rounded the curve and started up the middle hill, Agony Two. No languid grasshoppers leaped out at me today since we'd had that overnight frost they'd been predicting on the news.

I spit and looked at my watch. Eleven-ten. If I pushed it I could probably catch George before he went to lunch.

Chapter 20

"So that was the missing Mexican you were looking for, eh?" George asked me, reaching for the catsup. He and Doug had been out trying to serve a warrant on a suspect in the Beverly area and we agreed to meet for lunch.

"Actually he was from El Salvador," I said. "And, yeah, it was him." I poked around at my salad as he took a big bite of his hamburger. Doug had ordered a Reuben sandwich. I could feel my mouth water as I watched them eat. "So you know anything about the guy who'll be assigned to the case?"

"Huh-un," George said with a mouthful. Then, after chewing and swallowing, "It's state police jurisdiction. DCI. If you left a card at the morgue the investigator will get ahold of you."

"Your part should be pretty well finished anyway, shouldn't it?" Doug asked.

"Well, I sorta told a friend of mine I'd keep looking into it for a while."

George gave me a stern look and I knew what was coming.

"Listen," he said. "It's an active police investigation. They might not appreciate some private dick butting in."

The waitress came by and asked us if we needed more coffee. She smiled charmingly as she topped off each of our cups. When she left I answered him.

"Yeah, well, I still plan on touching bases with them. You know, sort of like an informal helper."

George snorted and shook his head.

"I know better than to try and talk you out of something once you've made up your mind," he said. "But watch your ass on this one."

When Doug got up to use the washroom, George leaned over the table and stared at me.

"I meant what I said."

"Yeah," I answered. "I know. Can you run some criminal histories for me?"

His stare got harder, and his head began a slow nodding.

"Criminal histories," he repeated. "For this case I just advised you to stay out of?"

"What other case would I be working on?" I said with a grin.

He heaved a sigh and rubbed his fingers over his temples.

"Give me the names," he said.

I handed him the names and license plates that I'd copied down from my last visit to Space Oddities.

"These are the names of the guys I need."

"Where are the dates of birth?"

"Don't have those yet. But the plates there can probably give you some more info."

"Christ, Ron," he groaned. "You know how long this'll take?"

"Maybe all of about five minutes," I said. "And besides, you'll probably have some cute little babe in the records division do it for you anyway."

He stuffed the list into his pocket.

"I'll see what I can do. But don't expect miracles."

"Thanks, buddy," I said as Doug came back to the table.

When we walked out to the parking lot Doug asked me how the Beater was running. I didn't have the heart to tell him about all the problems that I'd had with it, so I told him it was running fine. That was basically true now that I'd gotten the battery and the charging system squared away. Except for the heater being on strike. We said goodbye and I waved as they took off in their unmarked. I walked down to the corner drug store with the icy wind whipping right through my clothes. Why does it always seem so much worse during the first cold spell in the fall?

The clerk at the register was a heavy-set woman with thick glasses. The lenses distorted the size of her eyes, making them seem unusually large. Her nostrils flared when I asked her for change.

"We're not supposed to give out change, sir," she said.

"Aww, come on, can't you help me out?" I said, smiling my most winning smile. "My car was stolen and I have to make an important phone call."

"Well," she said. "I suppose it would be all right."

It must have been the smile. She pressed the appropriate buttons and opened the register. After getting change for a couple of dollars, I went to the rear of the store to the public telephone.

The first call I made was to Maria. Her cool voice on the answering machine said to leave a number and she'd return the call. I waited for the tone and told her to beep me when she had the chance. She was probably still with Juanita making funeral arrangements. Maybe she'd be available for a late dinner date or something.

Next I called the gym and asked to talk to Chappie. He came on the line with his usual cheerfulness.

"Where the hell were you last night?"

"Sorry," I said. "I got tied up on something."

"I'm gonna tie you up. Tie you in the middle of the ring and beat your ass. That's what Berger's gonna do if you don't get busy and start training for this one."

I sighed, knowing he was right.

"Sorry," I said.

"No you ain't," he retorted. "That's what you gonna be. You do your roadwork this morning, at least?"

"Yeah. And I'll be in shortly for a workout. But I might need tonight off."

"Well, we can see about that when the time comes," he grumbled. "What time you coming over?"

I glanced at my watch. It was almost two.

"How about four? I've got things to do."

"You got that right," he said. "Like training for a fight."

I grunted an okay and hung up, figuring I'd be in for a real ball-breaker.

My third call was to Midwestern Olympia. The receptionist put me on hold while she located Mr. MacKenzie. I had to put two more nickels in the slot while I waited. Finally, Dick came on the line with his usual verve.

"Dick MacKenzie. May I help you?"

"Dick," I said, opting for the subdued approach. "It's Ron."

"Oh. Yeah. How's it going?"

"I thought you could tell me."

"Well," he said. "I'm working on it."

"Working on it? Is that all you can say?"

"Aaah, yeah. I'm afraid it is, at this point." He suddenly sounded deflated. Without his usual self-assurance.

"Is there some problem?" I asked.

His gruffness returned. "Look, Ron, I told you I'd take care of it, and I'll do my level best. Now I'll get back to you later, okay?"

He hung up. I stared at the receiver for a few seconds before replacing it in the cradle. Scooping up the remaining change from the metal shelf, I was hit with a wave of dread.

A feeling that things were probably going to get worse before they got better. A lot worse.

I'd just gotten in the Beater and was turning the key when my beeper went off. It was Maria's number. God, I missed my cell phone. But, not wanting to keep her waiting, I made the trek back to the drug store and got more change from the clerk. This time she eyed me suspiciously. Maybe she thought I was a bookie or something. The phone's computer voice wasn't suspicious at all, however. It just wanted me to deposit "ten cents more, please."

Maria answered on the first ring. The sound of her hello was cool and crisp.

"Bet you didn't think I'd call back so soon," I said.

"Oh, Ron, hi. You're right. I didn't. Did you get another cell phone?"

"Not hardly. I'm still hoping the insurance will cover the last one. What's up?"

"Juanita and I went down to that awful place again, this morning with Father Felipe," she said. "But can you believe it, they won't release the body till next week now."

"Yeah, I figured as much," I said. "They'll have to schedule an autopsy and, being this close to the weekend they're probably swamped."

"Did you find out anything yet?"

"Not yet," I said, not wanting to tell her that I'd pretty much decided to go through the motions and let the state police handle things. "But I've started a few things. Gotta wait till I get some information back."

"Juanita's still very upset," Maria said. "But she's so glad that you've agreed to look into this."

Great, I thought. Just what I needed. More pressure.

"So can you come by tonight?" she said. "I told the

Valdezes that we'd come over for dinner."

"Well, I don't know," I said slowly. "I already made plans to work out tonight."

"Work out?" she said, after a second of silence.

"Yeah. I've got that title fight coming up and I've got to train for it. I missed my regular sparring session last night."

"I suppose I can go alone and tell them you're busy," she said. "But I just thought that since it's Friday night we could do something together."

I'd forgotten about it being Friday. Lately all the days had been running together.

"How about we go out tomorrow night?" I asked. "I'll take you to a fine restaurant and a movie."

"Hmm, sounds okay," she said coyly. "But, how about coming over tonight after your workout?"

"That sounds better than okay."

I was set to say good-bye when she said my name rather tentatively.

"Yeah?"

"Last night. Was it special for you?" she asked.

I didn't get to answer. The computerized operator broke in and told me that I needed "five cents more for the next one minute."

I frantically searched through my change for a nickel. Finding none, I dropped in a dime. The voice thanked me and informed that I had "five cents credit toward overtime." There was a clunk as the money was recorded and stored.

"Ron?" Maria said. "Are you still there?"

"I'm here," I answered. "And last night was special. Very special."

When I hung up the phone rang. I picked it up and the

computerized voice told me that it wanted five cents for overtime. Since it had just told me I had a credit I didn't deposit anything. Then a real live operator came on the line and told me she needed five cents.

"I deposited a dime before," I said. "I thought I had a credit."

It was a small thing, but it was the principle.

"No, sir," the operator said. "Five cents. I show no credit."

I looked down at my remaining change. Two quarters and a dime. I dropped in the dime.

"Now you have a credit," the operator said sarcastically. She terminated the connection before I could respond, but her rudeness left me pissed. What happened to the vivacious, friendly operator they always showed on the TV commercial?

I headed up to the front of the store and was buying a pack of sugarless gum when my beeper went off again. This time it was a totally unfamiliar number. The clerk gave me more change, and eyed my beeper closely. Maybe she thought I was a drug dealer. This time I made sure I got plenty of nickels.

After three rings a man's voice answered identifying itself as Investigator Tremain.

"This is Ron Shade, you beeped me."

"Who?" the voice asked. Then, "Oh, Mr. Shade. I'm Andrew Tremain with the State Police, Division of Criminal Investigations."

"Okay," I said, not wanting to volunteer information over the phone when I wasn't sure who I was talking to and for what reason.

"I've been assigned to the case of that dead Mexican that they found floating in the Cal Sag," he said. "The morgue told me that you helped identify the body."

"Right. But he wasn't a Mexican. He was Salvadoran."

"Hmm, that's interesting," Tremain said. "Got any theories?"

"None that I'd discuss over the phone."

"Yeah, you're right. Why don't I come by your office?"

"Well, I'm sort of between offices right now," I said. "But we can meet someplace, if you want."

"All right. I'm out in Palos Heights right now."

"The DCI office on Austin?" I asked. "I know the place. I could be there in about twenty-five minutes."

"Fine," he said. "I'll be waiting for you."

Chapter 21

Tremain turned out to be a young guy in his mid-twenties, with curly dark hair and a quick, reassuring smile. He had on a gray sport jacket and dark trousers, which fit his trim frame well. He was about five inches shorter than I was and apparently didn't like looking up at me. He ushered me into an office where we both sat down, with him taking the seat behind the desk. Obviously he'd read the books on proper techniques for conducting an interview.

"So what can you tell me about the dead man, Mr. Shade?"

"His name was Carlos Sanchez. He was an illegal alien from El Salvador. He was twenty-four years old." I handed him a piece of paper with Carlos's date of birth.

"You have his address?" Tremain asked.

"Not with me," I replied, not wanting to give it out yet because of the other illegals. "But I know he lived in Lincoln Estates. Worked at a place called Space Oddities."

Tremain made some notes on a legal pad.

"Just how did you get involved in this?"

"I was hired by Carlos's fiancée to find him. He'd been missing since last Friday."

Tremain looked at me and set his pen down. After a few seconds he said, "Mr. Shade, I did some research before I called you. I know you used to be a cop, and you were fired after a SWAT operation went bad and a bystander got killed."

"Somebody's head had to roll over that one," I said, feigning indifference to try and cover my discomfort. "I was the squad leader."

"Well, I'm not trying to drag up unpleasant memories," he said. "And, for what it's worth, everything else I heard about you was extremely favorable."

"You must've been talking to my uncle," I said with a grin.

Tremain didn't grin back.

"What I'm getting at," he continued, "is that I'm sure you're a very competent investigator. I'd appreciate it if we could sort of cut through all the bullshit and level with each other."

I didn't have anything to lose by leveling with him. If anything, he might be able to put some pressure on Big Frank that I sure couldn't.

"Sounds good to me," I said.

"Okay, what did your investigation find out?"

I gave him everything I had. The disappearance, Juanita hiring me, the discrepancies in the stories about Carlos's last day at work, and our identification of the body at the morgue. After I was finished Tremain scratched his head.

"That's not really a hell of a lot to go on," he said.

"Well, you got the fact that Bristol, that's Carlos's boss at the plant, lied to me about his last day."

Tremain sighed. "That's kind of tenuous."

Tenuous? What the hell did this guy want? Perry Mason to walk up and flush out the guilty party?

"I've got to ask you something," he said. "Have you come across any indication of a drug connection?"

I shook my head. "Why?"

"Well," he said, leaning forward, "we've been finding in a lot of these cases involving illegals that they'd been used as mules for transporting narcotics."

"I kind of doubt that," I said. "Carlos fled from El Salvador for political reasons. He'd been targeted by one of those right-wing death squads. Besides, he'd been in this country a while. Over a year. And he was going to get married."

Tremain sighed, obviously disappointed at my dismissal of his drug-mule theory. He leaned back and put his hands behind his head.

"So your theory is what?"

"I don't form a theory right off the bat," I said. "I sorta look around for inconsistencies when I try to fit things together."

"And so far the only one you've found involves his ex-boss."

"I gotta wonder why he lied to me."

Tremain rose and extended his hand.

"Well, thank you for all your assistance, Mr. Shade," he said. "I'll get back to you if I have any more questions."

I debated whether or not to tell him now that I'd be staying on the case, rather than risk not telling him, and maybe cross paths later on.

"The man's fiancée asked me to stay on the case," I said. "I just wanted to let you know that I'll be nosing around on my own a little."

He raised his eyebrows.

"I hope that doesn't mean that we'll be working at cross purposes," he said.

"Not at all. If I turn up anything I'll get hold of you. Detective George Grieves on CPD can vouch for me. He's a dick in the Second District. Area One Violent Crimes."

Tremain nodded and reached in his shirt pocket.

"Sounds fair enough," he said. "Here's my card, in case you do turn up anything."

"So, what would be the chances of me getting a peek at the autopsy report?"

"I'll have to check on that," he said. "It's not scheduled till Monday. There's not much we can do before then, anyway."

"All right," I said, turning to go.

"Mr. Shade."

I stopped.

"Just remember what I said about sharing information."

I wanted to say that it was a two-way street, but I just nodded and left.

After my interview with Tremain, I shivered my way over to Bob's Service Station and told them the heater wasn't working. Todd checked the radiator and put some anti-freeze in it. He said if that didn't correct it, they might have to look at the radiator or the heating system.

Marvelous, I thought, as I headed home to face my hungry cats and pack for the workout.

Chapter 22

Chappie had been waiting for me with three sparring partners lined up. After a warm-up workout, he had me go through three rounds with each of them. Usually, I didn't try to go nine rounds until I'd been training for a few weeks, but he kept reminding me, all the way through, that we didn't have the luxury of time for this one. Toward the end the last guy clipped me with a couple of good left hooks. I was too drained to slip them properly and thought the round would go on forever. At the end of it I felt totally drained, sore all over, and ready to sleep for a week. Chappie wanted me to sit in the steam but I told him I just couldn't do it. All I wanted was a hot bath to ease out the kinks. It was close to seven-thirty, and I felt like I'd been run over by a tank. I pulled my jacket on over my sweats, loaded my stuff into the Beater, and headed for home without even taking a shower. The heater worked for part of the way, then seemed to give way to the cold air again. I felt chilled to the bone when I walked in the door.

The cats regarded me curiously while I dropped my clothes in various rooms as I stumbled around. I filled the ice bag and held it to my face. After starting the hot water running, I went to the phone and dialed Maria's number. I got her answering machine. The message I left was short and concise: "I sort of overdid it at the gym. Regrettably, I won't be able to see you tonight. Sorry. I'll call you tomorrow."

I left any replies to my answering machine and, now completely nude, padded into the bathroom. My body felt like the White Sox had used it for batting practice. The tub was almost full and I tested the water with my foot. It felt hot enough to scald. After sprinkling in some Epsom Salt and letting it cool for a minute or so, I slowly lowered myself in. I managed to fold my legs into a semi-yoga position so I could submerse as much of my body as possible. Then I put my head back and returned the ice pack to my face. I was in for about twenty minutes and the phone started ringing. I let the answering machine take it.

As I lay there regretting my own stupidity at skipping the previous workout this close to the biggest fight of my career, my muscles were starting to loosen up as the water began to cool. I tried to tell myself that this might not have been so bad after all. If I could go nine rounds like I did tonight against three separate opponents, I must have been in better shape than I thought.

But there was still that lingering doubt: Anthony Berger was no sparring partner. He was a tough pro. I had time to prepare, but I couldn't afford to get hit as many times as I'd gotten caught tonight. My head ached with one of those headaches that wouldn't quite go away. I wished I'd taken some aspirin before I'd gotten in the tub. But aspirin thinned the blood, which, if I got cut, would impede clotting. God, I hoped I didn't get cut. Or take a lot of head shots.

That was another consideration. How much longer did I want to keep fighting? When I'd started my comeback, I'd made a pact with myself that I'd quit after two years or winning the title. That had been four years ago. I was still fighting. I hadn't won the title, and I'd taken a lot of punishment in some real ring wars. My fighting had been a sore spot between Cathy and me. She'd always give me articles on pugilistic dementia and the criticism of boxing by the

American Medical Association. I'd counter by saying that I was a kickboxer, and that would usually trigger one of our arguments.

I'd tossed it over and over in my mind why she left and always wondered if my fighting was part of it. Besides my failure to commit. Maybe, after a while, she felt that I was never going to change, and the only thing she could do was walk away. I blew out a long, slow breath. Hell, when I won the title from Berger I'd send her a copy of the headline. On the other hand, of course, it was doubtful that any of the major newspapers would even carry news of the fight. Maybe I could convince my newspaper buddy, Rich Staford, to have something printed up to look like a headline.

Thinking of Rich made me remember that I still had a case to solve if I was going to keep Maria happy. I'd have to do something on Carlos's murder. Assuming that he was murdered, that is. Now I was starting to sound like Tremain. I had him figured for the type of guy who would work real hard convincing himself that the solution lay with the path of least resistance, regardless of the truth.

Bristol seemed to be the key. He'd lied to me about the circumstances of Carlos's last day. But what was he hiding? When I found that out I'd probably have it all. Hopefully something would turn up on those criminal histories that George was running for me. Not a helluva lot I could do till then. Besides Big Frank, I had Enrique, Security-Nick, and Harold Jordan who tied in some way. It was as if they were all hiding something. Like some perverted family, conspiring to keep Granny buried in the basement while they kept cashing her social security checks.

The phone rang again. The answering machine clicked on. Shasha came to the edge of the tub and meowed, debating whether or not to investigate further. I flipped some water at her with my fingers and she took off like a shot. The water was getting real cold now, and I still had my headache. Even the ice bag was slushy. Pulling the drain with my toes, I felt the water start to go down. I stood and tossed the ice bag into the sink and grabbed a towel.

After drying off I wiped the steam off the mirror and took a look at my face. It was still red and just a little bit puffy. But at least I hadn't been cut. I took two aspirins and went straight to bed.

Chapter 23

I slept until almost eight the next morning. Just a tad less than twelve hours. Remembering it was Saturday, I called Bob's Service Station and asked if they had time to look at the Beater again.

"What's wrong with it now?" Bob asked me.

"No heat."

He told me to bring it over, but to check the antifreeze level first. It was low, and Todd had just filled it up yesterday. After dropping it off, I started in on my morning run. The cold weather had held on and, along with the wind, whipped unmercifully at my already tender face. My feet felt like hell too, and the rest of my body ached with each step. I went pretty slow, but at least I ground out the five miles.

At the end of the run I felt worse instead of better. I practically collapsed in a kitchen chair and drank three glasses of cranberry juice. After watching the second hand on the clock go around three times, I decided it was time to get up and take a shower.

As I was shaving I assessed my face again. The only noticeable swelling was around my left eye. The area was a little bluish. My jaw hinge clicked when I opened my mouth real wide, but it almost always did that. In the shower I let the hot water run over the back of my neck for a long time. It did little to alleviate the soreness.

After starting the coffee and heating up a bagel for breakfast, I remembered that I had some calls to check on the answering machine. The first one was from George. He said that he had those items for me and would get back to me later. That meant don't call me, I'll call you. The second one was from Maria, sounding concerned as to what had happened to me at the gym. I called her first.

She answered on the third ring.

"Hi, babe. It's me."

"Ron? Are you okay? After I got your call I was worried sick. What happened?"

I was both amused and pleased at the series of questions. They seemed to reflect care and interest.

"I was doing some sparring and we got a little carried away," I said. "I'm feeling a lot better now, but last night I was a wreck."

"I missed you at the dinner," she said. "So did Juanita."

"Sorry. Why don't you let me make it up to you? What's the rest of your schedule for today?"

"Shopping and laundry," she said. "After that, *nada.*"

"Well, how about tonight then? Dinner and a movie?"

"Let me check my appointment book," she laughed. Then added, "What time?"

"Six-thirty or seven?"

"Well, which is it?"

"That depends on how long it takes me to find a parking place in front of your building."

She laughed again. I was getting real fond of that sound.

After we hung up I tried George's house. No answer. Not even an answering machine. I thought about Dick MacKenzie and wished I had his home number. The son of a bitch hadn't even called me back. While I was mulling this over the phone rang. It was Bob Matulik.

"We got it pinpointed, Ron," he said. "The heater core was leaking. That's why you had that leak inside on the passenger side."

"Great, Bob. How long we talking about to fix it?"

"Well, I got Todd trying to find the part," he said. "That's the only problem with driving them old cars. But we should be able to get it squared away by two or three at the latest."

I looked at my watch. It was only ten o'clock. I told Bob that would be great and hung up. I had some time on my hands so I did some well-needed housework. Vacuuming, dishes, laundry, and the cat pans. By the time I finished I needed another shower, and it was only noon. But I wanted the place looking ship-shape, in case Maria and I ended up here tonight.

I gathered up my gear and put some clean clothes and a towel in the bag. Then I walked down to the bus stop and waited for the big green machine. I wasn't planning on doing a real heavy workout after last night, but I had to make an appearance.

On the bus I tried to concentrate on the case, but there were so many intangibles that I had to nail down it didn't make sense to think about it too much. At least that's what I told myself. The smartest course to follow was to let Maria think I was doing something, but to just keep in touch with Tremain. He would be able to check things out a lot faster than I could.

But was that fair to Maria? I didn't want to think too much about that either. After the pain that I'd gone through when Cathy left, I wasn't so sure I was ready to enter into another serious relationship. I wondered if that was what we were heading for. The bus went by Chan's Chop Suey Shop, and I knew it was getting close to 99th Street. I got up as we passed the next light and made my way to the front. The bus hissed to a stop and I slowly descended the steps.

Lee, the Korean kid who taught most of the karate and kickboxing classes was watching the front door. Brice must have either been off or inside pumping iron.

"Hi, Lee," I said. "Chappie here?"

He nodded and pointed to the back.

I went through the door to the inside. I decided to look for Chappie before changing, but he wasn't in his office. Instead, his daughter Darlene was leaning over the desk with a ledger book and a calculator. She looked up and smiled.

"Ron. Hi," she said. "Just catching up on the bookkeeping for Daddy."

She still lived at home with Chappie. His wife had died a few years ago. Darlene was so picturesque she could have been one of the top fashion models in the Midwest, but she was so devoted to her father that she never actively pursued it. She was going to law school though, and at night taught the aerobics classes at the gym.

"Where's he at?"

"In the gym. Working out," she said. "He said he'd be waiting for you."

"Yeah," I said. "I'll bet he is."

I went through the aerobics section and into the boxing gym. It was deserted except for Chappie pounding out a rhythm on the speed bag. He was wearing a gray sweat suit and boxing shoes. I waited for the round to finish. As the bell rang he turned and faced me.

"Get dressed. We got a work out to do," he said.

"Say, could we take it easy today? I'm still a little sore from last night."

"Take it easy?" Chappie said. "After all them left hooks you was getting clipped by last night?"

"Yeah, I was a little bit off at the end there."

He snorted. "Just remember, the only easy day was yesterday."

"Isn't that a Navy SEAL's saying? How did you hear it?"

His hand swooped up and punched the bag, sending it into a series of rhythmic bounces.

"*G.I. Jane* was on TV last night," he said. "And after watching that broad kick that big old master chief's ass, I figured you might have a chance against Berger. *If* I can get you trained right." The bell sounded and he raised his fist to begin the next cycle of punches. "Now get your ass dressed. We gots work to do."

Chapter 24

The workout went well, as workouts go. Chappie didn't push me like he usually did, I guess in deference to my sore body. We used the focus pads for about four rounds, then he recruited Lee to work on my kicks. He told me to finish out by skipping rope and using the bags.

"I'm gonna try to find another sparring partner for you," he said. "Somebody who's good at kicking. Berger likes to use his legs a lot."

Before the Elijah Day match I'd concentrated mostly on boxing with only occasional kicks. That had really hurt me in the fight that followed. In full-contact karate there's a minimum number of kicks required for each round. I'd failed to make the minimum during the fifth round and was assessed penalty points. If I hadn't managed to knock Day out, he would have surely won the decision.

When I'd finished the workout I spent some time in the steam room. It felt good to relax in the moist warmth. After my shower I felt pretty refreshed. I said good-bye to Chappie and told him I'd see him Monday. We normally skipped a workout on Sunday. The bus was running on its usual weekend schedule, which was hardly at all. After waiting for what seemed like forever, I said the hell with it and started walking down Western. I got almost to 111th Street before the bus zoomed past. At least the weather wasn't too bad. It was still a little nippy, but they were predicting an Indian summer–like warm-up. By the time I got to Bob's it was getting close to four. The Beater was parked on the street.

"You're all set, Ron," he said. "Replaced that heater coil for you. She's workin' like a charm now."

"Great, Bob," I said accepting the bill. "I've got an important date tonight."

He raised his eyebrows and looked at the Beater. "Oh, yeah?"

I grinned. "I'll have to impress her with my wit."

"You know, Ron, there's a lot of things ready to go on that car. You planning on keeping it?"

"Not any longer than I have to," I said. "Hopefully, I'll get this insurance problem sorted out by Monday."

"Those old cars are hard to get parts for, too."

"How come Spenser never had this trouble with his Mustang?" I joked, recalling the old TV show.

"Who's Spenser?" Bob asked.

Driving home I made a mental note to figure out exactly how much money the Beater had cost me for this case. If nothing else, I could write it off under expenses. Doug was getting the best of this deal, that was for sure. And I'd have to make sure I told George that I filled it up before I returned it.

Maria and I stood in the short line in front of the Biograph Theater. The weather had warmed slightly, as predicted, and we were comfortable in light jackets. She squeezed my hand as the line inched forward.

"All right," I said. "Let's do a little trivia quiz while we're here."

"What kind?"

"Famous places in Chicago," I said. "In fact, we're standing in front of one right now. What famous gangster was killed here?"

"That's easy," she said. "John Dillinger."

"Very good. Now what movie had he just seen?"

"Oh, right. Am I really supposed to know that one?"

"That's part of the quiz. Give up?"

She nodded.

"It was *Manhattan Melodrama.* Who were the stars?"

Maria shook her head and smiled. "You got me there."

"I'll give you a hint," I said. I leaned back and squinted and said, "Frankly, my dear, I just don't give a damn."

"Clark Gable?"

"That's correct," I said. "How about his co-star?"

"Male or female?"

"Male. He also played a famous detective in a series of movies."

"Peter Falk?" Maria asked.

"Nope. It was William Powell. You know, *The Thin Man.*"

"Wow, you really are into old movies, aren't you?" she said. "But I was thinking of Columbo. He kind of reminds me of you."

"Thanks a lot. Is that your impression of me? That I stumble around and ask a lot of stupid questions?"

"Actually, I was thinking how you always seem to have the tenacity to get things done," she said. "That you're a lot smarter than you pretend to be, and that people tend to underestimate you sometimes. And that's their mistake."

"Thanks for the compliment."

"You're welcome. Did I pass?"

"Only if you answer the following question correctly."

"What do I get if I do?"

"Then I pay for the tickets," I said. "What does the following sentence mean in English: *Pienso que eres muy hermosa?*"

She pulled close to me and squeezed my arm. We were

almost at the ticket booth.

"You think I'm beautiful," she said, smiling.

"Congratulations. You passed," I said, taking out my wallet.

"That last question was pretty easy," she said, her dark eyes sparkling as they looked up at me. "How about if I ask you a question?"

"Sure."

"Do you know what *ojos negros* means?"

"Black eyes?"

"Right," she said with a giggle. "Just like yours."

I'd forgotten about the discoloration that was now really getting noticeable under each eye. I was starting to look like a raccoon. I paid for two tickets and we moved to the doors.

"I guess I should have asked you what July 22, 1934 was," I said.

"Was that the date he was shot?"

I nodded.

"I never realized you were such a history buff," she said.

"Actually, I'm not," I said, pulling open the door. "I couldn't sleep and there was this old movie called *Dillinger* on the other night with Warren Oates and Ben Johnson."

The movie was just the kind of sweet entertainment that Maria needed to take her mind off the depressing events of the past week. It sort of put both of us in the mood for romance, and after a quick bite at a nearby restaurant, we went back to her apartment.

This time we moved purposefully to the bedroom and undressed quickly. In the mirror above her dresser I caught a glimpse of her standing in her bra and panties. She sat on the bed, after turning down the covers, and held up her long, dark hair for me to unsnap her. My hands roamed over her body as I drew her to me. Our mouths locked as she pulled the sheet over us, and I felt her strong legs circle around mine.

It was much later when we were still lying entwined in each other's arms, that I felt her stirring to free herself. I let her go and she got out of bed and retrieved her terry cloth robe from behind the door. She padded out of the room and went to the bathroom. I glanced at the clock. It was close to midnight. When she came back in she sat on the edge of the bed and picked up the alarm clock. Winding it, she leaned over and kissed me gently.

"Ron, are you going to stay?"

I was surprised by the question. I'd assumed she wanted me to.

"Do you want me to leave?"

She pulled her mouth tight and looked at me. Then she kissed me again.

"Of course not," she said haltingly. "But, it's just that this is Saturday night."

"Yeah?"

She set the alarm clock down and snuggled beside me, her arms around my neck.

"We've known each other for so long, but in some ways, you don't know me at all," she said.

"Meaning?"

"Meaning, my parents are very protective of me. They never have approved of me having my own place, and still look at me as their little girl, even at my age."

"So what is it you're trying to tell me?"

"They'll expect me to go to mass with them tomorrow morning. In fact, they'll probably be over early to take me out for breakfast."

"And my being here would be somewhat uncomfortable."

Her teeth closed over her lower lip.

"I'm sorry, Ron. I hope you aren't offended."

"I just have one question," I said, pulling off the covers and swinging my legs out. "Is some priest going to hear all about this tomorrow in confession?"

It turned out to be the wrong thing to say. I felt her stiffen, and she said, "Ron, please, don't make fun of my religion."

It's a good thing I'm such a hit as a detective, I thought, because I'd never make it as a comedian.

Chapter 25

As I was driving back I flipped on the radio and that old Lionel Ritchie song came on about the guy who wanted to win the girl's heart, but didn't have a clue. It set me thinking about Maria. I had been a tad insensitive toward her when she was trying to broach a difficult subject. And I'd told her so before I left. But as I was getting on the Ryan to head back south, I realized something else: how different we were in a lot of ways. I'd been raised in a home where religion wasn't stressed. My times in a church could maybe be counted in the double digits, but many of those were weddings and funerals. With Maria her faith was obviously more important. Something to consider in a relationship.

Not that I wanted to stop seeing her. Hell, I really enjoyed her company, and she was gorgeous. But was I ready for a serious relationship right now? *A serious relationship,* I repeated to myself. In modern terms I guess that meant close enough to go to bed together, but nothing more committal. I'd have to be sure of Maria's feelings, too. I wondered if she felt the same way, because I knew I didn't want to hurt her. But I also wondered what her expectations were about us. I'd been thinking a lot of what I wanted, but what was it she wanted? I'd have to figure that out before any answers would come to me.

The heavy Saturday night traffic gave me plenty of time to mull things over as I drifted from one bottleneck to another after the express lanes ended. But one thing the Beater was good for was expressway driving. The pick-up was good, and the size of the car made people tend to get out of my way. I felt like I was driving Battlestar Galactica.

When I turned off the Ryan to go south on I-57, I figured why not get a jump on the case and head out to Lincoln Estates. It was only about twenty minutes out of my way, and sometimes you just got to act on impulse. The traffic had thinned out considerably by the time I passed 147th. I practically flew the rest of the way there.

I decided to take a quick ride-by first to check out Space Oddities. As I passed it I was surprised at the way it was lit up. Pretty extravagant for a storage facility. There were a couple of cars in the lot too. Another surprise for this late hour.

I went down to the next intersection and turned, stopping in the all-night gas station. After draining my wallet to fill up, I headed back for another look. The property was adjacent to a railroad track. I knew that most railroad tracks had parallel frontage roads for their police patrols and maintenance trucks. This one was a wide macadamized lane. I slowed as I went over the tracks, scanning the frontage road. But something else caught my eye. A camera on the corner of the building. It focused on the parking lot. I continued to go straight and went down to the next light.

One good thing about the Illinois highway system is that nearly all major roads are laid out in perpendicular fashion. Lincoln Estates was still in Cook County, and most of the major highways were about a mile apart from each other. I turned left and went down to the next road. Another left and I was approaching the same railroad tracks from approximately one mile west of Space Oddities.

At this crossing I slowed again, but turned down the gravel road that ran parallel to the tracks. The tires of the Beater crunched as they went over the stones. Luckily, it was deserted along this stretch and I made pretty good time. To my right I saw some enormous cement pillars extending upward from a sloping embankment, and I realized I was passing under the expressway. After I'd gone a little farther I switched off my lights. That proved to be a mistake because I began hitting some enormous potholes. I turned the lights back on and crept forward. The haze from the bright parking lot lights was visible up ahead.

I decided to go the rest of the way on foot, took out my mini-mag flashlight, and started at an easy jog.

I wasn't really sure just what I was hoping to find, or even what I was looking for. But at least I was doing something, even if it was only checking the place out late at night. The stones on the road were large and I slowed down so not to twist an ankle. It took me a few minutes to get there.

The frontage road was about five feet lower than the tracks. The moon was hidden behind some dense clouds, but I still got down on my belly as I went over the tracks so I wouldn't be silhouetted. Old military habits die hard. There were two sets of tracks, then another embankment. I slid down that one and found myself about thirty feet away from the high cyclone fence that enclosed Space Oddities. The top of the fence was covered with three strands of barbed wire. I didn't see any need to try to scale or go under it, especially in my nice clothes, so I crept to the fence line. After all, I was just reconnoitering.

There were a lot of shrubs, but I managed to keep my footing. The rear of the place wasn't nearly as well lit up as the front, but I could discern a road around the building and several loading docks in the back. I crouched down so my form would be blocked against the background.

Squatting on my heels, I was thinking what a colossal waste of time this trip had been, when I heard it. A big diesel engine rumbling in the quietness of the night. One of the dock doors raised, folding itself into the building, the light spilling out around the body of a large truck. It looked like I wasn't the only one working on a Saturday night.

I moved down farther to try to get a better look at it, but could still only see the darkened outline. The tractor was a cab-over. It began pulling out of the dock, its lights still off. As it came out of the building I could see it had a tanker-trailer. Instead of pulling toward the road, the big metal monster swung around and headed toward the back fence area.

The truck's lights snapped on, and I scanned the fence line and saw there was a gate about forty yards east of me. The truck stopped at the gate and a figure got out of the passenger door. I could tell it was a man. A big guy. Big Frank?

The truck's lights snapped off again and the sounds of clinking metal echoed toward me in the darkness. I heard the gates creak open and the truck pulled out and swung up over the tracks. There must have been a crossing there to facilitate the railroad when the plant was in operation. After crossing the tracks the truck angled toward me and stopped.

I scrambled up the embankment to the area between the tracks and began running as fast as I could. It was obvious that the truck was going to head out west down the frontage road where I'd parked the Beater.

I had my flashlight on, shining down just in front of me. Even so the footing was terrible. The large stones seemed to twist under my feet, but I had to keep going at top speed if I had any hope of getting to my car—Doug's car—before the truck did. I knew I'd never hear the end of it from George if I let it get wrecked.

I tried to judge how far I'd come by using the distant expressway overpass as a frame of reference. But bouncing as I ran, that was pretty hard to do. The pathway between the two sets of tracks was slightly depressed and that made it difficult to see. I might also run past the Beater because I didn't know where to stop. Risky, or not, I had to get back on the frontage road.

I went up over the track to my left, and down the embankment. I tried to descend sideways, but lost my footing and went tumbling down. The heavy gravel hurt all the way and I was sure that I'd torn my pants. I heaved myself up and began running again. I could hear the rumble of the truck behind me.

Luckily, I hadn't lost my flashlight in the fall. I shone it in front of me and began to quicken my pace. A rapid glance over my shoulder. No lights behind me. But I could hear it coming. They were running without lights. But why? Why take the frontage road in the first place? Had they seen me and decided to investigate? No, they could have taken one of their cars for that rather than a tractor and trailer.

Suddenly my light beam swept over a glint of chrome. The front bumper of the Beater. It was just up ahead, maybe thirty feet more. My fingers dug frantically for the keys. I grasped them and stopped by the fender. Winded, I kept moving toward to the door. Locked. Force of habit. After a couple unsuccessful tries, I finally got the key into the lock and popped the door open. Sliding in I jammed the ignition key into the slot and twisted.

Oh, God, please let it start.

It turned over once without starting. I pumped the gas a few times and tried again. I could hear the sound of the truck, but still no lights. It was getting louder by the second. Should I jump out? Too risky. I twisted the key again and heard the engine catch. Now what? If I tried to out run them on this gravel, I ran the risk of blowing a tire, or getting stuck in some pothole. And since I was facing them, if I switched on the lights and tried to turn around, they'd see me for sure. I slammed it into reverse and began backing up as fast as I could, hitting every pothole and large rock in the roadway. As I went under the expressway I still hadn't seen the truck's headlights, but I could hear the heavy rumble of the diesel engine in the distance. This driving in reverse was killing me. I slowed down slightly, and looked to my right. A grass incline rose up between the towering cement support pillars of the expressway. Twisting the wheel, I turned and backed between them, going up out of sight. I stomped on the emergency brake and sat there idling in the darkness.

The blacked-out truck rolled by about a minute later. I waited until they were about a hundred yards ahead and drove down to follow them, glad to be going forward again. I appreciated how much easier it was, even without lights, but still managed to hit every damn pothole in the road. I hoped the Beater would hold together.

I saw a flash of red as the truck braked and turned right. They were at the highway, but they still hadn't turned on their lights, which meant that they weren't authorized to use the frontage road and didn't want to be seen either.

I bottomed-out getting back onto the highway and went after them. They still hadn't turned on their headlights, so I kept mine off, too. They were moving north. I pressed on the gas pedal and the big engine responded. Finally, I heard the distant whine of the truck's engine and suddenly their lights came on, and I saw them.

Might as well see where this baby's heading, I thought.

Chapter 26

The truck continued north. I kept behind it only long enough to get the plate number on the trailer. I didn't want to risk getting in front of them to try and get the plate off the tractor. There was no other lettering on it that I could see. The diamond shaped placards had nothing displayed. The highway was pretty deserted and I figured it would be easy for them to spot a tail. The truck seemed to be sticking to the highways rather than cutting over to the expressway where it could make better time.

But there usually were no state troopers on the highways. Since taking over all the Chicago expressways, they were spread pretty thin. Most local coppers receive little training in truck law enforcement. The driver was keeping well below the speed limit. I wondered what his game had been, using the frontage road instead of pulling around to the front of the building to the main road. And why hadn't he turned on his lights until he'd driven a good distance on the roadway?

There were enough questions to keep me guessing. I dropped back farther until the truck's taillights were like small red dots. We took Central Avenue north through the expansive forest preserves that proliferate in the south suburbs. At 159th the truck coasted up to a stop light and I turned off into a Dunkin' Donuts so they wouldn't see me pull up behind them. When the light changed the truck turned and went east. I waited a few seconds then followed.

They turned north again when they got to Cicero. The traffic picked up slightly as we entered a more populated area and I was able to stay slightly closer. But at Route 83 the truck veered left and went through the intersection going in a northwesterly direction. Route 83 was one of the few major roadways that ran on an angle and this particular stretch was only two lanes. If I followed they'd surely pick up the tail. Instead, I pulled into the parking lot of a shopping center and doused my lights.

This time of night the center was deserted so I was able to run somewhat parallel. I was doing great keeping them in sight when I saw the red and blue lights behind me. A spotlight hit my rearview mirror and the siren sounded. I pulled over and watched the truck continue out of sight on the roadway.

It took me about ten minutes to talk my way out of a ticket for driving without my lights. I explained to the cop who I was and that I was attempting to follow a truck. He listened patiently and went back to his car to run me through the computer. When the license plate came back to Doug Percy, he came up and ran the VIN. I showed him the police stickers on the window and explained why I had the car. By the time he let me go the truck was nowhere to be found.

I spent about twenty minutes driving around looking for it before realizing it was hopeless. It was almost two in the morning and I was feeling really fatigued. I debated the feasibility of going back to Space Oddities and setting up a stake out, but there was no assurance that the truck would return. Besides, it might not be related to the case at all. But the circumstances of the late night, back road exodus didn't smell right to me. I had a feeling that there was something rotten at 2001, and when I found out what it was, I might then know the full story about what happened to Carlos.

When I got home both the cats had apparently given up on me and gone to sleep. Or maybe it was an intentional snub. I didn't know and was too tired to try to figure. I undressed as I walked to the bedroom, dropping clothes on the floor as I went. After taking the time to unload my gun and stow it in its usual hiding place, a hollow section in my dresser, I made a quick security check. It was not something that I always did, like brushing my teeth and washing my face, but this case was starting to make me jumpy.

The next morning I woke up with the two cats comfortably ensconced around my legs. I assumed that all was forgiven. It was close to ten. Maria would probably still be at mass, and then at her parents' house for Sunday dinner. I got up slowly and stretched. Outside it was bright and sunny. Maybe Indian summer was making a comeback. Thinking of my own comeback, I changed into my sweats and running shoes without further delay. I knew if I didn't get my roadwork in sooner rather than later, I'd regret it.

It was one of those cool and crispy fall days, so I just settled into what I call one of my relaxation runs. I kept up a decent pace, but allowed my concentration to drift from imagined combinations and pacing to my previous night's date with Maria. She was really beginning to get special for me, and I wondered if that was good. The differences between us kept popping up. Were there too many?

I decided that it was too early to be thinking about the relationship in those terms and began to concentrate on the case. The interlude with the truck had proven intriguing, but what did it really mean? I had to get hold of George and have him run that trailer plate for me. Maybe that would shed some light on things. By the time I reached the top of Miss Agony, I had the rest of my day mapped out.

When I got back the light on my answering machine was blinking. Figuring it might be George returning the call I'd left on his machine I played it back. But it was Chappie, inviting me over to his house for a chicken dinner—after I'd done my road work, of course. I dialed his number and told him I'd be there.

"Good," he said. "I got some tapes of Berger we can watch after the Bears' game."

"Okay," I said. "I'll be there as soon as I shower."

"What you doing running so late?" he demanded.

"I went an extra couple of miles," I lied. He grunted a response and hung up. I dialed George's home number, got his answering machine again, and left another message for him to call or beep me. Then I called Maria and left a message on her machine, telling her where I'd be, and for her to beep me when she had a chance. As I soaped up in the shower I thought about how many conversations I was having with answering machines and computerized telephone voices lately.

The Bears managed a struggling win over the equally shaky Detroit Lions. Chappie shook his head and moaned about how the cheap bastard that owned the franchise had let the championship team that had once won the Super Bowl slip away.

"You ain't blaming the new coach?" I asked. "He seems to be everybody's favorite whipping boy lately."

"Nah," Chappie said. "I like him. The man's got heart."

"How 'bout Berger?" I asked. "He got heart?"

Chappie turned to me and grinned.

"If he do, we gonna punch it out of him."

When we got around to watching the tapes Chappie showed me the things he noticed. Small weaknesses, like

Berger's tendency to step in with an uppercut. He'd barely outpointed Elijah Day. And every time Day had him on the ropes, he'd just cover up and stand there.

"That's where we gonna kill him," Chappie said. "We gonna start working on body shots. See how he keeps his arms." He froze the motion on the TV. "You kill the body and what happens?"

"The head will die."

Chappie nodded approvingly.

"Instead of trying to come at him head on, like Day did, we gonna grind him down slow. Otherwise you gonna wear yourself out and have nothing left in the tank."

I watched him as he got up and threw some imagined body punches. Darlene came in and brought us both some coffee. She looked at her father and smiled at me.

"I got some better sparring partners lined up too," Chappie said. "Raul's gonna help us out. And there's a couple of new guys that I met look pretty good."

"Those last guys weren't so bad."

Chappie shook his head. "A bunch of chumps. We gonna get some real rough boys for you to mess with."

Marvelous, I thought. Somebody else trying to knock my block off.

"That'll give me something to look forward to," I said.

"Look forward to winning. Nothing else matters," he said.

Later that evening I went over to Maria's. We went out for a snack and then watched a TV movie together. I didn't mention anything about church. Neither did she. The movie was just about finished when George beeped me. He sounded tired when I called him back.

"Where the hell you at?" he asked me. "I tried your

house a couple of times."

"Where the hell am I at? I've been leaving messages on your machine for two days."

"You must need something real bad," he chuckled. "I took the family to the Holiday Inn in Merrillville for the weekend."

"How'd it go?"

"Great," he said. "I spent the weekend in one room with my wife, three kids, and a dog."

"Well, did you find anything on those guys I asked you to run?" I said.

I heard him yawn before answering. "Yeah, one of 'em had a pretty good sheet."

"Which one?"

"I don't remember. I left the stuff at work. Come by tomorrow and I'll give it to you."

"What time?"

"I don't know," he said. "Depends on how busy we are. Call first."

"Okay, but I need another plate run," I said, taking out my notebook.

"Christ, Ron, you think I'm your private pipeline to the Secretary of State? I could get my ass in a sling doing this stuff for you."

"My, aren't you cranky. I figured you'd be all relaxed and in a good mood after your mini-vacation."

"Listen, after that weekend I'm lucky I'm not in a psych ward. What's the plate?"

I gave it to him.

"What is it? A semi-trailer?"

"Yeah."

"Okay, I'll see what I can do. But this is it. No more. Understand?"

I said I did and hung up without reminding him that he said that every time he helped me. Maria asked me why I was smiling.

"Just thinking about George," I said. "He's so predictable."

"Aren't friends usually predictable?" she said. "Otherwise, we wouldn't be able to count on them."

"I suppose," I said, walking over to her. I cradled her face in my hands and kissed her softly. We never did get to see how the movie turned out.

Chapter 27

George didn't look too rested after his weekend in Merrillville. I told him so, and he stared at me balefully.

"One thing I don't need on a Monday morning," he said, "is a goddamn smart ass."

We were sitting in the large room that he shared with Doug and several other detectives. The battle-scarred desk was cluttered with stacks of papers. He was searching through them for the printouts that he'd run for me. Doug came in and slapped me on the back.

"Hey, Ron," he said. "You taking care of my car?"

"Like it was my own," I said.

Doug smiled, then told George that he'd seen Bielmaster lurking around the hallway.

"Great," George groaned. "All I need is for him to catch you in here." He pointed an accusatory finger at me as he glanced furtively toward the door.

"I can come back," I said.

"Nah," he grunted with a wave of his hand. He withdrew some papers from one of the piles and winked quickly. "Let's go get some coffee."

George got to the doorway first and stuck his head out, glancing both ways. After deciding that the coast was clear, he motioned for me to follow. We went down the hall and George hit the elevator button.

"For one floor?" I asked incredulously. "You got to be kidding."

"I ain't," he said. Then, as the elevator doors popped open, he gestured for me to get in. After the doors closed he gave me the computer printout sheets and told me to stick them inside my coat. I did.

"If Bielmaster ever found out all the shit I do for you I'd be walking a beat around the projects," he said.

"Thanks, buddy," I said sincerely.

The doors opened and we went to the coffee machine. I dropped in the coins for both of us and we sat at one of the tables away from the group of other coppers who were laughing and joking about their cases.

George sipped from his cup and set it down.

"That guy Bristol has a sheet," he said. "Strong arm robberies, aggravated assault, a couple weapons offenses."

I raised my eyebrows.

"The only other guy that came up with anything was named Jordan," he continued. "And the interesting thing is that he's clear through Illinois. The CQR did show some arrests from New Jersey for the same kinds of things. Battery, assault, extortion. But that was over ten years ago. Nothing recent."

"Sounds like another career criminal type who rehabilitated himself," I said facetiously.

"Irregardless, these guys don't sound like they're lightweights, Ron. What's this all about, anyway?"

"That missing illegal that I was working on for Maria's friend."

"Maria? That foxy chick from DCFS who was at your last fight?"

I nodded.

"Shit, now I know why you're knocking yourself out on this one," he said with a grin. He eyed me as he took another swig of his coffee. "So you said that floater was the kid you were looking for?"

"Yeah."

He sighed and set his cup down.

"You remember that advice I gave you?" he said. "Back off and let the state police handle it. This ain't nothing for you to get tangled up in."

"I appreciate the advice."

"In other words, you're gonna do what you goddamn well please anyway, right?"

I just smiled.

"Did you run that trailer plate for me?"

"Oh yeah," he said, reaching in his pocket. "I almost forgot." He took out the folded paper and slipped it across the table to me. "Comes back to some oil company in the Joliet area. J and D Oil, or something like that."

I nodded my appreciation. "I don't know what I'd do without you."

"I don't either, but sometimes I think we'd both be better off if we found out." He cleared his throat. "By the way, Doug was asking about the Beater. Not that I think he needs it back right away, or anything, but it would be nice if I could tell him how much longer you think you'll be needing it."

"Okay, fair enough." I stood up. "Just let me make a call."

I went over to the pay phone and dropped in enough coins to call downtown. Dick MacKenzie's secretary answered on the second ring.

When Dick came on the line his voice sounded tired.

"You get everything taken care of on that policy?" I asked.

"Ron, I uh didn't get a chance to do that yet," he said. "I'll see what I can do today, if I have time."

"Look, Dick," I said, trying not to sound as pissed as I felt. "I'd really appreciate it if you could expedite it a little.

I've borrowed a car from a buddy and I've been using that. Plus I still owe the bank a big old car payment at the end of the month."

"Look, I been busy," he said gruffly.

"That's the same line of bullshit you gave me last time," I said. "What the hell's going on?"

I could hear his sonorous breathing. Finally, he spoke. "Okay, I'll level with you. There's some major problems in the company right now."

"Major problems?"

"Yeah," he said. "There's a rumor of insolvency. It's just a rumor, now." I didn't know if he was trying to convince me or himself. "Midwestern Olympia's a big company, and I'm confident we'll weather this thing. But there's a lot of things happening. We're all going to have to tighten our belts."

"Mine's about as tight as it can get," I said. "And I sure can't afford to pay out five hundred bucks to you if I'm going to be paying for a non-existent car for the next three years."

"Listen, pal, that ain't my fault," he snapped.

"I'm not saying it is," I answered. "But I got to know. Can I count on you to help me, or not?"

I heard him swallow before he answered. "I'll try to let you know by this afternoon."

When I walked back to the table George read my expression like a book.

"Bad news?" he asked.

"Yeah," I said. "My insurance company's going under. And I'm not sure if they're gonna cover me for the Z-28."

He nodded thoughtfully.

"Dammit," I said. "This was the worst fucking time for my car to get stolen."

"You mean there's a good time?" George grinned.

I managed to get out of the building without seeing Bielmaster, so I didn't feel that the morning was a complete loss. And the expressway wasn't real crowded as I got on and headed downtown. I tried to cheer myself up by thinking that things could always be worse, but that didn't work. I started to worry that maybe they would. I needed to settle this car mess fast, or I'd be one step away from insolvency myself. And as a bonded, small businessman that would be all she wrote. I'd probably lose everything and end up working for some uniform security-guard company for minimum wage. And if Midwestern Olympia did go under, I'd lose the yearly retainer that they paid me as an on-staff investigator.

I blew out a long, slow breath and decided to try to concentrate on clearing this case as quickly as I could. Maybe that way I wouldn't feel so guilty about asking Juanita for my fee. Hell, I told myself. I shouldn't feel guilty about it anyway.

I decided to make some calls before I met Maria for lunch. As I got near the Loop I pulled off and went to a small restaurant near the Metropolitan Correction Center. It was a favorite hangout of coppers and the service is great. After getting a large coffee I went to the pay phone and called Tremain.

"Mr. Shade," he said, sounding glad to hear from me. "I was just looking for your card. I wanted to call you."

"I hope you find it. Those cards cost money, you know."

"I'm sure I'll run on to it," he said. If he appreciated my humor his voice didn't show it. "What I wanted to talk to you about was that address you were supposed to get for me."

"Carlos's? I've got it here someplace. Did you get anything back on the autopsy yet?"

"Hopefully I'll hear something by this afternoon," he said.

I found the address and gave it to him.

"You know," I said. "The roommates don't really speak English. I'd be glad to go with you. I speak some Spanish and they already know me. Plus I've got a friend who—"

"I appreciate your offer, Mr. Shade," he said, cutting me off, "but I think I'm perfectly capable of handling the interviews myself."

"I'm sure you are," I said, trying to sound diplomatic. "But my point is, these guys are illegals and they might be a little scared."

"I see what you mean, but I was planning on taking someone along who speaks Spanish."

"That'd be wise," I said. "When can we meet? I've got some theories I'd like to discuss with you."

"I'll have to get back to you on that," he said flatly.

"Well at least let me give you something to check out," I said, taking out the printout on the trailer that George had given me.

"Mr. Shade, I'm afraid I'm going to have to be blunt with you. While I'm sure your interest and efforts in this case are considerable, I find your interference somewhat distracting."

"Meaning?"

"Meaning that I've been assigned this investigation and I will proceed as I see fit. Now, as I said, I can appreciate your interest, but I can't have you running around jeopardizing the investigation."

"So you're telling me to butt out?"

"I didn't want to use those terms, but yes." He paused,

as if to let it all sink in, then added, "I'm sure I don't have to remind you that there are some very severe penalties for interfering in a police investigation. Especially for a state-licensed person like yourself."

"I get the picture," I said. "Give me a call if you need anything else. Provided, of course, you find my card."

I hung up and stormed out of the restaurant, determined now, more than ever, to crack this one.

Chapter 28

Maria and I ate a quick lunch at the same restaurant where my Z-28 had been stolen, but for some reason I didn't feel worried about going out and not finding the Beater there when we were done. The food tasted bland, though. Maybe I was lamenting about my missing car, or because of the bombshell about Midwestern Olympia that Dick had dropped on me earlier. My phone conversation with Tremain hadn't helped any, either.

"Ron, is something troubling you?" Maria asked.

"No more than the usual troubles," I grinned. I gave her a run-down of my morning conversations.

"That's terrible about the insurance company," she said, the space between her eyebrows furrowing. "Does this mean they're not going to pay for your car?"

"It might," I said. "But I'm trying to conjure up some positive vibes."

She smiled slightly.

"But the attitude of that state cop doesn't surprise me," she said, the anger seeping into her voice. "I'll bet if Carlos had come from Kenilworth they'd be falling all over themselves to investigate. That's why I'm glad you're working on it too." She reached over and squeezed my hand.

"Speaking of which," I said, picking up my coffee cup. "Do you think Juanita can advance me some money on this?"

"I can ask her," she said with a shrug. "But I'd prefer to wait till after the funeral, at least."

"Yeah, sure. But, I mean, I can't keep draining my bank

account to work this case I'll go broke. And I've got enough money worries right now."

"Of course you do," she said rubbing her fingers over my hand. "Which is why I'm going to pay for lunch today." Her smile dazzled me.

"I can handle lunch," I said. "But talk to Juanita soon, okay?"

"I promise," she nodded.

Maria and I decided that we'd eat tomorrow night at her place, after the wake. Hopefully that wouldn't be an all day affair. But Juanita was her friend, and I felt I'd better give her some extra room on this one. I told her I'd meet her at the wake around seven-thirty or so, and we could figure out what we wanted to do then.

"What about tonight?" she asked. "You want to come by?"

I smiled. "I've got to work tonight."

After I dropped her off I sat in the parking lot and unfolded the print-out of the trailer plate that George had given me in the lunch room. J & D Oil, Joliet, Illinois. I had a feeling that this was significant. Why had they sneaked out the back way that night? And with an unmarked tanker-trailer from an oil company that wasn't even in the immediate area. Something didn't smell right. At the very least, I needed to follow up on a few things. And to do that I'd need access to an information base. I glanced at my watch. One-fifteen. I'd catch all the rush hour traffic coming back if I made a trip out to Joliet to dig through the hall of records. Probably miss my Monday workout, too, and Chappie wouldn't be very forgiving.

I had to be realistic with my time management, but I also wanted to get something solid to make Tremain sit up and take notice. By the time I pulled out of the lot I had rationalized putting the records check off until tomorrow. But tonight would be another story.

I went home and started assembling things I'd need for some more late-night reconnoitering. This time I'd go there prepared. And hopefully get some answers, or at least the basis for some more questions. After putting together my ditty bag it was close to five. I fed the cats, changed their litterpans, and made a protein drink.

Laurel Ann Dean was anchoring the five o'clock news. The top stories included bits about the upcoming elections for county-wide seats and the latest attempts by the Feds to indict Sergio DeKooning. They flashed pictures of DeKooning, who was covering his face with a newspaper, and my old buddy Lawrence C. Peck, the pre-eminent sleaze-bag lawyer. Peck made some statements about the federal government's feeble attempt to harass his client as the camouflaged gangster made a rush for his Cadillac. Peck's face looked haggard hanging in front of all those reporters' microphones. Maybe the "Gee" actually had a good case against Sergio this time.

I made an imaginary pistol with my fingers and shot Peck through the forehead as he spoke. Ah, what would life be if it weren't for our fantasies?

I got to the gym about seven and began pounding the bags. Around eight Raul Reyes, one of my kick-boxing buddies, came in and Chappie told us to go a couple of rounds.

Sparring with Raul was always challenging. He'd been a world champ himself, winning the vacant cruiserweight title last year, only to lose it in his first defense. At thirty-four he was getting a little bit past it, but was still in great shape.

We went five quick rounds, then Raul slipped off his

headset and got the focus pads on. He led me through a couple more rounds of both punches and kicks, with Chappie shouting instructions. When the last bell rang he sprayed my face with water and stripped off my gloves. I sat on the edge of the ring.

"Chappie called me the other day," Raul said. "So you got a shot at the title?"

I nodded.

"You'll win," he said.

"I appreciate your confidence. And your help."

"Oh, hell, Ron, it's the least I can do. All the help you've given me. Besides," he grinned at me, "you'll beat the shit out of Berger."

"Not if he don't start working harder," Chappie said, slapping his shoulder. The round bell rang, oblivious to our fatigue, reminding me that time waits for no man. I glanced at the clock. It was close to ten. After a scorching in the steam for a few minutes the cold shower felt good as I lathered up and rinsed off. I let the water pour over the back of my head. By the time I dried off and got dressed, Darlene's aerobics class was ending.

"You're sweating more than I did," I joked as I approached her. She delicately wiped the rivulets of perspiration from her chocolate brow with a towel.

"Isn't that what you're supposed to do around here?" she asked.

"Yeah," I said, "but not everybody looks as good doing it as you."

She smiled. "So where you running off to?"

"Night maneuvers," I said.

Chapter 29

I stashed my workout gear in the trunk and took out my ditty bag. Once inside the Beater I took off my jacket and slipped on a black wool sweater. I put my Beretta in the pancake holster on my right hip and made sure my mini-mag flashlight had strong batteries. The ski mask and black leather driving gloves could stay off until I arrived. This time I was going to see if preparation would make a difference.

The expressway was pretty deserted so the drive out to Lincoln Estates only took me about twenty-five minutes. I went the speed limit, too. I wasn't in any hurry and didn't want to take the chance that some trooper would pull me over and see my ski mask, dark outfit, and weapon.

I took a slow cruise by 2001. There were a couple of cars parked in front, and the place was lit up like a Christmas tree again. I drove down to the railroad tracks and made a U-turn. As I passed it going the opposite direction I glanced at the odometer. I hoped that it was working correctly. Down the road to the intersection was three-quarters of a mile. The rest of the way to the strip mall and the restaurant where Kelly Lipton and I had eaten showed a total distance of one mile from Space Oddities. Not a bad distance for a midnight run.

The restaurant was right off the expressway and open twenty-four hours. It didn't look crowded, but there were enough cars in the lot so that the Beater didn't look conspicuous. Nobody seemed to notice me as I pulled up and got out. I went in and used the facilities. It was a hold over from my SWAT days: never go on an operation with a full bladder.

Instead of going back to the car I walked the other way. About fifty yards to the west was a large hotel. I slipped on the ski mask, but left it rolled up on my head like a stocking cap. A five-foot cyclone fence ran parallel to the roadway. I jogged over and vaulted it. The highway was wide and had a high median strip down the center. I hit my stride as I crossed the road and headed for the strip mall directly south of the restaurant. Beyond it, about a mile away, lay Space Oddities.

The trek took me fifteen minutes. An abysmal time for a runner like me to cover a mile, but after I cleared the southern edge of the parking lot the area became very woodsy. Uneven ground, high grass, and a maze of trees. I cut on an angle toward the railroad tracks so I could approach the place from the back. I had on my jump boots to protect my ankles from the unstable footing. It was a good thing, too, because I hit a marshy patch and was ankle-deep in water.

Finally I made it to the tracks. I was beginning to regret my caution and wished I'd parked on the railroad access road again. There was a full moon and no cloud cover tonight. Rather than risk being silhouetted on top of the tracks, I went over them and got on the road. From there it was easy going for the last hundred yards to the rear of the old plant. I rolled the ski mask down over my face and went along the embankment on all fours, angling toward the fence-line.

I knew from my previous visit it was one of those twelve-foot cyclone jobs with the three strands of barbed wire along the top. Much too high to try and go up and over. The rear of the building was well lit by flood lights at intervals of several feet along the edge of the roof. Ahead, inside the fenced-in yard, was a row of parked trailers and beyond them the overhead dock doors. Keeping the trailers between me and the building, I advanced to the fence. It was caked with rust, but still much too sturdy for me to detach from the post. Luckily the ground had eroded in several places making it possible to slip underneath.

I did a low crawl to the trailers. The loading docks were about fifty yards away, and it was all cement with no place to hide along the way. My only hope to get a closer look was to make a run for one of the docks and hide under the overhang. I settled next to the trailer's axle and pulled out the small, collapsible binoculars that I had in my pocket.

Not a creature was stirring. I snapped the binoculars closed and was just getting ready to make a dash for the closest loading dock when I heard the sound of a motor. The headlights of a Jeep swung around the north corner and headed slowly along the perimeter of the building.

It was an old Jeep Wrangler with a plastic top and no doors. Two men rode in the front seats. The passenger shone a spotlight around randomly. I stayed real still as they practically came up next to me. The passenger was good old Nick the security guard. The guy I'd had the run-in with at that sleazy bar. They rolled by and went around the south side of the building.

I hadn't anticipated the roving patrol. Even though they didn't appear to be real professional, they were out there to watch for somebody. Maybe my impetuous late-night visit of the other night didn't go unnoticed after all. This was a new wrinkle that I hadn't figured on. I decided to wait. Time the rounds of the Jeep. If they were bored, they probably had an established routine, even if they didn't consciously think about it. I looked at my watch. Eleven o'clock.

I waited ten minutes. Nothing. Just when I was debating whether or not to make a move, I heard the Jeep again. They rounded the north corner but this time headed to the fence line and drove along it. The Jeep bounced over the grass as Nick aimed the spot-light along the fence. I flattened against the tires as they went behind me.

The Jeep rolled to a stop and the lights went out. Shifting around I peered from behind the tires. A lighter flared twice and the embers of their cigarettes floated around like fireflies in the darkness in front of them. I strained to hear their voices as the words floated toward me. The fragments of their conversation seemed inane. Then I heard a radio.

"Nick, you out there?"

"Yeah, Frank," Nick said, holding up the portable to his mouth. "We're out by the back fence."

"Well get your ass over to the front gate and watch for the truck."

"Okay," Nick said into the walkie-talkie. He set it down and added, "That asshole."

The Jeep's lights came on and they sped over to the paved area and then disappeared around the corner. I stayed put and waited ten more minutes. Finally, one of the large overhead dock doors began rolling upward. I got out the binoculars again and focused on the dock. Two men stood there alongside one of those golf carts that I'd seen on my last trip. Even if I hadn't heard his name on the radio, the huge proportions of the man on the right made it obvious that he was Big Frank.

I couldn't hear what they were saying, but the smaller man left the area by the door. Big Frank said something into his walkie-talkie. He scanned the rear yard intently. For a moment I was sure that he'd seen me, but I stayed still. One thing I'd learned about evasion was not to move. It isn't your position that gives you away so much as the movement.

Big Frank got into his golf cart and backed it out of my view. The overhead door stayed open. Something was coming in, that was for sure. But did it have anything to do with my case? I couldn't be sure yet, but I had a hunch. And sometimes you just have to follow your gut.

I waited about ten more minutes. There wasn't much I could tell about the inside of the dock area from where I was, but I didn't like the prospects of moving up for a closer look. For one thing I didn't know how close they were to the door on the inside. And with no cover between me and the building, I'd be a sitting duck if someone spotted me. The ground was hard and growing colder, but it was the best position available. Besides, I figured the truck they'd talked about would get there soon.

Another ten minutes passed. The overhead door began to roll downward, making me think maybe the truck wasn't coming after all. But the Jeep abruptly wheeled around the south corner, and the large door stopped descending and began raising upward once more. This time Big Frank was there without his golf cart. Next to him was a guy in an idling fork-lift.

A big semi rolled around the corner and I tucked my gloved fingers over the binoculars. Didn't want to risk the headlights reflecting off the lenses. The truck pulled beyond the dock area, stopped, and then began backing up. I tried to read the license plate, but it was too dark. The side of the trailer had some lettering which was made visible by the roof lights. WASTE ELIMINATORS, JOLIET, IL, it said in large red letters outlined in black. Then underneath, in smaller print, was Responsible Waste Management.

I logged this in my notebook. It was enough to go on, but I really would have liked to have the plate. The truck had a diamond-shaped placard on the front bumper, but I couldn't quite make that out either. Frustrated, I mentally debated the risk of trying either to focus my flashlight at the front of the truck or maybe doing a low crawl to get closer.

The driver opened the door and climbed down. Just then the Jeep, which had continued around the building, pulled up in front of the tractor, and in the glow of the headlights I could see the placard number was 1115. Security-Nick got out and began bullshitting with the driver. They were too far for me to hear them, except for an occasional loud word or laugh. Nick spoke into his walkie-talkie, got in the Jeep, and started prowling again. They made a circle right in back of me, hitting the spotlight all around the perimeter. After they'd gone down to the far end I decided that I had all that I was likely to get, and that it was a good time to get out of there.

The Jeep turned and went east along the fence line and out of my view. I crawled back to the low spot in the fence and worked my way under it. Just to be on the safe side, I crawled several yards into the brush before assuming a crouched position. Instead of working over to the railroad frontage road like I had coming in, I went on an angle into the field and started heading toward the lights of the highway. I used my flashlight to check the way. This far in the field they wouldn't be able to see it.

It took me about twenty minutes to get through the woods. Usually it's easier going out, but I hit a couple of marshy patches again. My feet felt soggy and cold as I squished across the highway and wondered if this should take a couple of miles off my run in the morning.

Not a chance, I thought.

It was close to one when I got back to the Beater, and was glad, at least, that I'd gotten the damn heater fixed.

Chapter 30

The next morning I did something that I seldom do: I turned off my alarm and went back to sleep. It'd been close to two by the time I'd gotten home, stripped off my clothes, and washed my feet. I figured I'd earned a couple extra hours. At nine my beeper went off and woke me up again. It was my answering service.

"Sorry to wake you up, Mr. Shade," the girl said. "But the man who called was most insistent."

"That's okay," I said. "Who is it?"

"A Mr. MacKenzie from Midwestern Olympia Insurance."

I hoped it was good news, after all the grief they'd caused me lately. I hung up and dialed the number. Dick came on the line after a few minutes.

"Ron," he said. "I've got some good news. The company's filing under Chapter 11 for reorganization."

"Great. I take it to mean that you still have a job then. What about my claim on the Z-28?"

"I sort of snuck that in this morning," he said. "Pre-dated the paperwork and everything. Shouldn't be a problem. Of course, don't expect immediate payment, now."

"Huh?"

"Well, it stands to reason that the company's going to have to secure some big time credit to keep functioning, doesn't it?" His voice was getting stuffy again.

"What about the extra money that I paid to oil the system?"

"Look, Ron. I did you a favor, remember? I really put

myself on the line for you."

I decided it was better not to argue at this point.

"How soon can I expect the check?" I asked. "I want to let the bank know."

"I'll do my best to push it through as quickly as possible," he said. "But don't expect miracles, okay?"

"I won't, but I still need to let the bank know. Give me a date."

He hemmed and hawed and finally said he'd get to it by the end of the day, ending with, "I only called you because we're friends, and I knew how worried you've been about this."

Gritting my teeth, I managed to thank him and hung up.

Friends! Him and me? Never. But it did feel good to at least have the car worry attended to. Or, at least, almost attended to. I got on my sweats and went for a real good run.

After I'd showered and eaten my usual bagel and cream cheese, I made calls to Chappie and Maria. Chappie was at the gym. He said I could just train light with Raul for a couple of days until he got a few more sparring partners lined up. I talked briefly to Maria about last night so she was familiar with the situation. I told her that I'd be gone most of the day working on the case.

"Do you think this might be a good lead?" she asked.

"Could be. But it might just be a false trail, too. I'm not sure yet."

I told her that I'd meet her at the funeral home tonight and we could talk more then.

"I'll be looking forward to seeing you," she said. There was a nice hint of promise in her voice.

"Me too."

I'd noticed on my run that the weather was settling into

a cold, but sunny pattern. It was still nice enough—probably in the fifties, but the crispness in the air made me think of winter. The thoughts of the bitter sub-zero temperatures and the snow depressed me. Especially when I realized how much I had to accomplish before it got here. I'd have my title fight out of the way by then and hopefully be champion. And the car business should be settled too. A myriad of other little worries crept into my mind as I headed west on I-80 toward Joliet. I decided to concentrate on one thing at a time, solving this case being number one.

Joliet started out in the eighteen hundreds as another farm town along the railroad tracks. The city struggled, grabbing at every opportunity for investment from Will County Jail to Stateville Penitentiary. In the 1990's they struck oil when the gaming commission okayed a riverboat casino on the Des Plaines River that set off a sprawling urbanization, and turned it into sort of a mini-Chicago. Then the city fathers began clearing historic buildings in favor of a voracious annexation campaign. So now, besides being the center for all the old Will County offices, it was also the site of a nice new NASCAR racetrack. I wondered how much longer the rest of the old Joliet's heritage would stand as I parked and made my way to the County Clerk's office.

The building on Jefferson Street was relatively new and rather well crafted with fine wood counters and marble floors. Inside the Hall of Records there were rows and rows of shelves with stacks of books imposingly arranged. The woman behind the counter was an attractive, forty-something brunette. She pushed her glasses up on her nose and smiled.

"May I help you?" she asked. Her name tag said C. Beaumont.

Ms. Beaumont proved very helpful in assisting me in finding the corporate records for J & D Oil and Waste Eliminators. The only thing I was able to find about J & D was that it was a subsidiary of Victory Oil Corporation in Newark, New Jersey. Waste Eliminators listed B. Travens and Associates as its owner.

That sent me back to find out more about B. Travens, which, in turn, led to another company. After following the paper trail for about thirty minutes, even nice Ms. Beaumont was getting a little perturbed. I finally zeroed in on a firm called Carriers, Inc.

"I hope this is the last one you need," she said after dropping the book on the counter.

"Me too," I answered, trying to impress her with my smile just in case it wasn't.

As it turned out, Carriers Inc. had some familiar names on its list of corporate officers: Harold D. Jordan and Thomas P. Lipton. And, wouldn't you know it, L & M Trucking had good old Harold listed too.

I thanked Ms. Beaumont and went for the nearest public telephone. As I was looking up the address of L & M Trucking I found a printed political pamphlet urging the reader to vote for Thomas Lipton for President of the Will County Board. *Experience, Leadership, Integrity* the pamphlet said. On the front was a picture of a smiling Tom Lipton. Inside were pictures of him working at a desk with rolled-up shirtsleeves. On the last page was a family shot of him with Kelly and an attractive woman whom I assumed was Kelly's mother.

I tried to think back on my lunch with Kelly. She'd mentioned that Lipton was actually her stepfather. What did she say her real father's name was? I remembered that it started with an M. An Irish-sounding name. Mc something.

McKay. That was it. And she'd said that he'd disappeared. I looked back down the hallway.

I was in the right place to find out about marriages, births, and deaths. I copied down the address of L & M Trucking and put the political pamphlet in my pocket.

After exploring everything available about Kelly's birth to Vivian and Wayne McKay nineteen years ago, I checked on Wayne's untimely departure and Vivian's subsequent re-marriage. She and Lipton had waited for two years after McKay's disappearance. An appropriate length of time, but I wondered if there had been more to it.

I stopped by the library and looked through the old copies for anything I could find on Wayne McKay. That was no easy trick since all the old newspapers were on microfilm. Finally, I found a small article on his disappearance. It read:

Local Businessman Missing

> Authorities are baffled at the disappearance of local businessman Wayne McKay of L & M Trucking in Joliet. McKay's auto was found abandoned on Southwest Highway three miles east of Gouger Road. The blue Cadillac was found by Will County Sheriff's Police at one-ten Saturday morning. There were no apparent signs that the auto had been stolen and McKay's whereabouts are not known at this time. His disappearance is being investigated. Authorities are requesting that anyone with any information about McKay contact the Will County Sheriff's Department or the Joliet Police Department.

A few weeks later there was a follow-up article:

Local Businessman Still Missing

Local businessman Wayne McKay has been missing since July 10, and authorities admit they still have no leads as to his whereabouts. McKay, 33, who is part owner of the troubled L & M Trucking in Joliet, was last seen heading to a business meeting at six o'clock in the evening. His car, a blue Cadillac El Dorado, was later found by Will County Sheriff's Police abandoned near Gouger Road.

Authorities would not comment on rumors that a substantial amount of money was purported to be missing from L & M Trucking bank accounts, however, unnamed sources have alleged that bank records do show substantial withdrawals of the company's funds over the past three months. McKay's partner, Thomas Lipton, also refused to comment on the situation, stating only that he was "very concerned," and hoped the questions about McKay's disappearance "would be answered soon."

And two years later Vivian McKay filed for desertion, was granted a divorce, and married her former husband's partner. Kelly was adopted by Lipton and everybody lived happily ever after. A real storybook ending. Or was it?

For the sake of the completeness of my file, I positioned the first article between the brackets and slipped a dime into the slot. It disappeared as the machine copied it. I did the same for the second one. After returning the microfilms, I took out the political pamphlet again and looked at Lipton's smiling face. Time to meet Mr. Experience, Leadership, and Integrity, I thought.

Chapter 31

Since it was getting close to lunch time, I found a decent-looking restaurant near the Will County Courthouse and had a salad and an iced tea. Then I went looking for L & M Trucking. I found it in the northeastern section of the city near Silver Cross Hospital.

It was an impressive-looking place with a large, brick building surrounded by a high, cyclone fence. Rows of trailers were parked in back of the building and beyond that were several rows of parked tractors. On the front of the building L & M was spelled out in big white letters. A uniformed security guard stopped me at the front gate and asked who I was. He was a heavy-set guy with a florid face and a big gut that hung over his pistol belt.

"I'm here to see Mr. Lipton," I said.

"You got an appointment?"

I shook my head.

"You need an appointment," he said. "The boss don't see nobody without an appointment."

I was trying to figure out an appropriate move to counter his obstinacy when a car pulled up behind the Beater and honked. I looked around and saw Kelly Lipton getting out of the maroon Lincoln Towncar.

"Ron," she said. "I thought that was your car. What are you doing here?"

The guard seemed taken aback that we were on a first-name basis.

"I was trying to get in to see your father," I said. "But I wasn't having much success." I gestured toward the guard.

"Oh, Henry," she said to him, "he's a friend of mine."

"I'm sorry, Miss Lipton, I didn't know."

"No need to apologize, Henry," I said. "I can appreciate a man who takes his job seriously."

"Come on," said Kelly. "I'll follow you in."

We pulled in and parked in front of the building. Walking up the concrete steps, Kelly was smiling and telling me about a political luncheon that she and her father were going to.

"I'm going to write a paper about it for my political science class," she said.

"I hope your father's not too busy to see me."

"Relax," she said. "I'll get you in."

Kelly said hello to a middle-aged woman sitting behind a large metal desk. She stopped typing on a computer monitor and smiled.

"Mrs. Walden, is Dad busy?"

Mrs. Walden picked up the phone and spoke softly into the receiver. After a few seconds the office door opened and Lipton came out. His shirt sleeves were rolled up and his tie was undone, just like on the pamphlet. The perfect picture of a working-man's candidate.

"Daddy, you should be getting ready for the dinner," Kelly scolded. She made a half turn toward me. "This is Ron Shade."

Lipton reached out and shook my hand.

"Good to meet you, Mr. Shade," he said. "Kelly's told me about you."

"Daddy," Kelly said, flushed with embarrassment. Lipton glanced at her, then added, "You're quite a martial artist, she tells me."

I gave my best aw-shucks look and nodded.

"She said you're also some kind of a detective," he said.

"Investigating the disappearance of some Mexican who used to work at Hal's place."

"Salvadoran," I said. "He was from El Salvador."

Lipton gave a fractional nod and flashed his patented politician's smile.

"Well, I'll let you two guys talk," Kelly said. "I've got to pay a visit to the ladies' room, but we've got to leave soon, so don't forget."

"Okay, honey," he said. She smiled again as she walked away. We both watched her depart, then Lipton stepped to the side and invited me into his office. It was nicely decorated with the rear wall covered in fine wood. Numerous pictures and awards hung in frames behind the desk, and Lipton's face, blown up on a political poster, with the words *Experience, Leadership, Integrity* lettered beneath it, was hanging behind his chair. Off to the right was a large credenza and next to it a liquor cabinet. Lipton went right for it.

"Drink, Mr. Shade?"

"No thanks."

He poured himself a small shot and replaced the bottle.

"Have to get in the mood for the dinner," he said, grinning again. "You got kids?"

"Un-uhn," I said.

He gave a quick nod and swallowed some of his drink.

"Well, Kelly and her mom were the best things that ever happened to me," he said. "Now, what can I do for you?"

"I was hoping you could clarify a few things for me."

"Such as?"

"Such as, what's the connection between you and Space Oddities?"

He snorted slightly and flashed an amused grin.

"Connection? I'm friends with Hal Jordan, who owns the place."

"A little bit more than friends, I'd say."

The grin faded.

"We share a few business concerns," he said. "I do own a trucking company, after all. But what's that got to do with a missing illegal?"

"That's what I'm trying to figure out."

"There's a high turnover with those kind. Probably ran off, figuring Immigration was breathing down his neck."

"Actually, he's not missing anymore," I said. "He turned up. Dead."

Lipton raised his eyebrows and swallowed the rest of his drink.

"I still fail to see how any of this involves me," he said, irritation creeping into his voice. "Ask Hal if you want to know something about the Mexican, or whatever the hell he was. He was *his* employee, not mine."

"Isn't Jordan one of your partners for this place?"

Lipton's neck muscles tightened for a moment as he made a show of setting his glass down on the desk.

"Sounds like you've been doing some checking up on me, Mr. Shade."

"Just looking into Carlos Sanchez's death."

"That was his name?"

"Yeah."

"So how do you figure that I factor into any of this?" Lipton asked.

"I was hoping you could tell me just what your involvement is with Jordan and Space Oddities."

"I told you, Hal and I have been friends for years," he said, angrily. "Not that it's any of your business."

"Just exactly what is Hal's business?"

"I told you, I don't answer for Hal."

"Ever hear of a company around here called Waste

Eliminators?" I asked.

Lipton's bottom lip jutted out and his face began to redden. I thought he was contemplating trying to throw me out. But he knew better. His eyes darted toward the door as Kelly came in.

"Daddy?" her voice was quivering with concern. "What's going on in here?"

Lipton breathed hard twice before he answered. "Nothing, honey."

She looked at me questioningly.

I took out one of my cards and dropped it on Lipton's desk. "If you do think of anything, Mr. Lipton, I'd appreciate it if you'd give me a call."

"Daddy, what's going on? You look flushed."

I turned to leave, but Kelly ran up to me.

"Did you say something to upset my father?"

"I don't know," I said. "Ask him."

She compressed her lips and glared at me.

I continued walking. Why was it that there always seemed to be some innocent person who ended up getting hurt in situations like this?

Chapter 32

I felt bad about upsetting Kelly, but I knew that her father was involved in this somehow. Something was rotten in this whole big mess, and it was beginning to stink. If I could get enough proof, I could go to Tremain and spoonfeed it to him. Right now, all I could do was take out my frustrations on the heavy bag.

I made the drive back in about an hour. The traffic was still pretty light going into the city. After stopping at home to feed the cats, I grabbed my stuff and went to the gym. Chappie wasn't there, but I conned Brice into holding the focus mitts for me. It was a tedious workout, having to stop every few seconds and tell him how to hold his hands so I could vary my punches and kicks. After about twenty minutes I gave up and went to the heavy bag.

"Jesus, Ron," Brice said. "You're really killing that thing."

"It doesn't punch back," I grunted.

"Well, don't look at me," he said, throwing up his hands as he walked away. "I ain't getting in that ring with you."

He'd made that mistake once before, a couple of years ago.

I ground some body punches into the middle of the bag, purposely dropping some down, practicing liver shots. Lipton's query about kids had started me thinking. Maria and I had reached the stage in our relationship where we'd stopped the usual precautions. But with her being such a devout Catholic, would she be on the pill? I'd assumed that she was, but what if she wasn't?

I also had to think about where the relationship was going. She was gorgeous and nice to be with, but did we have the same expectations about everything? Obviously, the religion thing was a major factor. I had nothing against Catholics, but didn't think I could ever fit in as one of them. Organized religion as a whole just didn't appeal to me. But it did to her. And was I sure I was ready for another serious relationship so soon after Cathy's departure?

The round-bell rang and I sat down heavily on the floor. The bag was still swinging and smacked me on the side of the head. Upside the head, as Chappie would say. I sure missed him not being here for this workout. When the bell sounded again, I hoisted myself up and dragged my sorry ass to the showers.

A shower and change of clothes didn't do much for my disposition. I still felt gloomy as I drove to the funeral home. I was supposed to meet Maria there, pay my respects, and, hopefully, we could leave and get something to eat. I've always hated wakes and funerals, but I guess you'd have to be a little weird to enjoy them.

The funeral home was an old house. What had once been the living room had been converted into a large reception area. A sign with an arrow indicated which of the rooms Carlos was in. I tightened my tie and went in. The room was full of people. Juanita's father stood near the door, talking with some other Hispanic men. A glimmer of recognition flashed in his eyes as he nodded to me. Maria sat with Juanita and her mother on a sofa near the coffin. It was closed-casket. Being in the water does that to you.

Maria didn't see me come in and I paused for a moment and looked at her. She'd pulled her raven hair back into a bun, and had on a black suit with a white silk blouse. Her neck looked long and slender as she turned her head toward Juanita in conversation. Then she saw me and rose. As we met she kissed me softly on the cheek and grabbed my hand to lead me over to the sofa.

After the mandatory introductions, we retreated to the kitchen area and I asked her how soon we could get out of there.

"Ron, I have to stay," she said. "How would it look, me leaving. Juanita's like a sister to me."

I glanced at my watch. It was only seven thirty. That meant at least an hour of sitting around.

"Father Felipe's coming by to hold a prayer service at eight," she said. "Come on, I'll fix you some coffee."

We went into the big room adjacent to the visitation rooms. It must have originally been for dining. There was a long table and a group of chairs. All made of fine wood, with a crafted design ornately carved on the legs and backs. Maria poured some coffee from a fancy silver pot into a Styrofoam cup. I appreciated the irony.

I told her she could go back and sit with Juanita if she wanted to, but she poured herself one and sat opposite me.

"My parents were here earlier," she said. "You just missed them."

Thank God for that, I thought.

I took a swallow of the coffee and smiled at her.

"What are we doing after this is over with?" I asked.

She smiled back at me.

"We could go over to my place and watch TV," she said. "I rented a movie for tonight."

"Oh? What is it?"

"One of my favorites," she said. "*Casablanca*."

"One of my favorites, too. I can hardly wait."

I managed to drink three more cups in the large dining room before Father Felipe finally showed up for the prayer service. Maria came and dragged me into the other room to say hello to him. He shook hands with me politely.

I drifted toward the back as the priest made his way through the crowd. When he took his place by the small lectern, the room fell silent. He spoke in slow, deliberate Spanish, extolling the brief life of Carlos. How he escaped from the land of terror to live his dream in America. Surprisingly, I was able to understand a lot of it, but I'm sure if he would have been speaking faster, I wouldn't have caught much.

Then he began to recite the rosary. The sound of the whole room mumbling something in unison was unnerving. Even though I knew what it was, I felt uncomfortable. I was alone in a roomful of people all chanting a litany in a foreign tongue, reminding me that I was an outsider in their religion as well as their nationality.

Much later I found myself entwined in Maria's bed sheets as she lay against my side. I should have felt like I was in heaven, but even that didn't turn out right.

"Are you okay?" she asked, tilting her head back ever so slightly to look at me.

"Yeah, why?"

"Nothing. I was just wondering." She paused, then added, "You seemed distracted."

"I wasn't," I said haltingly.

"Are you sure?" she asked. "You felt distant. Almost like you weren't here with me. Like your mind was a million miles away."

I hadn't purposely held back. But the fears and worries from earlier were still tagging me.

"You were, weren't you?"

"What?"

"Holding back. Why?"

I took a deep breath. "I've been worried. A little."

"Oh?"

"I haven't exactly been dressing for the occasion these last few times," I said, trying for a smile.

"And that worries you?"

"Well, yeah. You know."

"No, I don't," she said. "Suppose you explain it to me."

My jaw sagged and I searched for the words.

"You're worried you might catch something, is that it?" she said angrily. "You think I jump into bed with everyone? That I'm some kind of easy Latina whore. Another simple but risky conquest for the big, strong, blond Anglo?"

I felt her start to pull away from me so I tightened my arm around her.

"Let me go," she said. "And get out."

"Hey, I think you're misinterpreting what I said."

I stared at her defiant face in the semi-darkness.

"What I meant was—" I began.

"I trusted you," she said. "I thought you were different. Better than most of the men I knew."

She tried to pull away again, but I held her even tighter.

"Will you listen to me? What do I have to do to get you to listen?"

She relaxed slightly, but her face still held its defiance.

"I've been worried," I said. "I just got out of a serious relationship, and not sure that I'm ready to start another one."

"Oh, so that's it. You're trying to get rid of me now?"

I blew out a long breath.

"I'm trying to talk with you," I said. "Make sure we're

on the same wavelength. Or at least that we understand what we expect out of each other."

"Haven't I given you enough? Let me go."

I held on.

"Look, everything I'm trying to say is coming out wrong. I've been worried that you'll end up pregnant, being the good Catholic girl that you are."

"You think I'd try to trap you?"

"I don't know," I said. "This religion thing never seemed to matter much to me, but to you it seems real important. It's been weighing heavily on my mind."

I felt her relax slightly and I released my grip on her. She turned away and immediately started crying. When I touched her shoulder she pulled away.

Great job, Shade, I thought.

I sat up in bed and untangled myself from the sheets.

"I'm sorry," I said. "Nothing came out the way I meant it. I just want you to know that I never wanted to hurt you."

She continued crying into the pillow.

"You still want me to leave?"

No answer. Just more crying.

I slowly got out of bed and went to the pile of my clothes. As I started to get dressed I saw her reach for a tissue. She blew her nose a couple of times, then looked at me.

"I guess I have a real way with words, don't I?" I said. "I don't suppose I could rewind the tape back to the part where Bogey says that this is the beginning of a wonderful friendship?"

"Too bad we can't rewind our lives," she said. "It would make things a lot more simple, wouldn't it?"

I nodded and started getting dressed.

"Ron, come here," she said, patting the bed next to her. "Sit down. Please."

I did.

"First of all," she said, "there's no need for you to worry. I'm on the pill."

"But I thought . . ." I left the sentence unfinished.

"I know," she said. "I'm Catholic, but I live in the real world." She swallowed hard. "I never told you that I have a daughter, did I?"

"No," I said. I was shocked. I'd seen no sign of any child in her life at all. And how long had I known her?

"I know what you're thinking," she said. "How come I never told you, right?"

"Right."

"It was a mistake I made a long time ago. When I was sixteen. My parents made me give her up for adoption as soon as she was born. I never even got to know what they named her."

I saw the tears rolling down her face now.

"So I made a pact with myself that I'd never make that mistake again, no matter what the church says."

"I'm sorry," I said. "It must have been very difficult for you." My hand traced over her shoulder. "Is that why you started working with disadvantaged kids?"

"You're the first person who's ever realized that," she said.

"It explains a lot," I said. "And makes me feel like an even bigger jackass, if that's possible."

Her hand caught mine as it skimmed her shoulder. "No, I overreacted. I'm sorry."

"Hey," I said. "You don't have to apologize to me."

She smiled. "Why don't you stay?"

I smiled back. "You're sure it's okay?"

She nodded. I brought her face close and kissed her gently, then held her as she continued crying against my shoulder. I realized then that we needed to talk. But she was still crying and this didn't seem like the right time. I had to find out what she wanted out of our relationship. She'd reached out for me in a time of crisis in her life. I was sure that was part of it. Still, I had to make sure that I didn't repeat the mistakes of the past.

Chapter 33

The next morning we went to the funeral together. I was curious if anyone realized that I had on the same clothes that I'd worn to the wake, but figured if they did they'd just assume that I was either cheap or poor. I convinced Maria that I wouldn't mind if she sat up near the front with Juanita and her family. Then I judiciously took a seat in one of the rear pews, away from all the people who would periodically kneel and re-seat themselves.

After the funeral there was a luncheon at a local restaurant. I managed to sidestep that one, saying that I had some special things to check out regarding the case. Maria seemed to accept that and told me to call her later. I said I would, but left wondering silently how things were going to turn out between us.

After our argument we'd kissed and made up. Neither one of us was in the mood for any more heavy conversation, so we just let everything drop, rewound the movie, and made out with Bogey and Ingrid. The worries about our relationship still nagged me, but I was content to leave them on hold for the present.

I got into the Beater and headed downtown. I'd have to get something concrete on this case to take to Tremain. And to do that I'd need access to an information base. The mid-day traffic was starting to pick up, and I suddenly found myself creeping along in a slow-moving cluster.

My philosophy was not to fight the traffic, since there's nothing that you can do about it anyway. Instead, I turned on the radio and went with the flow. Unfortunately, none of the FM stations were coming in very well on the converted system in the canyons of steel and big buildings. So I switched to an AM news channel and listened to the announcer talk about the latest charges in the upcoming elections.

Chicago politics were never boring, and always provided plenty of fodder for the news commentaries. I found myself wondering about good old honest Tom Lipton and his Will County crusade. But Will County politics were seldom discussed on Chicago area stations. I was hoping to hear something about the Sergio DeKooning indictment, but that, too, was absent from the features. The announcer did mention that there'd been another large fish-kill in the Des Plaines River. The second one in two weeks. The cause, he said, was being investigated.

Miraculously, the traffic thinned and we started moving again. I was able to get off at Roosevelt and take that to Michigan. From there I went north till I found an unoccupied loading zone near the Chicago Metro Building. Even though there were signs posted warning that it was illegal to park anywhere in the Loop where there wasn't a meter, I figured that the Beater'd be safe enough with all of Doug's FOP stickers plastered on the windshield.

The *Metro* was one of the smaller newspapers trying to compete in the shadow of the two Chicago giants, the *Tribune* and the *Sun-Times*. It had more of a business orientation to it, but devoted a lot of space to crime issues and suburban topics. And one of its star reporters, Rich Staford, was a buddy of mine.

It had been gray and overcast at the funeral, but the sun had burned through and the air felt crisp and sunny. I walked leisurely toward the front doors. A pretty woman in a dark business suit smiled as we passed. I took that as a good omen. Maybe my luck was about to change.

I found Rich in his office on the fifth floor. He was hunched over his computer, staring intently at the screen. A cigarette burned alongside him in a crowded ashtray.

"I thought they outlawed smoking in public buildings," I said as I walked in.

His big, shaggy head twisted in my direction, and I could see a grin under the unkempt mustache.

"Yeah, except for designated smoking areas," he said, rising to shake my hand. "Which this is. Long time no see. That must mean you want something."

"You been talking to my police buddy George?"

"Oh, you got another friend you take advantage of?"

He reached over, picked up the cigarette, and took one more drag before stubbing it out.

"Thank you," I said, nodding toward the ashtray.

"Don't mention it," he said, taking another out of his pack. He grinned, but didn't light it. Just put it between his lips. "Got something crucial to discuss, or should I fire this up and chase you out of here?"

"I'm not sure exactly what I got," I said. "Let me run it by you and see if you find it interesting."

Rich leaned back, his arms behind his head, as I brought him up to date on the case, from Carlos's disappearance to my conversation with honest Tom Lipton. Except for an occasional raised eyebrow, it didn't seem to pique his interest much. When I finished he leaned forward and took the disk out of his computer.

"Let me see what I have on Lipton," he said, sorting through a box of more disks. He found the one he wanted and slid it into the machine. After scrutinizing the screen for a couple of minutes he turned back to me. "Ron, what you say is interesting, but I don't have a lot on this guy.

And, frankly, I can't get real excited about this one either. We don't really push stories about the Joliet area much."

"He's mixed up in this somehow," I said. "I can feel it."

Rich sighed. "Yeah, but is it something big that I can sink my teeth into, or is it business as usual in politics? A candidate with ties to private industry is pretty standard stuff in Chicago. What makes you think Will County's any different? It's just not as well publicized."

"So what you're saying is that you're not interested?"

He held up his hands, palms outward. "Now I didn't say that. This tie-in to that waste disposal company might be something."

"You got a line on them?"

"No," he said. "But I got a friend who's been working on a story along those lines. He lives out in Lockport."

"Great. When can I meet him?"

Rich turned and flipped through his Rolodex. "I'll see if he's home."

"What is he, a freelancer?"

"Sort of," Rich said, cradling the phone on his huge shoulder. "Works out of his house. Emails his articles to us. He's kinda sick now."

"What's wrong with him?"

"Cancer," he said as he was dialing the phone.

Lockport, one of the far-western suburbs, was all the way out by Joliet and Stateville Penitentiary, and about thirty or forty miles from downtown Chicago. Rich had introduced me to Bob Cassidy over the phone. His voice sounded weak and was punctuated by a frequent, hacking cough. Nonetheless, he seemed interested to meet me, and gave me directions on how to get out to his house. He did request that I make it before three, when he had a doctor's appointment. It was twelve-thirty, so I left right away. Rich walked me down to the elevator and told me that his friend liked to be called Hoppy, after Hopalong Cassidy.

When I got back to the Beater I saw a parking ticket stuck to the windshield wiper. So much for the FOP stickers, I thought. I plucked the ticket off the windshield and stuck it in my jacket pocket. Maybe George could fix it for me.

The quickest way to Lockport from the Loop was the Stevenson Expressway. I got on and made pretty good time once I got away from the downtown area traffic. Per Hoppy's directions, I got off at Route 83 and went south to Archer, which angled southwest into town. An hour and a half later I was pulling up in front of his house.

It was a single-level frame structure with a dull gray siding covering it. The yard was unfenced and a rickety swing set sat in the back. A cement driveway extended from the street and abruptly stopped. There was no garage, and a rusting, blue Ford station wagon was parked next to the side door. When I rang the bell a thin blond woman answered.

"Hi. I'm Ron Shade. Here to see Mr. Cassidy."

She smiled and opened the door wider. I guessed her to be in her late thirties. There was a drawn, sad look around her eyes.

"Come in, Mr. Shade. Hoppy's been expecting you."

I walked into a living room that was littered with newspapers, magazines, and a child's toys. The coffee table was stacked with papers and a bunch of VHS tapes. There was a console TV in the opposite corner with a VCR on top. A huge gray-and-white tom cat slept next to it, his long legs dangling over the edge of the TV.

"Please, excuse the mess," she said. "I just got home from work."

"It's no mess," I said. "Reminds me of my place on a good day."

Mrs. Cassidy smiled and led me into a bedroom. There was a hospital-type bed set at a right angle. Next to it was an oxygen tank, a wheelchair, and a movable bed-stand. On the bed-stand was a computer monitor and keyboard. The man on the bed had the tubes from the oxygen hooked in his nostrils. His hair and beard looked grayish and he was bone-thin.

"Glad to meet ya, Shade," he said, extending a thin hand.

I shook it and he grimaced. "You're squeezing my hand too hard," he grunted. I let go immediately and apologized. He shook his head and twisted, after considerable effort, to face me. "Ain't your fault," he said.

"Honey," the woman said. "I'm going to pick up Dorrie. I'll be back in a minute."

He nodded and watched her leave the room.

Hoppy reached over and shut off the valve that was connected to the neck of the oxygen tube. Then he slipped off the hose.

"You look pretty strong," he said. "How about helping me into the chair. Don't want to be in bed when my daughter gets home."

I moved the wheelchair over beside the bed and asked him what he wanted me to do.

"Just guide my legs onto the seat," he said. I did, but he started to slip. I held him under the arms and slowly lowered him onto the chair.

"Thanks," he said, after shifting himself. "Now, how about we go into the kitchen?"

I pushed the chair through the doorway. In the kitchen we sat at the table. The first thing he did was have me get a cup from the sink and fill it with water. He dug out a cigarette hidden in the seat of his chair.

"You smoke, Shade?"

I shook my head.

"Good," he said, rolling over to the stove and turning on a burner. "Don't start." He drew on the square and exhaled a cloud of smoke. "Do me a favor, okay? When my wife comes home tell her it was you, if she asks who was smoking, okay?"

"All right, but should you be smoking in your condition?"

"My condition," he laughed. The laugh turned into a coughing fit. Finally he got it under control. "Already got lung cancer. Everything else is being eaten away, too. Don't matter much now."

I said nothing as he took another drag off the cigarette.

"So whatcha got?" he asked, cocking his head.

I spread my notes out on the kitchen table and started at the beginning. Carlos's disappearance. Space Oddities, Big Frank, Lipton, Waste Eliminators, and the strange things I'd seen on my surveillances. That seemed to pique his interest.

"Never heard of that Space Oddities outfit," he said, tapping some ash into the cup. "But J & D Oil and Waste Eliminators are old friends. Doesn't surprise me that Lipton's tied in, either."

"That's *honest* Tom Lipton," I said with a grin.

"Yeah. Right." He took another drag on the cigarette. "Old J & D was involved in a little mini-scandal of sorts last year. Seems they submitted a bid to provide heating oil for some of the low income housing around the Joliet area. The bid was so low that one of their competitors accused them of rigging it. Turns out they were legit. Just had the cheapest oil in town."

"How about Waste Eliminators? Ever hear about them?"

He inhaled one last time on the cigarette and dipped it in the water. It went out with a quick hiss. I felt relieved for both of us.

"Got some stuff on them," he said. "I know they were involved in some kind of lawsuit with a trailer park north of here. Settled out of court. Haven't been able to get any of the particulars. The file was sealed as part of the settlement. All it reads is 'Suppressed vs. Suppressed.' "

"Why would a trailer park sue them?"

"Apparently they had a landfill near the place." He picked up a pencil and his nervous hands began playing with it. "The people in the trailer park charged that PCBs had leaked from the site and tainted the ground water. Ruined all their wells."

"You know any more about it?"

"Wish I did," he said. "But like I told you, the file's been sealed. They had some high-powered attorney that blew the trailer park's lawyer right out of the water."

"Is the park still there? Maybe I could go over and find somebody to talk to."

"Nope. All of them relocated." He looked down at my notes, which I'd spread out on the table. "What's that?"

I looked down at the paper. He was pointing to the symbol that Paco had drawn when he was describing Carlos's argument with Big Frank.

"It's some sort of symbol," I said. "Paco said that Carlos got into an argument with Big Frank over this type of symbol being on one of the drums."

"Looks almost like the chemical symbol for benzene," he said. Hoppy used his pencil to draw a hexagon with a circle inside.

"What exactly is benzene?"

"A toxic hydrocarbon," he said. "Usually used as a solvent or mixed with gasoline."

"You know, Carlos had a degree in chemical engineering."

Hoppy's eyebrows raised. "So then he'd know if they wanted him to load drums of a toxic substance like benzene, wouldn't he?"

"That's just what I was thinking."

"And that little nighttime, back road ride you saw that tanker truck going on," he said. "Bet they were going to do a little midnight dumping. Yeah, it's all starting to fit together. J & D saves money by not paying the extra freight on toxic waste disposal by storing the stuff in the warehouse and dumping it little by little."

"But wouldn't they have to have permits for hazardous waste disposal?" I asked.

"Waste Eliminators does," he said. "Supposed to have a specially constructed landfill near Crown of Victory, Indiana, where they take all that shit. Or so they tell me. Never been there myself."

"Can you tell me where it's at? I think I'll take a ride out there tomorrow."

"I'll do better than that," he said. "I'll go with you."

"I don't know, Hoppy."

"Hey, come on. Shade," he said, an almost pitiful tone seeping into his voice. "I wouldn't be no trouble."

I looked at him. "You sure you're up to it?"

He snorted and swallowed hard.

"Look, I won't be any trouble. I promise. I just gotta go in for my chemo today and that's why I'm feeling kind of crummy. But I been hoping for a break on this article I been working on. It's called 'A Killing Frost.' I want to finish it while I still can . . . with something good."

I heard a car door slam and then another. Hoppy still looked at me imploringly. Through the window I saw his wife and a small, blond girl about ten moving toward the house.

"Dump this for me, will ya?" He held the extinguished butt toward me. His eyes twitched.

"What time tomorrow can you be ready?" I asked.

Chapter 34

"I been doing some heavy thinking since we talked last night," Hoppy said as we sped along I-80 toward the Illinois-Indiana border. He paused long enough to take out one of the cigarettes he'd requested that I buy for him before we'd left Lockport. I told him if he insisted on smoking to crank down the window.

"That symbol on the drum that you said Carlos was arguing about," he continued. "The more I think about it, the more sense it makes."

"How so?"

"Well," he said, inhaling on the cigarette. "You said you saw a tanker truck taking the back way out of that place, right?"

"Un-huh."

"And the plate came back to J & D Oil out of Joliet, right?"

"Yeah."

He paused to take another drag, then suddenly began a coughing fit. It was a deep, heavy sounding cough. I asked him if he was all right.

"Are you kidding?" he said between gasps for air. "I'm dyin'." More coughing, then he added, "From the toes on up."

He tossed the cigarette out the window and after a few minutes got his breath back.

"I told you that J & D was involved in that bid-rigging controversy, didn't I?" he said. "Well, the investigation revealed that they actually did submit the lowest bid.

Now I got an idea how."

I waited for him to continue, but he seemed to be concentrating on his breathing.

"How's that?" I finally asked.

"That other truck you saw, the one from the waste disposal."

"Waste Eliminators," I said.

"Right. J & D is supposedly paying them to dispose of their hazardous waste, see. But instead of disposing of it like they're supposed to, they mix the benzene with the regular heating oil, and dump the rest."

"So they save money from the disposal and on the heating oil."

"You got it, Shade," he said. "There was an outfit doing this type of thing in New Jersey a few years ago. I'll have to look that one up."

"What's the effect of mixing the benzene in with the regular heating oil?"

"Let me put it this way," he said. "Benzene is a carcinogen. By diluting the heating oil with it you're exposing the people to a big health risk. They're probably tossing in other waste products like xylene and PCBs, too. But since nobody's aware of what they're doing, and they're delivering the diluted oil to low income slumlord apartment buildings anyway . . ."

"In other words, nobody gives a shit."

"Shade," he grinned, "you'll never make it as a journalist with a vocabulary like that."

After getting off the expressway, we took the highway south past the small town of Crown of Victory. I stopped at a gas station to fill up and asked directions. The attendant eyed me suspiciously, but pointed down the road.

"It's down there a couple of miles," he said. "Away from everything."

When we got to the landfill it was a pretty impressive sight. A pretty impressive smell, too. It was an old abandoned quarry about a mile in diameter and probably about a hundred-and-fifty feet deep. But now half of it was filled with mountains of garbage.

Big trucks pulled in and out at a furious pace, going down macadamized dirt roads to dump their loads and hurry back up as bulldozers labored to cover parts of the trash mountain with dirt. A large group of sea gulls hovered overhead, crying like babies. Some of the braver ones swooped down to pick among the rubble. The main entrance was an asphalt road that met the highway. An office building was farther down the road. Looked to be an old abandoned factory of some sort. Probably from when they sold stone or bricks. A ten-foot cyclone fence surrounded the perimeter and a husky, uniformed security guard lounged on a bench inside a shack at the main gate. A big pump twelve gauge sat across his lap.

I kept driving down the highway and pulled over after about a mile.

"Well, Hoppy," I said. "We're here. Any ideas on what to do now?"

"Christ, you're the detective," he said with a grin. "Go detect something."

"I've already detected that I don't like the smell of this place. Literally."

"That's methane gas. A bi-product. You know, they've found all sorts of things preserved in these landfills," he said. "Sort of like a time capsule."

"Yeah, once you get past the smell."

"What would you do if I wasn't with you?"

I considered the question for a moment.

"Probably try to bluff my way in," I said.

"No shit? You really do that? Just like on TV?"

"Actually, it always seemed to work a little better when it was done by James Garner or Tom Selleck."

"Ah, Rockford and Magnum," he said wistfully. "Two of my all time favorites. Well, let's give it a try. I'm game."

"It's not that simple, Hoppy. As I said, things don't always go as planned."

"What usually happens?"

"I usually end up getting caught and beating the hell out of somebody."

"Hey, sounds like fun," he said, grinning again. "Rich told me about you. I'd like to see you in action."

"Be better to watch ESPN next time I'm on. Besides, I'm not on my home turf here. We go down there and try to buffalo our way in, that guy's sure to notice our Illinois plates."

He pursed his lips. "We could say we're from Chicago and we're interested in buying the landfill. You know how fast Illinois' landfill space is disappearing?"

"Is that feasible? I mean going out of state?"

"Real feasible," he said. "The Supreme Court upheld the right to transport garbage across state lines regardless about how the receiving state feels about it."

"I don't know. They might see through that one in a hurry. We need something more universal. An easier scam."

"We could say we wanted to donate your car."

I frowned.

"How about insurance salesmen then?" he said.

"I said easier, not obnoxious."

"Shade, you ever been anywhere where some asshole didn't walk up to you and try to tell you that you needed to increase your insurance? Believe me, I know."

"Maybe it does have possibilities." His wheelchair was in the trunk. "You gonna be able to make it?"

He nodded.

"Since this place is supposed to be set up to take hazardous waste, proper insurance coverage should be very much in demand. Just get me in there, Shade, and I'll ask all the right questions."

"Okay, buddy, we'll give it a try."

I made a U-turn and headed back toward the entrance of the landfill. A big garbage truck was swinging into the place and I fell in behind it. The big, fat security guard didn't get off his butt until we were rolling past the gate-shack. In the rear-view mirror I saw him come out, look at us, and then go back in. I drove to the office and parked in front. It took me a couple of minutes to get Hoppy's wheelchair out of the trunk and get him into it. But once we had that accomplished we opened the door to the office building and went inside.

It wasn't much to look at. Dingy walls that looked like they hadn't been painted in years. There was a little corridor and several doors with frosted glass. The one closest to the door was open and a man was leaning against the frame. He looked to be in his fifties, heavyset, with shirt sleeves rolled up to his elbows. His reddish hair was swept back from an expansive forehead.

"What's the idea of running the gate?" he asked.

I smiled ingratiatingly as I pushed Hoppy forward.

"Sorry about that," I said. "Forgot my glasses today and can't see a damn thing without 'em." I extended my hand, but he let it sit out there.

"MacKenzie's the name," I said.

"Bill Pearl," he said noncommittally, as he finally shook my hand.

I fished one of Dick's cards out of my wallet.

"My associate, Mr. Cassidy," I said, indicating Hoppy, as I handed over the card. "We're with Midwestern Olympia Insurance."

Pearl looked at the card, then back at us.

"This still doesn't tell me why you barged in here," he said, handing it back to me.

I grinned and held up my hands. "No, no. The card's free." I smiled again.

"So what do you want?" Pearl asked, putting the card in his shirt pocket.

"Ah, Mr. Pearl. Bill . . . May I call you Bill? Fine. What myself and my associate want to do is improve things for you." I let him munch on that for a few seconds, then added, "Is that your office? May we go in?"

Pearl's brow wrinkled, but he stood aside and let us in. I wheeled Hoppy through the doorway.

"Are you married, Bill?" He nodded. "Good, good. Kids?" He nodded again. "Excellent. I have a great opportunity for you. One that's perfectly suited for a family man like yourself." I reached in my pocket and took out my notebook. Flipping it open I said, "Now, if I can just get some preliminary information. Who is the owner of this facility?"

"Waste Eliminators," he answered.

"And, Bill, how long have you been employed here?"

"Since it opened," he muttered. "Two years."

"You're the foreman?" I asked, making furious notes.

"Assistant foreman. The regular guy's out to lunch."

"Well, I can see you'll probably be the top man before too much longer," I said. "I've got a feeling for these things, you know."

"So what is it you're selling, Mr. MacKenzie?" Pearl asked.

"Dick," I said. "Call me Dick. Please."

"Okay, Dick."

He waited for me to speak.

"What we sell is security, Bill. Security for the future."

"We already got plenty of security," he said.

I forced a laugh. "I'm aware of that. We saw him at the gate. No, Bill, this is security for the unexpected. Peace of mind. For you. For your family."

"Life insurance," Hoppy blurted out.

"I already got that," Pearl said.

"Most places do offer a policy on their workers, this is true, but have you read all the fine print, Bill?" His eyebrows furrowed. "Are you covered in case of accidental death or dismemberment off the job?"

He shook his head. "I ain't sure."

"How about for catastrophic illness that may be job related?" Hoppy asked. "Working around hazardous wastes has its dangers."

Pearl looked at him questioningly. "Hazardous wastes?"

Hoppy nodded.

"We ain't got none of that shit here," Pearl said. "We ain't licensed for it. Just regular garbage is all we take."

"Are you sure?" Hoppy asked. "I was under the assumption that this facility was specially designed to dispose of toxic waste."

Pearl shook his head. "The company's got another landfill in Illinois that handles that stuff."

"Oh? Where's that?" Hoppy asked.

"That's none of your business," another voice said from behind us. We turned and saw a slender guy in a brown sports jacket.

"Hi, boss," Pearl said. "These guys are from Midwestern . . ." he paused to take the card out of his pocket and read from it. "Midwestern Olympia Insurance."

"We don't need no more insurance," the slender guy said. I rose and extended my hand.

"Dick MacKenzie's the name."

"Beat it," he said. "Like I said, we don't need no insurance." His mouth drew into a tight line. "You know better than to discuss company business with strangers," he said to Pearl. Pearl's face reddened.

"You guys still here? I told you to beat it."

I gave a conciliatory nod. Mr. Milquetoast. No Problems. I gripped Hoppy's chair and began wheeling him out. Maybe this would be a first for me, I thought. Getting in and out without getting into a fight with somebody. Pearl followed us out, watching as I helped Hoppy into the Beater and folded the chair to stash it in the trunk. As we pulled toward the gate Hoppy began laughing.

"Shade, that was great. I ain't had so much fun in years."

"If we can just get outta here without any problems," I added.

At the gate the security guard was waiting for us, holding the shotgun at port-arms. A scowl twisted across his lips. I rolled to a stop, and he came around to the side of the car.

"The boss wants me to check your ID," he said. "Get out of the car."

I put it in park and opened the door. His chin jutted out as he scrutinized me.

"Him too," the guard said, indicating Hoppy.

"I'm handicapped," Hoppy said. "Want to see my wheelchair in the trunk?"

"Just give me some ID," the guard said.

I handed him one of Dick's cards.

"Driver's license too," the guard said. "This ain't shit."

I smiled and gave an "aw-shucks" type of shrug. Suddenly the guard looked over at the gate. A brown, mongrel dog prowled by the roadway.

"There's that son of a bitch," the guard said. Dropping the card, he raised the shotgun to his shoulder and aimed at the dog. I brought my hand up quickly and shoved the barrel into the air. The blast was deafening.

The guard started to say something, but I was already grabbing the barrel with both hands. I pulled as I pivoted, just the way we'd practiced in the Army in Saudi, and the rifle slipped from his grip. Then I pivoted back the other way and drove the stock into his gut. He sagged forward and I brought it up under his chin with enough force to close his mouth hard as he tumbled the rest of the way to the ground. I looked for the dog. It'd taken off running.

"What was that all about?" Hoppy asked as I got back into the car.

"I like dogs," I said.

"Oh, I thought maybe you just didn't like Hoosiers," he said. "Anyway, he'll probably just shoot it tomorrow."

"Not with this gun he won't," I said, tossing the shotgun in the back seat. "Let's see if we can catch him." I drove down the road after the dog. He was walking now, furtively glancing over his shoulder every few steps. As soon as we got close he began running again. I got out of the car and called to him, but he only ran faster. Finally he disappeared into an adjacent field.

"What were you going to do with him if you caught him, Shade?" Hoppy asked as I got back into the car.

"I don't know. Take him to the animal welfare, I guess."

Hoppy snorted. "So they could gas him? You got a thing about lost causes, don't you?"

I didn't answer. We rode back to the expressway in silence.

Chapter 35

It took us a good hour to get back to the Lockport area. I offered to buy Hoppy some lunch, but he declined.

"I gotta go in for another chemo today, so what's the use? I'll just throw it up anyway." He took out another cigarette and lit it. After a long drag and some more coughing he seemed to be exhausted.

"Want me to drive you home?" I asked.

He shook his head.

"Nah. What I'd like to do is find that other dump site that old Bill mentioned."

"Ever heard of it?" I asked.

He inhaled some more smoke before answering. "Uh-uh. The information I had said that they were using the Indiana site. Unless . . ." He paused and thought for a moment. "You game for a trip to that trailer park that I told you about?"

"The one that was closed down?"

"Yeah. It's on the way," he said with a grin. "If these bastards are doing what I think they're doing we might just have 'em."

The trailer park was set off Route 53 on an arterial road. A large fence surrounded it and a big sign was posted on the gate warning of danger. We stopped in front and looked at it. The trailers were still there, for the most part. But they were boarded up and patches of long, wild grass and weeds crept out from every opening.

"Looks pretty much deserted," I said.

"Totally deserted, I'd say. Sure like to know what kind

of settlement these people got."

"This is the law suit you told me about? Where the court file was sealed as part of the settlement."

"Yeah," Hoppy said. "Like I told you, all you can find out about it now is that it's listed as 'Suppressed vs. Suppressed.' Supposedly Waste Eliminators had a landfill adjacent to the park. On the west side."

I put the Beater in drive and pulled back onto the road.

"Let's see if we can find it," I said.

We found an old abandoned farm directly west of the trailer park. A gravel road cut in from the highway. The Beater's tires crunched as we made the turn and drove toward the dilapidated farmhouse. A pair of barns stood just beyond it. They looked in pretty bad shape, too. Sections were missing toward the bottom and the same wild growth of shrubbery sprouted through the openings. The road extended beyond the barns, but the plant life seemed to abruptly end. A few trees were there, but they had no leaves. And the same wild grass that flourished around the house had turned to a sea of dead yellow, as if the field had been struck by a premature winter.

"Sure smells pretty," I said.

"Like rotten eggs," Hoppy added. "That's from the hydrogen sulfate that's being produced by the chemicals that were dumped here. Let's see if there's an address on the house. Then let's find out who owns this place."

Our trip into Joliet put us dangerously close to the time of Hoppy's chemo appointment so we stopped to call his wife. I pulled into a gas station with one of those public phones on a post, designed so he didn't have to get out of the car to call. While he was talking I put the guard's shotgun in my trunk. The side of the conversation I heard wasn't pleasant. Hoppy told her that we were going to be late and to call and reschedule the appointment. Apparently his wife was upset and told him so. He finally just exploded into the phone and yelled, "Well, just cancel the goddamn thing then."

After he'd hung up I told him that I'd be glad to drop him off and check on the information myself and get back to him. He shook his head.

"If I'm gonna get anything done on this, it's got to be before I go in for that damn chemo," he said. "I'm not fit for shit after going through that."

I tried to think of something to say, but couldn't.

"I haven't got much longer, Shade. A couple of months at the most. If that." He swallowed hard. "Just want to write one more good story. Something important. Something that my wife and kid can be proud of me for."

"I'm sure they've got lots of reasons to feel proud of you."

He closed his eyes and a tear rolled down his cheek.

"Let's go," he said.

At the township tax office we found out that the farmland was in trust. All the record said was the bank and trust number. That was where the trail ended. There was no way of finding out who the real owner was. No legitimate way, anyway. Banks don't normally give out that kind of information. But Hoppy said he knew someone in the bank who could maybe help us out. We went to the row of phone booths and called him. Hoppy looked ecstatic when he hung up. It was getting close to three, and he said he'd better get home as quickly as possible.

"The owner is listed as a John H. Suttor," Hoppy told me as I pushed him toward the Beater. "My friend remembered when Waste Eliminators paid Suttor to fill in his land. It was an old family farm and Suttor had a bad heart and no inclination to work it himself. Supposed to be a C and D dump—construction and demolition."

"How long ago was this?"

"About fifteen years. They filled it in five and left. But the smell and the problems stayed. Then the trailer park people complained that their wells had been tainted. They filed suit. Waste Eliminators brought in some high-priced lawyer, and they settled out of court."

"So where does that leave us?" I asked.

"I know from my own information that there were no criminal charges filed. The company was fined ten grand, but that's a drop in the bucket to them. The farm's on the Superfund list of toxic waste sites to be cleaned up, but there are about six thousand sites on the list and it's growing every day."

We got to the car and I helped him in, then put the chair in the trunk. He seemed a lot weaker than when we'd left. I got in and started it up. He continued to talk.

"According to the information Waste Eliminators gave me when I first approached them about this story, they told me that all the toxic stuff was being dumped in Indiana at this specially designed site. Supposed to be lined with plastic to prevent groundwater contamination." He got out another cigarette and lit it up. Surprisingly, this time he didn't have the accompanying coughing fit.

"I'm beginning to wonder if they really have a special site at all. Maybe they're just mixing the toxic stuff in with the regular garbage and dumping it in their Indiana landfill."

"Is that profitable?"

"Yep," he said. "They charge the company the special

rates for disposing of toxic wastes, then bypass all the expensive safeguards that they're required to do by the EPA, and just dump the stuff."

"Or mix it with oil and send it into low income housing."

"Right. Pure profit. So what if people get exposed to millions of PCBs and carcinogens. I wish there was some way to check on the disposition of the toxic waste they pick up from the different sites."

"I might be able to find something out along those lines," I said. "DCI, that's the Illinois State Police, have got a man investigating Carlos's death. I'll see what he can find out. I'm sure they have to have papers and permits and all that shit."

"Yeah," Hoppy said. "They gotta fill out the form in triplicate. One from the company that has the waste, one from the contracted waste disposer, and one for the final site of disposal. That'd be all we need to nail 'em."

"I'll see what I can do," I said. "In the mean time, can your sources find out anything on this Suttor guy? I'd like to talk to him."

"I'll see what I can come up with tomorrow," he said, taking out another cigarette and lighting it off the old one. "God, I miss these things. Promised my wife I wouldn't smoke anymore. Not that it's gonna make much difference at this point." He inhaled more smoke.

"Maybe you should try thinking more positively."

He squinted at me through the haze.

"Yeah, Shade. You sure do have a thing about lost causes, all right."

When we got to Hoppy's house he slipped two cigarettes in his shirt pocket and tossed me the pack. His wife came out to meet us and gave me a stern look.

"I'm glad you're finally home," she said.

"Jeannie, I think Mr. Shade and I are on to something big," Hoppy said.

I went around to open the trunk and get his chair.

"We're already so late for his appointment, Mr. Shade. Would you mind driving him over to the hospital. I'll follow you in our car?"

"No problem, Mrs. Cassidy," I said. Hoppy grinned as I got back in the car and started it up. He lit up one of the cigarettes that he'd stashed in his pocket and slumped down in the seat.

"Remember, if she asks you at the hospital, tell her you smoke, okay?" he said. "In case she smells it on my clothes."

I nodded, and told him to crank down the window.

Chapter 36

Luckily, Jeannie Cassidy didn't ask me about the cigarette odor as we unloaded Hoppy. I helped her put him in the chair. Hoppy told me to take off, but to let him know as soon as I found anything else out. I said I would, and pointed the Beater back to Chi-town. When I got back it was close to four-thirty and my stomach was reminding me that I'd skipped lunch. I stopped at a restaurant and had a steak and salad. Then I tried to call Maria, but all I got was her answering machine. I left a message that I'd like to see her and for her to beep me. I tried calling Tremain, but got no answer at his office.

Since I'd missed my morning run and my workouts had been generally low-key this week, I figured it was time for a tough one. When I got home I fed the cats and got my gear together. On the way out I checked the messages on my machine. One of was from Maria telling me to call her after six. I glanced at my watch. Five-twenty. I could call from the gym, finish my workout, and hopefully head over there afterwards.

The second message was from my answering service. They told me that a Mr. Lipton had called several times and requested that I call him back as soon as possible. I jotted the number down. It was an 815 area code, which meant it was probably in the Joliet area. Lipton's honey-voiced secretary answered on the second ring.

"This is Ron Shade. I'm returning Mr. Lipton's call."

"Oh, yes, Mr. Shade. Just a moment."

I was on hold for no more than twenty seconds when Lipton's voice came on the line.

"Shade? Tom Lipton." His voice seemed unusually loud.

"You don't have to shout," I said. "I can hear just fine. What can I do for you?"

"Sorry," he said, after a slight hesitation. "I had the phone set for a conference call. I had my hands full. I appreciate you calling back."

I was bothered by his solicitousness and waited for him to continue.

"My daughter was pretty upset about our last meeting," he said finally.

"I'm sorry to hear that."

"Well, she and I sat down and discussed the situation and came to a decision."

"Oh? About what?"

"Shade, I've always considered myself to be a fair man," he said, lapsing into his politician's voice. "And I've always prided myself in doing the right thing, even when I was under no obligation to."

"I'm afraid you're losing me."

Lipton laughed, although if it was from something he'd found humorous or just to give himself more time, I wasn't sure.

"Well, like I said, Kelly told me about the case you're working on," he continued. "I was very moved by the whole thing and, frankly, she brought out some facets that I was not aware of earlier. I discussed the matter with Hal, and, well, what we'd like to do is provide some monetary compensation for the poor boy's widow."

"They weren't married yet. Just engaged."

"That doesn't matter," Lipton said. "I'm sure he would have named her as beneficiary anyway."

"I thought you told me you weren't that connected to Space Oddities?"

"I'm not," he said, clearing his throat. "I do advise Hal on certain business matters from time to time, since we share some mutual concerns, so I suppose I am an investor, of sorts, in his company."

I didn't reply. This guy had a politician's gift for double-talk, that was for sure. Sometimes it's best to let the other guy sweat a bit.

"Shade? Are you there?"

"Yeah. So what kind of money are we talking about?"

"Well, their standard policy for accidental death of an employee is ten thousand."

"Ten thousand?" I repeated.

"But, considering the tragic nature of these circumstances," he interjected, "we'd be willing to consider a higher figure. Say . . . doubling the award."

"Twenty grand?"

"That seems more than fair, doesn't it?"

"I'll run it by my client," I said.

"Good, good," he said, confident that he had me sewn up in his pocket. "You'll let me know? Then I'll contact Hal."

"I'll call you tomorrow," I said.

"Well, I'll be working late at the office tonight," he said. "If you can get back to me tonight, I'll be able to get the ball rolling on this first thing in the morning."

"I'll keep that in mind," I said, and told him good-bye.

He was willing to buy us off with twenty grand, I thought as I headed out of the house. I must be getting close to something.

I kept thinking about Lipton's offer during my workout, and Chappie seemed to sense that my concentration was off. The bell rang signaling the end of the round and he motioned for me to sit down on the stool.

"Somethin' on your mind, or what?" he asked as he toweled me off. "Cause it sure ain't fightin'."

I tried to catch my breath.

"Listen," he said. "I told Raul to dance around, like Berger's gonna do. What you gotta do is cut off the ring on him. He's lighter and faster than you. So you gotta keep your left foot between his, and when he tries to move you can go either way and cut him off. You can steer him like a racecar. Understand? That's the only way to fight a guy that keeps dancing around the ring. Otherwise, you just end up following him around and getting hit."

He sprayed some water over my face and then smeared on the Vaseline. The bell rang and I got up. Raul was bouncing around, looking fresh as a spring breeze, but he wasn't carrying the thirty extra pounds that I was. I moved to the center of the ring and waited for him to come to me.

I concentrated on keeping my left foot in the center of his, like Chappie'd said. Soon I was able to catch him in the corner and give him a pasting to the body. That slowed him up and when he tried dancing away I just went with him, cutting off his escape route.

"Now you got it, baby," Chappie yelled. "Now you got it."

It was after seven when I managed to stop long enough to call Maria. She didn't seem too happy.

"I thought you were going to call me at six," she said. "Do you know how long I've been waiting?"

"Sorry. I'm at the gym and sorta lost track of the time."

"Is that supposed to be an excuse?"

I thought it was, but didn't say so.

"Look. I'm sorry," I said. "I must have misinterpreted

your message. You busy tonight?"

"You mean for what's left of the night?" she said sarcastically.

"Yeah," I said. "I'd like to see you, if that's all right."

After a moment of silence she said, "Okay, we do have a lot to talk about. What time can you fit me in to your busy schedule, Ron?"

I had a feeling that I should have told her that maybe it'd be better to wait till tomorrow, but instead I told her that I'd rush right over to see her. "Unless you want me to take a shower first," I joked.

"Suit yourself. I'll be here," she said flatly and hung up.

I stared at the phone and wondered what the rest of this night would be like.

By the time I finished showering and drove over to Maria's it was almost an hour later. Time enough for her to have cooled off, I hoped. Just to make sure, I'd stopped at the 7-Eleven and picked up a small bouquet for her. Say it with flowers, the sign said. Even if you're not sure what you actually are trying to say. I found my usual parking space near the alley and pulled in, hoping that Doug's police stickers would keep me from getting any more tickets. I didn't really want to waste more time looking for a legitimate parking spot. I rang her buzzer and was glad when I heard her ask who it was. Her tone sounded almost neutral.

When I came bounding up the stairs with the flowers she opened the door quickly. I could tell from her expression that she was still upset so I handed her the bouquet right away.

"I'm not sure why you're mad at me," I said. "But I want you to know that I hope we can work it out."

She looked at me, then at the flowers and bowed her head. I could see that she'd started crying, but when I reached out to hold her she stepped back with an emphatic, "Don't."

"Are you at least going to tell me what I did to make you so upset with me?" I said.

She raised her face and looked at me.

"You don't know?"

I shook my head, as perplexed as all hell.

"Your friend from the State Police," she said. "He raided the apartment with I.N.S. They took everybody downtown to deport them."

"I'm sorry for being so . . . so mean to you, Ron," she said. "But everything's turned out so terrible."

I patted her arm. We were sitting at her kitchen table drinking coffee. The flowers were in a vase on the sink.

"Part of it's my fault," I said. "I should have called you earlier."

"And I should have known that you didn't have anything to do with that damn I.N.S. raid," she said.

"I'm not too happy about it, either," I said. "Tremain's made a really dumb move this time. The only witness to the argument that Carlos had with Big Frank is going to be down in Mexico somewhere."

"Do you think you can do anything?"

"I don't know," I said. "I'll give Tremain a call in the morning. Maybe he'll listen to me about Paco. Maybe not."

"What about the others?"

I shook my head.

"It's just not fair," she said.

"Sometimes life isn't," I said. "Which brings me to another topic. Lipton's offered to pay Juanita twenty thousand for an accidental death settlement. Think she'd be interested?"

"Twenty thousand? Is that what he thinks the price is for a dead illegal Hispanic?"

"Regardless of his motive, we should run it by Juanita."

"Why? You looking for a way to get out of this case, Ron?"

I took a deep breath before answering.

"It's an opportunity for her to get something positive for herself out of all this mess," I said. "There may not be another chance."

"If you're worried about your fee," she said in clipped tones, "I can give you a check right now."

"I wasn't, but now that you mention it, it may be nice to get some advance money. I'm pulling all my expenses out of my pocket."

"Here," she said, getting up. "I'll give you your check and then you can leave."

"Is that what you want?"

"That's what you want, isn't it?"

She stood there staring at me defiantly.

"Maybe the best thing would be for me to leave," I said, standing up. I'd been party to enough domestics to know that nothing was going to be solved in an emotional climate.

"Fine," Maria said. "Go."

"I'll call you tomorrow," I said as I was moving toward the door. "And I'll let you know about the check. In the mean time, let Juanita know about Lipton's offer, okay? I have to tell him one way or another tomorrow."

I heard the apartment door slam hard behind me. I walked down the stairs reflecting on the argument. Unavoidable, or did it portend of a deeper problem? Maybe we didn't have the same expectations or hopes about the relationship. I still wasn't sure how I really felt about Maria. Did I want something serious, or was I secretly hoping to keep it casual? How casual should you hope for, when you'd been to bed with somebody? I liked her a lot, but did I dare consider the "L" word? I thought about how badly things had turned out with Cathy.

Maria and I needed to have a serious talk, before things went any further, that was for sure. The last thing in the world I wanted to do was hurt her. At least the Beater started right up. I flipped on the radio to keep me company. Yeah, the car was running right now, but it wasn't even my car—just my money tied up in fixing it. That Lionel Ritchie song came on again about how he wanted to win this girl's heart, but he didn't have a clue. It was somehow comforting to know I wasn't alone. And looking for clues was my livelihood, wasn't it?

Chapter 37

It was so cold when I got up at six to do my roadwork I could see my breath as I ran. Most of the wild flowers had disappeared, and it struck me that I'd been so preoccupied lately that I hadn't even noticed before this. Traffic was unusually heavy and I remembered it was Friday. Maybe everybody was getting an early start to their weekend. I began concentrating on my next move in this case. Logic told me it was best left to Tremain, but after all the work I'd put into it, I hated the thought of him blowing it off.

When I rounded the block to head home I'd decided to keep plodding ahead. Just like Chappie'd told me last night: cut off the ring. I was pretty sure that Big Frank had killed Carlos and dumped his body in the Cal-Sag. Probably because Carlos figured out that the symbol on the drum was toxic stuff. But proving it was another matter. If I couldn't get Tremain to listen to me, my chances were slim to none.

I finished showering and had a leisurely breakfast. Tremain probably wouldn't start till eight or so. As I read the paper I came across an article on the recent fish kills in the Calumet River. The Calumet had long been polluted by all the industry on the southeast side. In recent years an attempt to clean it up had been mounted, but it was like trying to paddle upstream with a teaspoon. The article had an accompanying map illustration that showed the location of the fish kills. Something clicked for me as I looked at it.

I set down my coffee and got my road atlas out of the bookcase. It showed most of the roads and rivers around the Chicago area. I found the Calumet and traced my finger down from the lake. Then I found the Cal Sag Channel and traced it. They intersected on the Blue Island/Riverdale border. A couple miles west of the fish kill, and a couple miles west of where Carlos's body was found. That would be a definite connection between Big Frank and Carlos's death if I could prove he was responsible for the dumping. But would Tremain buy it?

I glanced at my watch. It was a little after eight. I went to the phone and dialed Tremain's office. A secretary answered and told me he wasn't in yet. I gave her my name and asked to have him call me as soon as he arrived.

I called Hoppy, but his wife answered and told me he was still sleeping.

"He had a bad night," she said reproachfully. "All that traveling yesterday didn't do him a lot of good."

"Yeah, I was afraid of that. If you could tell him I called."

She said she would and hung up.

I called Maria's and left a message on her answering machine for her to call me. I thought about calling her at work, but decided to wait. About ten minutes later, just as I was getting my sport jacket and heading out the door, the phone rang. It was Tremain.

"What can I do for you, Mr. Shade?"

"You've already done plenty," I said. "What's the idea of raiding the apartment in Lincoln Estates?"

"It was part of an active police investigation," he replied.

"Is there any chance of holding up deportation of one of those illegals? He could be important to our case."

"Our case?"

"Yeah," I said. "Carlos Sanchez's murder. You are still working on that one, aren't you?"

"I'm still working on it, but I hardly consider it *our* case."

"So that's the way it is."

"I'm afraid so, Mr. Shade. I can appreciate your interest in the matter, but it is, after all, an active police investigation and I want to advise you again not to interfere."

"Interference is the farthest thing from my mind, Tremain. But I have been working this thing and have some definite ideas I'd like to discuss with you."

"Well," he said. "I'm afraid I do have a rather busy schedule."

"Yeah, I'll bet. Still chasing the phantom drug connection?"

"I don't feel that I need to justify, or reveal any of my findings to you."

"No," I said. "You sure don't." I hesitated and tried to regain my cool. It wouldn't do me any good to alienate him more than I already had. "Look," I said, trying to soften my tone. "I don't want to get into a pissing contest with you. What I'd like to do is sit down and discuss some things I've found out. Would you be agreeable to that?"

He didn't answer.

"How about this," I said. "Call Detective George Grieves at Area One Violent Crimes. He'll vouch for me. Tell you that I'm not some crackpot. I'll give you my beeper number and you can call me back, okay?"

I heard him take in a deep breath and let it out.

"Okay," he said. "What's your number?"

I'd just hung up when my beeper went off. I was hoping it was Hoppy, but it was my answering service. I dialed the number and the girl told me that a Mr. MacKenzie had called and said it was urgent. I hung up and dialed Midwestern Olympia. Maybe old Dick was going to come through with the check for the Camaro.

"Shade," his voice boomed when he came on the line. "What's the big idea?"

"Huh?"

"Using my cards and impersonating me at some dump in Indiana."

I covered the receiver to stifle a laugh.

"What you talking about? You want to lay it out for me?"

"I got a message to call a Mr. Pierce yesterday afternoon when I got back from a meeting," he said, some control seeping back into his voice. "A very important meeting, I might add. When I returned the call, this guy threatened to have me arrested for beating up some security guard at some dump. Naturally, I didn't have the slightest idea what he was talking about."

"What kind of a dump was it?"

"A dump dump."

"Hmmm," I said, mustering as much false concern as I could. "Sounds like you might have been the victim of an identity theft. I'll be glad to look into it if you want. For a nominal fee, of course."

"Don't give me that shit," he sneered. "The guy described you to a T. And anyway, this sort of thing has you written all over it. And I don't even sell life insurance."

"Dick, I haven't got the slightest idea what you're talking about, but like I said, I'll be glad to look into it as soon as my case-load drops off a bit. What's the story on the check for my car, anyway?"

"Forget it, buddy," he said. "If you think I'm helping you now, after what you did."

"Look, I don't know what exactly you think I did, but one thing I know for sure that I did was to give you some goddamned money to take care of a problem for me. If you can't or won't do that, Dick, I'll come down to your office in person and get my premium back. *Comprende?*"

"You can't do that," he stammered.

"Just watch me," I said like I meant it and hung up. It took me a few minutes to stop laughing so I could assess the situation. If Pierce and the boss were really concerned about having "Dick" arrested, I doubted if he would have bothered calling Midwestern Olympia. Why not just call the police? They probably just wanted to verify if the guy who paid them a visit was actually Dick, and when it was obvious that it wasn't, they tried blowing some smoke up his ass to see what they could find out. It did remind me that I'd have to get rid of the shotgun I'd taken away from the guard yesterday. It was still in my trunk.

I decided to run out to the Joliet area to check in with Hoppy. I also had to meet with Lipton to discuss the "insurance settlement." My next move was dependent on Tremain. If he called George and agreed to talk with me, maybe I could get his investigation of the case on the same track with mine. The traffic was pretty light on I-80 and I was in Lockport by quarter to ten. I stopped at a Dunkin' Donuts and called Hoppy's again. This time he answered.

"Where the hell you been?" he asked. "I been trying to call you."

"I was on my way out to see you," I said. "Don't you have my beeper number?"

"Nah, I lost it, or something," he said. "I did find out a couple of things, though. Where you at?"

"The Dunkin' Donuts on Archer Avenue."

"Great. Why don't you shoot over here."

"You sure you feel up to it?" I asked.

"Yeah. Why?"

"When I called earlier your wife said you weren't feeling good."

"What? No, I'm all right. She's just worried about me. And, Shade, how about stopping at the gas station on the way over and picking me up a pack of squares?"

Hoppy answered the door when I got there, looking up at me from his wheelchair. He was dressed in a bathrobe and pajamas, and he looked pretty haggard. His wife wasn't there. The first thing he did was ask me for the cigarettes, and then lit one up. He inhaled and held it down to admire it as the smoke drifted out of his nose.

"Not coughing as much," he said with a smile. "Must be getting used to it. Here's what I got." He wheeled himself over to the kitchen table and spread some papers out on the top.

"That guy Suttor, who owned the farm land. He died about six years ago. Left everything to the beneficiary on the trust. Some guy named Jordan."

"Harold Jordan?"

He nodded. "It gets better," he said with a grin. "Guess who ramrodded the permit through the Will County Board to allow the land to be used as a C and D dump?"

I raised my eyebrows.

"None other than Honest Tom Lipton," he said. "Of course, now that he's running for Board President he's on a soapbox promising to clean up all such hazardous waste sites, and make it more difficult for new ones to be opened."

"That hypocrite," I said. "How can he get away with that?"

"This was all about six years ago. Voters have short

memories. They tend to focus on the immediate issues, and nobody's squawking too much about that site. The trailer park residents are all gone. There's nobody around to make the connection to Lipton." He paused to take another long drag. "And even if there were, he could always push the blame on somebody else by saying that he thought it was only gonna be a regular landfill-type dump."

I shook my head.

"We need to get a line on where they're actually dumping that stuff," he continued. "The Indiana landfill's only licensed to take solid, non-toxic waste, and they claimed that the hazardous stuff was being disposed of in Illinois. But they told me before that they were taking it to a special site in Indiana, so somebody's full of bullshit. We got to find out where they're actually dumping the shit."

"I think I've figured that out," I said.

Chapter 38

"I appreciate you seeing me on such short notice," I said as I sat down in Lipton's office. We were alone. He sat behind his big, imposing gunmetal desk. Behind him, on the wall, the poster of his face looked down on us. *Experience, leadership, integrity.*

Lipton flashed his politician's smile.

"Perfectly all right, Mr. Shade. I feel an almost fiduciary responsibility in this case."

"That's very generous of you."

"Not really," he said, grinning again. "After all, as you know, I am a silent partner in Space Oddities, and Carlos was one of our employees."

Now it's Carlos, I thought.

"So I take it the sum we discussed was satisfactory to your client?" Lipton asked.

"She still hasn't okayed it."

Lipton's smile faded slightly. "Oh?" he said, his chin jutting forward.

"In fact, I haven't approached her about it."

Lipton leaned back in his big swivel chair and cupped a hand over his chin.

"Do I read you correctly, Mr. Shade," he said, "that the amount is not suitable?"

I leaned forward and smiled.

"The amount's probably fair, as things go," I said. "But my client's primary interest was discovering the circumstances surrounding her fiancé's death."

Lipton stared at me.

"I'm afraid I don't understand what you want, Shade."

"I'd like to ask you a few questions," I said.

"Questions," he repeated.

"Right," I continued. "Like how you helped Jordan get a permit to create a dump site on the old Suttor farm."

Lipton's mouth gaped slightly, then he recovered. "That was a number of years ago."

"Yeah, and nothing's been able to grow on it since."

"Hal wasn't involved in that," Lipton said defensively. "The company he sub-contracted to caused the contamination."

"Oh, right. And I suppose that you're going to deny any connection with Waste Eliminators, too."

"I'll admit that Hal's company sometimes leases trucks from L & M, but so what?"

"So," I said, "sooner or later I'm going to tie this sordid mess to Carlos's death. If you don't want to go down with them, you'd better start cooperating now."

He pursed his lips and looked at me.

"Sounds like I'd better contact my attorney, Mr. Shade. To tell him about these slanderous statements you're making." He tried to flash what I guessed was his confident politician's smile. But he just looked weak.

"I hope your attorney's a good one," I said. "Because you're not going to last ten minutes in Stateville. But at least it's close. Your family will be able to visit, and you can introduce them to your new friend, Bubba." I tried a sardonic grin of my own.

"Get out of here, Shade," Lipton said, his face reddening. "Before I have security throw you out."

I stood up and took out one of my cards.

"Mr. Lipton, I think we've had this conversation before. My advice is still the same: I wouldn't advise you or your security guards to try to throw me anywhere. Here." I handed him the card. He didn't take it so I let it fall on top of his desk. "My answering service's number is on the back. Call them and tell them to beep me when you wise up."

I turned and walked slowly to the door, where I paused.

"You're wading around in a swamp, Tom," I said, hoping that using his first name would put more of an edge on my words. "Pretty soon you're gonna find out that there's a bunch of crocodiles in the lily-pads."

It was mostly a bluff. Lipton might call it, but then again, at this point I had nothing to lose by trying to shake things up. The fact that they had tried to buy me out of the picture definitely said something. By forcing things I was cutting off the ring on 'em. Like Chappie'd told me last night. They were dancing around while Tremain was off in a corner chasing shadows.

I was heading back toward I-80 feeling pretty satisfied with myself, when my beeper went off. I looked at it eagerly, hoping that it was Lipton calling to tell me he was ready to spill his guts. No such luck. It was Tremain's number. I pulled into the next Dunkin' Donuts that I spotted and got change from the girl behind the counter. It cost me fifty cents for the call. Tremain came on the line after about thirty seconds.

"Mr. Shade," he said. "I spoke to Detective Grieves. He gives you very high marks."

Good old George.

"We probably should get together and talk," he said.

"That sounds good," I said. "I think I've got enough to tie this up for you. One thing, though. Do you think you can contact I.N.S. and have them put a hold on deporting one of those illegals from the other day?"

He was slow to respond. "I'll see what I can do," he said. "Is it that important?"

"It is. Look, you're going to have to trust me a little bit on this. Paco, that's the illegal, is a witness who can verify that Carlos was involved in an argument with Frank Bristol shortly before he disappeared."

"What do you have on this Bristol guy?" Tremain asked.

I looked up Big Frank's date of birth in my notebook and gave it to him.

"It might be a good idea to run a criminal history check on him," I said. "This guy, too." I gave him the date of birth for Harold Jordan.

"And what will I find out?" he asked.

"Run it and see," I said, not wanting to let him know that George had already run them for me. "I'm sure you'll come up with something." I decided to appeal to his vanity a little. "I need to tap into your expertise. You know anything about the transportation of hazardous material?"

Before he could answer the computerized operator broke in and told me I needed "five cents more." I dug in my pocket for a nickel as I heard Tremain say, "Shade? You still there?"

"Yeah," I said, depositing the nickel. The connection clicked again, and the computerized voice thanked me.

"I thought you hung up," Tremain said. "What'd you ask about?"

"Hazardous material," I said. "You know anything about it?"

"Yeah, I was a haz-mat officer before I got into DCI."

"Excellent. Maybe you can nail this down then. When a company transports hazardous waste, do they have to get any special permits?"

"Yeah," he said. "They have to be registered with the

EPA as a hazardous waste hauler."

"Oh great. Then the Feds handle that stuff?"

"No, I meant the Illinois EPA," he said. "We've got a division that works exclusively with them called Haz-Min."

"Are there records that show where the toxic waste goes?"

"Yeah."

"Who has them?" I asked. "The EPA?"

The computerized voice returned and requested five cents again, "for the past one minute." I dropped in another nickel.

"Where the hell are you?" Tremain asked.

"Joliet."

"You ought to invest in a cell phone, or something."

"I had one in my Z-28," I said. "But it got stolen. What about the records?"

"There's a hazardous waste manifest," he said. "It's about six copies thick and it's filled out prior to shipping. One copy goes to the company that's contracting for the waste disposal, one to the point of origin, one to the final destination. I'd have to check on where all the rest of them go."

"That sounds like just what we need to really tie this thing up," I said. "Could you put these Haz Min guys on a company called Waste Eliminators?"

"That's all tied into this homicide?"

"Yeah, it is."

"Shade, this sounds like it's pretty complicated. If I'm going to do all this I'll have to get it straight in my mind. Can you swing by my office?"

"Sure thing," I said. "What time?"

"It's close to eleven now. How about one o'clock?"

"Sounds good. I'll be there."

I hung up just as the computerized voice was asking for more money. The phone rang and I picked it up.

"You have a five cent charge for overtime." This time it was a real, live human voice.

"Lo siento," I said. *"No hablo ingles."*

I heard her exhale loudly into the receiver then the phone went dead. Things were definitely looking up.

I kept the Beater at a pretty steady pace all the way back. It was quarter to twelve when I pulled into a restaurant in Palos Heights. I figured I could grab a quick meal there and still be close enough to Tremain's office to make the one o'clock meeting. I went in, placed my order, and went immediately to the pay phone. I dialed Maria's work number as fast as I could, hoping I'd catch her before she left for lunch. I was lucky. She answered on the first ring.

"Ms. Castro," her cool voice said. "May I help you?"

"That depends."

"Ron?"

"Yeah. You still mad at me?"

She didn't answer right away.

"What do you think?" she asked.

"I was hoping you weren't. Did you talk to Juanita?"

"No, I haven't."

"Good, because the offer's been withdrawn," I said. "I went to see Lipton this morning. I think I might be making some headway."

"What do you mean?"

"I mean, I'm closing in on them. If everything that I've set in motion goes as planned, it could be over soon."

There was silence on the other end.

"Well," I said, "doesn't that make you happy?"

"Yes. Yes, of course. I'll talk to Juanita about your money."

"Oh, yeah," I said. That was something I wanted to get out of the way. "Say, what about dinner tonight?"

"Okay," she said hesitantly. "What time?"

"I'll pick you up at around seven-thirty, okay?"

"All right," she said.

When I hung up the phone I was thinking that the cards might finally be starting to fall my way.

Chapter 39

The meeting at Tremain's office went better than I thought it would. He introduced me to a Mr. Allen, from the Illinois EPA, and to the Haz-Min DCI agent, a sergeant named Stallworth. Both seemed pretty sharp as I laid everything out for them. We were in a mid-sized conference room with a large table. Tremain sat at the end. I was on his right and Stallworth and Allen sat across from me.

"Plus," Tremain said, when I'd finished, "I called a friend of mine on the Indiana State Police. He's running some checks for me, but he knows for a fact that the Crown of Victory landfill site is not licensed for toxic waste disposal."

"And if they're not dumping it there," Allen said, "where the hell are they putting it?" He looked about forty, with receding dark hair and black, horn-rimmed glasses. His head nodded several times, then he looked at me. "Mr. Shade, you're sure that they're dumping in the Cal-Sag?"

"As sure as I can be without catching them in the act. One of the nights I followed them, I lost them right in that area. The fish kill was right after that."

"Not to mention the earlier fish kill, which roughly corresponds to the projected homicide date," Stallworth said.

"Then we're going to have to notify the Metropolitan Water Reclamation District," Allen said.

"What we need to do is to put some pressure on them," I said. "Lipton's the weak link. He's the one we should go after."

Stallworth and Tremain exchanged glances.

"Mr. Shade," Stallworth said. "Don't take this the wrong way. We deeply appreciate your assistance in this matter . . ."

"But," Tremain said, leaning his upper body toward me, "I think you've done just about all you can do. Let us handle it from this point."

"Wait a minute," I said. "You guys would be absolutely nowhere on this if it wasn't for what I told you. I've earned a right to be in on this till the end. Besides, Lipton's ready to crack. I can sense it. When he does, he'll come to me."

"That's one of the problems with your involvement, Shade," Stallworth said. "Your methods are unorthodox. We work very closely with the State's Attorney's office. In fact, we have a special Assistant State's Attorney assigned to work with us."

"Good," I said. "Put him to work and issue a subpoena for Lipton's trucking company business records."

Stallworth looked at his watch. "It's getting kind of late. And this is Friday afternoon."

"Probably have to wait till after the weekend," Tremain added.

"God dammit, we can't afford to wait," I said. "If these assholes suspect we're on to them they'll destroy everything we need."

"They're required to maintain those records by law," Allen said.

"They're required to refrain from killing people, too," I said. "But that doesn't seem to have stopped them."

"Now we still haven't positively linked them to the homicide," Stallworth said. I looked at him and he read my expression. "Shade, I know how you feel, but try to see our point of view. We've got to have solid facts."

"Lean on Lipton a little and you'll get your facts," I said. "Trust me."

"We're troopers, not a goon squad," he said.

"I realize that," I said, trying to calm my voice down. "But I know it'll work."

"He did get rave reviews from the Chicago Police," Tremain said.

Stallworth massaged his temples with his fingers.

"I suppose," he said slowly, "I could use a few favors and get the subpoenas issued today."

"But then it still has to go out by mail," Allen said.

"Mail the others," I said. "You're the State Police. Have somebody in Will County hand deliver it. It's got to get there today, for the maximum effect."

Stallworth shook his head. "No, it's better if we go there Monday morning with subpoenas in hand and get the stuff we need. Otherwise, they'll be forewarned we're coming."

"I agree," Tremain said. "And, Ron, I'll do my best to keep you informed as to what's going on, but this is an official police investigation. We just can't have you tagging along every step of the way."

I was going to try and argue, but sighed instead. It was like trying to persuade a rock to get up and change positions. No matter what I said, it wasn't going to make any difference. Maybe it was better to just turn it over to them and hope they solved it. At least I could honestly tell Maria that I tried.

After the meeting I went home to pick up my workout stuff. The cats were both curled up on the couch together. Georgio raised his head sleepily, gave a half audible mew, then tucked his head back in place. The light on the answering machine was blinking. I rewound it and played back the tape.

"Ron, it's Dick MacKenzie." His voice sounded subdued. "I just wanted to let you know that the claim for your car went through. The check's in the mail."

Welcome news, even if it was a tired expression. It must have been my warning not to go down there and collect in person. Too bad I hadn't used that approach on Dick earlier. But, timing is everything. I dialed George's work number. He sounded in a good mood when he answered the phone. I told him so.

"That's because I *am* in a good mood," he said. "Or at least I was till you called. Do me a favor and don't ruin it by telling me you need something, okay?"

"Relax. I just wanted to call and thank you for vouching for me with that Tremain guy."

"No problem. I just repeated some of the bullshit I always hear you spouting off." His voice grew serious. "Ron, how's things going on this one? Run it by me."

I gave him a quick summary. "Should be wrapped up soon," I said. "As far as Tremain's concerned, my role in it is over with."

"That's a relief," George said.

"Oh?"

"Ron, homicide's not the same as some damn insurance fraud. These guys are heavy hitters."

"Meaning?"

"Meaning, I don't want to see you get in over your head."

"I've been in deep water before," I said.

"Yeah, but this time you're batting out of your league. This whole thing has the smell of mob involvement. Back off and let the professionals handle it. It's what we get paid for."

I was stunned. Did that mean he didn't think I was a pro?

"Yeah, well I'm getting paid for this too," I said.

I heard him sigh. "Look, I don't want to get you pissed off," he said. "We're heading up to the cabin this weekend. Why don't you grab your lady friend and come with us? On Monday we'll go talk to a buddy of mine in the Organized Crime Unit. Okay?"

He owned some property by a lake up in Michigan. It was peaceful, and he used it to get away from all the bad things he was exposed to in the city.

"No wonder you're in a good mood," I said, trying to change the subject. "Thanks anyway, but I'll have to pass."

"Well, the invitation stands. You know the way, if you want to pop up there tomorrow."

"When you leaving?"

"Right after work," he said. "And watch your ass on this other thing, okay?"

"Sure thing. Have a good trip."

After hanging up I considered the possibilities. It sounded like a good deal, and there was a small town with a nice motel near his place. Maybe, if Maria wanted to, we could go up there tomorrow. Hopefully, everything'd be back to peaches and cream after our date tonight. It would probably do her good to get away from the city for a while, too. I packed my bag and headed for the gym.

I took my time and went through a by-the-numbers workout. I worked on the bags, shadow boxed, and did sit-ups until Raul got there. Then we sparred for about seven rounds. I was dead tired toward the end and he was catching me with everything but the kitchen sink. Finally, the bell rang ending the round.

Raul went to sit on his stool, and I went to mine. Chappie sprayed me with some water and wiped the sweat from my arms and shoulders.

"You looking better today," he said. "Starting to cut that ring off, like I told ya. Give me one more good round and then you can hit the steam."

"Can't I skip that today? I got a date tonight."

"In that case," he grinned. "Let's make it two more rounds."

The buzzer rang, and he rinsed off my mouthpiece and shoved it back into my mouth. Across the ring, Raul was already up and bouncing on his toes.

Skipping the steam didn't seem to help my date with Maria. I picked her up a few minutes later than I planned, and she seemed miffed. I apologized, but she just shook her head. She looked great in a white silk blouse and dark skirt. A silver chain delicately peeped out from her open collar. She slipped on a gray jacket to suit the somewhat cool evening air, and we were off.

I'd reserved a table for us at the Beverly Woods Restaurant. It was an elegant place, with just enough subdued lighting to be really romantic. And it was close to my place so I could suggest that we go there afterwards to look at my etchings.

She had a glass of white wine as an after-dinner drink, and I had my usual tonic water with a lime twist. Although she'd been polite and quiet through the meal, I was hoping that it was just fatigue after a long day at work.

"Ron, I've got something for you," she said, opening her purse.

I looked at the envelope she gave me.

"Hey, my birthday's not till the end of the month." I smiled. She didn't.

"It's a check for seventeen-hundred dollars. Your retainer fee plus money for the time you've put in."

My mouth sort of fell open. "You didn't need to give me this now."

"No. You were right. I shouldn't have expected you to work for nothing. I'm just sorry that I didn't give it to you earlier, like I should have. Is it enough?"

I nodded and put the envelope in my inside jacket pocket.

"I guess we need to talk," I said.

Her eyes were dark as obsidian.

"I've been kind of concerned at the way our relationship's been going," I said. "Lately I don't seem to be able to do anything right."

She tilted her head to one side.

"I've been worried that we . . ." I started floundering. "That we . . ."

"What are you trying to say, Ron?"

I took a deep breath and tried to begin again. Nothing I'd rehearsed earlier about defining our relationship was coming out the way I intended.

"I want to say that I really value our friendship, and—"

"*Friendship.* Is that how you think of us?"

"Well, I meant that we're very close. And I care a lot about you, and don't want to hurt you."

"So you're trying to dump me now?"

"No," I said, shaking my head. "I'm trying to explain something. I want to make sure your expectations and mine are along the same lines."

"Meaning?"

I took a deep breath. This wasn't turning out the way I wanted. "Meaning that I'm just getting over a long-term serious relationship. It ended badly, and I don't want to see that happen with us."

"So what are you trying to tell me, Ron? That you went to bed with me because you were on the rebound?"

"What I'm trying to say is that I don't want to end up hurting you if—"

"You've already said that."

I exhaled, trying to get a grip on things. "Maria, what is it you want from me? From us? I just don't understand."

"You're supposed to be the big, smart detective," she shot back. "Why don't you figure it out?"

I looked around. People at the surrounding tables were staring.

"Maybe it would be better if we finished this discussion someplace else." If only I can get her to my place, I thought.

"I really don't think there's anything left for us to discuss, Ron," she said, standing up. "I'll take a taxi home."

I managed to collar a waiter, pay for the meal, and still caught Maria before she took off in the cab. She was adamant about me not driving her home. The cabby accepted the last bit of my money as I shoved it through the window at him, and I watched the taxi drive off. You really blew this one all to hell, Shade, I told myself as I slowly walked back to the Beater.

Chapter 40

At ten-oh-five I was settling in to watch the news when my beeper went off. It was my answering service. I dialed them back, and the girl told me that a Mr. Lipton had just called saying it was imperative that I get back to him as soon as possible. She gave me the number, and I asked her if she was sure about the area code, which was local.

"That's what he gave me, Mr. Shade."

"Okay, thanks," I said and hung up.

I checked the number through name-and-address information before dialing it. It came back to a public phone in a restaurant in Lincoln Estates. So Lipton had come out this way to call me. He answered with a nervous hello on the first ring.

"What do you want, Lipton?" I asked.

"Shade." His voice was trembling. "This whole thing's getting out of control. You've got to help me."

"Help you how?" I could hear his rapid breathing.

"Look, I've got connections in the clerk's office," he said. "I know about the subpoenas coming down. I can't afford to be drawn into this. Believe me, I didn't have anything to do with that boy's death."

"I never figured you were directly involved, but knowing about a murder and failing to report it puts you in the thick of things."

Another heavy, trembling breath. "Okay, Shade, look. I can give you information that will tie the real killers to the crime. But if they catch me I'm done for, understand?"

"I'll do my best to see that you're protected," I said.

"What kind of information you got?"

"Not over the phone. Meet me out here in Lincoln Estates now. I'm at a restaurant called Athena's. It's right off the expressway."

"I know where it's at," I said. "I'll be there in twenty minutes."

After I hung up I tried Tremain's office, but there was no answer. The State Police Chicago District was no help, either. All they did was give me the number for the DCI Office in Palos Heights, which I already had, and told me to call back during regular business hours.

I changed into some blue jeans, a dark T-shirt, and my Nike cross trainers. If things went bad, I wanted to be able to move. I strapped on the pancake holster for my Beretta, and put an extra magazine in my jacket pocket. The thought that it could be a trap ran through my mind. Not being able to get a hold of Tremain, and with George out of town, I didn't have anybody I could call for a back-up.

Pausing as I picked up my jacket, I thought about George's advice on the phone earlier. Maybe it would be best to just hold off. But I'd set everything in motion, and now it was coming around just like I'd predicted. I was a big boy. A pro, even if some people didn't think so. And I wanted to crack this one. Have enough evidence to plop down on Tremain's desk Monday and watch his eyes pop out. And George's too.

I'll just have to be extra careful, I told myself. And if it looked like a trap, I could always backpedal.

Lipton's maroon Lincoln Towncar was parked in front of the place, and through the window I could see him hunched over one of the tables in the atrium section near the entrance. On the drive there I'd regretted I didn't have the presence of mind to tell him I'd call him back at the pay phone in an hour and give him the location for the meet. Hindsight's twenty-twenty, as they say.

I circled the lot and the parking lot of the adjacent shopping plaza before going in. He saw me immediately and waved. I went to his table. The place was mostly deserted, and we were the only two in the smoking section. The ashtray in front of him was overflowing with cigarette butts. He immediately stubbed out the one he was smoking and lit up a fresh one.

"What the hell took you so long?" he said. His voice was raspy. "You said twenty minutes."

"Heavy traffic," I joked. The waitress came over and I ordered a cup of coffee. When she left I asked him, "What you got?"

"You alone?"

"Yeah. Are you?" I said gruffly.

He studied me as he blew some smoke out of his nostrils.

"First I gotta know if you can keep me outta this," he said.

"I'll do my best. But you've got to realize that things have gotten a little out of hand."

He nodded and took a long drag on his cigarette. We stopped and waited as the waitress returned with the coffee. She set my cup down and poured fresh ones for both of us.

When she'd left, he said, "You don't have any idea who we're dealing with here, do you?"

"I could venture a guess, but why don't you tell me?"

He quickly looked around, then back to me. "Okay," he said, hunching forward. "Ten years ago my partner, Wayne McKay, and me were in business together with L & M trucking."

"That's Kelly's natural father, right?"

He nodded. "We had an okay business. Nothing spectacular. Times were hard. We were making it, but just barely. Then things started getting real bad. The economy, you know? We needed a loan to keep things going. Otherwise, we were headed for bankruptcy court. Well, that's when I got put in contact with a guy."

"A guy?"

"Right." He swallowed hard and took another drag on his cigarette. "A guy who offered to loan us the money. The interest rates were unpayable, but nobody else would touch us."

"In other words, a juice man?"

"Yeah, I guess that's what you'd call it. Wayne was against it. Said we'd lose everything if we got in bed with those people. So we told them no." He looked at me and took another heavy drag, before stubbing out that cigarette. "Then Jordan approached us with another offer. Let his company buy in with us as a silent partner, and he'd float us some money."

"His company?"

"Yeah. They called it B. Travens and Associates."

"Sounds too good to be true."

"That's what Wayne said." He wiped some sweat off his upper lip with one of the paper napkins. "Jordan badgered us for a while. Wayne wouldn't even talk to him, but me, like a fool, I called him. He set up a meeting. Told me that the deal would go through. We'd re-form the corporate charter under the name of Carriers, Inc, but keep the name L & M Trucking. Jordan told me that he'd talk to Wayne about it. A couple days later, Wayne disappeared."

"That's when he supposedly absconded with part of the company funds?"

"Yeah," Lipton said weakly. "But I knew they'd killed

him. Wayne never would've left Vivian and Kelly. She was all he ever talked about."

"So, in other words, there was a hostile take-over," I said. "You allowed them to use your company to launder money, in exchange for staying in business."

"It was more than that," he said defensively. "I knew that if I didn't go along, they'd kill me too. Then where would Vivian and Kelly be?"

"Okay, so then what happened?"

He bowed his head slightly and ran his hand through his hair. "It kept getting bigger and bigger. Back East, Hal ran this toxic waste scam, where they'd set up a waste disposal company, contract to haul the stuff, then just dump it in some farmer's field at night, or something. Pretty soon they had the same setup here."

"Where does Space Oddities fit in?"

"Space Oddities, L & M Trucking, and Waste Eliminators are all interrelated," he said. "The whole thing's run by the DeKooning mob. That's what Carriers Incorporated really is. They use our trucks to haul the sludge that they've picked up from oil refineries back to J & D Oil. They reuse it in low income housing in the Joliet area. Makes them a ton of money, because they can undercut the market prices. But they need a place to store it. And to store the part they have to dump off."

"So what you're telling me is that they're using Space Oddities for toxic waste storage?"

He nodded again.

"And Carlos?"

His eyes drifted downward. "They hire a lot of illegals. Mexicans, Polacks, those types, because they don't want anybody talking about things. But this Carlos guy, he was smart. Figured out what was in the barrels. What they were doing."

"So who killed him?"

"I'm not sure."

"Come on."

"I'm not," he said defensively. "Hal just said that Big Frank had to take care of a problem."

A problem, I thought. Is that what Carlos was? Thoughts about Maria's intensity flashed in my mind.

"Are you willing to testify to all this?"

"Won't do any good," he said, shaking his head. "They'll destroy all the pertinent records when the subpoenas come out. The only thing this'll accomplish is to kill my chances of winning the election."

"I'd be more worried about staying out of prison if I were you," I said. "There must be a way we can nail the bastards. Help me out and I'll talk to my buddy Tremain for you. Tell him you cooperated."

"Tremain? Who's he?"

"He's the DCI investigator I've been working with. We're like this." I held up two intertwined fingers. "He'll take it seriously if I tell him you helped out." I realized I was stretching the truth a little, but, what the hell, I was talking to a politician.

"You'll really help me, Shade?"

"You got my word. I'll do my best."

He pursed his lips, then pulled out another cigarette.

"Okay, there might be a way," he said. "All the real records are kept on computers. If we could get those disks . . ."

"Where they at?"

"Space Oddities," he said.

"Can we break in there?"

"Don't have to," he said. "I'm on the access list. We can use my keys. I'll have to call the alarm company first and give them my authorization number so they don't call anybody else when the alarm goes off."

"Okay," I said.

He got up abruptly and went to the register. He handed the clerk a dollar and asked for change. When she gave it to him, he turned and handed me the check and said, "Get this, will you?"

He moved quickly to the foyer where the pay phones were. By the time I paid the bill and got next to him he was already dialing. I watched him as he gave his name and read his authorization number off the card.

"Okay," he said. "We'll have to call them again as soon as we get inside."

"All right," I said. "We'll take your car, and I'll drive." I held out my hand for the keys.

Chapter 41

The parking lot was dark as I swung Lipton's big Lincoln off the main highway and onto the private drive. The building itself looked black, except for the big lighted Space Oddities sign and the perimeter lights spaced along the roofline. The glass doors where the office section joined the main factory area were lit up. There were no other cars in the lot, but I wanted to make sure.

Circling around, we sloshed through a big puddle of standing water, and I went to the gravel road that ran parallel to the railroad tracks. As I drove down it I could see the rear of the place. The perimeter lights shone above each loading dock, but all the bays were empty. Nothing but the row of trailers that I'd used for cover on my previous visit.

"What the hell you doing, Shade?" Lipton asked me.

"Just a little recon," I said. "You sure this place is empty?"

"Yeah, it is. They don't run the night shift on Fridays," he said. "Unless there's a special order."

"And we both know what those are," I said as I swung the car around and went back toward the front.

The high beams swept over the deserted expanse of asphalt. Little rows of weeds had begun to force their way up through the cracks. I saw the fading tracks of our tires from the big puddle that we'd gone through on our way in. A rabbit darted across our path and made for the high grass. Lipton told me to hurry up.

"I've got to call the alarm company as soon as we go in," he said.

"Okay," I said, and headed for the main entrance. It looked all right, but I wished that I had more time to scout the back. In and out, as fast as we could make it, I thought. I repeated that to Lipton.

"You think I like this?" he asked.

I parked the Lincoln and we walked to the doors. Lipton was fumbling for the keys so I took out my mini-mag flashlight and shone it on his hands. They were wet with sweat. He went through several keys before finding the right one. When his hand went to the lock I noticed he was trembling. That should have told me something.

"Relax, Lipton. You're doing the right thing."

He nodded and twisted the key. The lock rotated upward and the door opened.

"I'll have to call the alarm company," he repeated nervously. He re-locked the door and walked briskly toward the hallway where the offices were.

"Where're the computer disks?" I asked, following him.

The hallway was semi-lit with what appeared to be some sort of firelights. Lipton turned and walked by the cubicles. He stopped at the door to Jordan's office and opened it. It was dark inside, but from the ambient lighting in the hallway I could make out a desk and some chairs.

"I've got to—" he stammered.

"Call the alarm company," I finished for him. "Yeah, I know."

He moved toward the big desk area, and as I stepped in behind him I felt a very unpleasant nudge in my ribs.

"Put up your hands, Shade," a gruff voice said. "Or I'll blow you in fucking two."

The lights came on and I saw Big Frank holding a sawed-off twelve gauge against my rear left side. I started to raise my hands and he swung the butt into my kidneys.

Hard. I sagged to the floor, conscious of Lipton standing there in front of me, frozen, holding the phone. Big Frank kicked me, and I tried to curl up, but he stuck the big circular barrel in my face.

"Don't move," he said. Then, to Lipton, "What the fuck took you so long?"

Lipton hung up the phone and started to mumble something.

"Never mind," said Big Frank. "Nickie, get your ass over here and search him. You're supposed to be the security guard."

"He's got a flashlight," Lipton said. "He used it to shine on my hands."

"He's got this too," I heard a voice say as I felt some strange hands pulling on my Beretta. "Shit, Frank, this is a beauty. Can I keep it?" It was Security-Nick.

"Shut up and finish searching him," Big Frank said, still poking the shotgun in my face. "Find me that flashlight, too."

I was slowly starting to recover from the blows. Being in top shape had its advantages. But I knew I'd have to make it to my feet if I was going to have any chance at all so I feigned like I was still hurt.

"I could take you out right now, Mr. Tough Guy," Nick sneered, his face close to my ear. As he straightened up he slapped my cheek with the Beretta. I curled into a fetal position on my right side, facing Big Frank.

"You told me I could leave after I got him here," Lipton said nervously.

"Shut the fuck up," Big Frank said. I could see his large work shoes a few inches from my face now. "The boss wants us to find out just what he knows."

That meant they were going to interrogate me. And from

the looks of things, that wouldn't be pleasant.

"Frank, look," Lipton pleaded. "I did my part."

"You ain't done shit, Lipton. Now shut up. Nickie, gimme those handcuffs."

I saw him handing Security-Nick the sawed-off. Nick set my Beretta on the desk, way too far for me to try and reach. If they got the cuffs on me I was dead meat. I had to move fast, while they thought I was still hurt.

My right hand curled around Big Frank's left foot at the ankle, and my left shot up and pushed hard against the inside of his knee. He started to go over, and I reared up, elbows flying, and was lucky enough to catch Nick in the balls. The big man flopped down on his side, and the shotgun roared, sending the blast toward the desk area. Lipton screamed.

I was moving out the door and down the hallway when I saw two other figures running toward me. Jordan and the Mexican. They looked shocked to see me. I slammed my fist into the Mexican's face as he reached out for me. Jordan just sidestepped back. I whirled around the corner and went to my right, into the factory area. I remembered that Lipton had locked the main entrance behind us. The big storehouse was dimly lit, and I could see row after row of stacked paper sacks. Looked like bags of cement or something.

An explosion, then the rush of a round whizzing by me.

"Don't shoot in there, you dumb fuck," Big Frank's voice boomed. "You hit one of those barrels of benzene this whole fucking place'll go up."

I zigzagged between more of the stacks, trying to get to the wall. There were no windows, but there had to be a door. Once I was outside I could make a beeline for the fence and the wooded area beyond it.

Footsteps behind me. I pivoted and went down another aisle.

"Jordan," I heard Big Frank yell. "Shut off the power so he won't be able to raise any of the big doors."

"That'll set off the fire alarm," I heard Jordan yell.

"So call 'em and tell 'em we're working on the system," Big Frank yelled back. "Enrique, Nickie, get a couple a them carts and spread out. But don't fucking shoot unless you're sure of your backstop."

I paused to get my bearings. I was roughly in the middle of the floor, with the wall about a hundred yards ahead of me. But it wasn't a straight path for me. The sacks of cement, or whatever the hell they were, had been stacked at angles so there were no straight aisles. I heard the acceleration of an electric motor. Getting louder. Those golf carts that I'd seen before. They were going to run me down. I turned and scrambled up the stack behind me. Maybe they wouldn't think to look up, and I could get an idea as to where they were.

Suddenly there was a humming sound and all the lights went off. Somebody yelled, "What the fuck!" After some popping and sputtering, a motor caught and the fire lights on the ceiling came on. Emergency generator. I flattened myself on top of the stack and peered cautiously in the direction of the offices. Big Frank got into a golf cart and went rumbling off toward the opposite wall.

Good, they didn't know which way I'd run. I checked to see what I was lying on and saw that it wasn't cement after all, but a hundred-pound bag of powdered milk. My breathing was still rapid so I tried to concentrate on getting it under control. Glancing in the other direction I saw that the closest wall to my position was the back one. The only doors were the large, overhead type. Electrically controlled, as Big Frank had said. They had me effectively caged, and time wasn't on my side.

One of the carts whizzed by my stack. I ducked as I heard it go past. Then looked. Enrique.

He turned at the end of the aisle and went down the other side, steering with one hand and holding a revolver in the other. I shifted around slowly. Near the dock doors were row after row of metal barrels.

That must be the benzene, I thought. If I could work my way over there, maybe they'd be more reluctant to shoot at me.

The ear-piercing sound of a shot exploded from below. I covered my face, thinking they must have seen me. But the follow-up shot didn't come.

"Who was that?" Big Frank yelled. "Did ya see him?" I estimated his position as down about seventy yards to my right.

"It was me, Frank," Security-Nick yelled back. He was to my right also, but farther away than Big Frank. "I thought I seen him over here."

"Well, don't shoot until you're fucking sure, you idiot. You might hit one of us. We got him trapped. We just gotta find him."

I heard the sound of the electric motor again and got a glimpse of Enrique steering his golf cart down the aisle toward the others. As I shifted, the stack of bags wobbled. A shiver went through me, then I regained my composure. Enrique turned and began heading down my aisle. If I could time it just right, maybe I could tip the stack next to me on top of him. It would be an all or nothing move, because they'd surely know where I was whether I hit or missed. But what other options did I have? Keep on hiding until they tracked me down?

I moved to the edge and peeked over. Enrique was moving toward me, his lower jaw protruding as he scanned between each stack. The cart edged forward, then he slowed.

"Hey, Frank," he yelled. "Put somebody in the floor office. That way they can look out over the tops of these things."

The floor office? I looked around and saw it about a hundred and fifty yards away. A wooden cubicle suspended from the roof in the center of the warehouse, with a set of stairs descending. They'd be able to spot me for sure from there. I had to make my move now.

Enrique crept forward. At this speed he just might see the stack falling and be able to stop. I needed some way to make him speed up. A diversion. I still had Lipton's car keys in my pocket. Rising to a kneeling position, I threw the tangled keys as hard as I could at one of the far stacks down the aisle.

Enrique must have heard the sound because he yelled and began accelerating in that direction. I shifted my position and shoved both my legs against the adjacent stack closest to the aisle. The stack listed, then fell away, sending a shower of powdered milk sacks raining down on him as he approached. But this was a hard rain. Enrique's scream was loud and abrupt. Like somebody snapping off the volume on a radio. I followed the pile down, trying to find his gun, but he was completely buried. I scrambled over the bags and ran toward the barrels.

Crouching down beside another stack, I listened. Yelling, then the whine of the motors getting closer. I ran back the way I'd come, away from the barrels, going stack to stack. My foot caught something and I went down hard on the concrete floor. As I pushed myself up I saw what had tripped me. A steel bar. Probably a lever of some sort. I grabbed it and tried to pick it up, but it was wedged under a wooden pallet.

The sound of a motor got louder. I wrenched the bar loose and held it in my hands like a baseball bat. At least now I had some type of weapon. Peering around the stack, I moved to the next one.

"It's Enrique," I heard Security-Nick yell. "I think he's dead."

"Son of a bitch," I heard another voice say.

"Come over here and spread out," Nick yelled. He was only a few stacks over to my left.

"Frank," someone called. "Where are you?"

No answer.

"Hey, Frank," he called again.

"Shut up, and keep quiet," Big Frank said. "You're giving up your positions."

"Huh?" I heard Nick say. I shot a glance around the corner. He was only about twenty feet away, and moving toward me now. Pulling my head back, I flattened against the stack of bags and waited. The golf cart sounded like it was almost on top of me. I cocked the bar in my hands. As Security-Nick rounded the corner, I whirled around, swinging the bar as hard as I could. It caught him on the forehead, and his head snapped back with the sound of a melon being smashed. He twisted and rolled off the cart, which kept going a few more feet, then ran into one of the adjacent stacks.

Nick wasn't moving. Frantically I searched for the gun. Where the hell could it have gone? Then I saw it. Next to his hand. A snub nosed revolver. Putting it in my belt, I checked Nick's body for my automatic. Blood was all over, and from his eyes I knew he was dead. I gave up looking for the Beretta and ran down toward the barrels again, still carrying the bar.

"Hey!" I heard someone yell. I switched direction and wedged myself between two closely stacked piles.

"Frank, he got Nickie," someone answered. It had to be Jordan.

"Shit," Frank grunted. He couldn't have been more than twenty feet to my right. I managed to climb up the paper bag wall. The stack went up pretty high. Higher than the others. Take the high ground. Good military tactics. On top I saw that I was only about fifteen feet from the ceiling. Then another idea hit me. The sprinkler heads. If I could knock one off, it would set off the fire alarm. Not just the fire alarm, but a water flow alarm. The fire department would have to respond then. If I could survive until they got here.

I held the bar like a javelin and threw it at the sprinkler head nearest to me. It missed by a mile, and I crouched down and tried to think of another idea as the bar clunked to the floor. The revolver was a six shot, with two rounds expended. Four shots left. I wished to hell I'd been able to find my Beretta. It held fifteen.

I glanced toward the floor office. There had to be a fire alarm in there. Hopefully a phone too. If I could make it over there maybe I could hold them off. I had four bullets, but they didn't know that. I decided to try for it. Sliding down the stack, I hit the ground running. I went from stack to stack, pausing at each one, hoping they wouldn't expect me to be working my way toward the center of the floor.

Then, as I crouched by one corner, from somewhere behind me I heard Lipton crying, "There he is! There he is!" Jordan appeared from farther down the aisle and took a shot at me. It went high, slamming into the bag of powdered milk about a foot above my head. The stupid son of a bitch was standing right out in the open, but then, as far as he knew, I was unarmed. I sighted in on him and squeezed off two rounds. He shot at me again, and, without thinking, I fired back. Twice. I saw a flash of sparks as one of my rounds hit the cement floor behind him. A wisp of yellow flame twisted crookedly along the floor as it wound back toward the stacks of barrels.

Jordan did a stutter step forward, clutching his chest, then twisted forward, shooting off rounds as he fell. An explosion went off behind him. Then, like a chain reaction, barrel after barrel began to explode, some of them hurling fifty feet into the air, filling the place with an incredibly noxious smelling smoke that swept over me, forcing itself into my mouth and nose with a blistering pungency. I tried to hold my breath. A bell began sounding intermittently and the ceiling sprinklers went on with a simultaneous clinking sound.

"Lipton," Big Frank's voice called, trying to be heard between the ringing. "Call the fucking fire department and tell 'em it's a false alarm."

I felt the concussive wave of another heavy roar as more barrels blew up. Despite the sprinklers, a heavy, thick smoke began to curl up from the flames. I caught a glance of something moving away from the fire. Big Frank's golf cart. I ran in the same direction down a parallel aisle, the inside of my chest tingling with a burning sensation. The aisle he was in was on sort of an angle, so I knew it'd eventually merge into mine. I was slightly ahead of him and got to a corner in time to see him coming. The spray from the sprinklers was making the floor slick, and the smoke was starting to fill up the whole place. The paper bags were slippery too, but I was able to dislodge one near the midpoint and that sent the whole corner stack tumbling toward the aisle. Big Frank tried to decelerate, but couldn't, as the pile of hundred pound bags crashed down in front of him.

The cart smashed into them and he flew forward. I swarmed over the sacks and tried to wrestle the sawed-off from his hands. He was strong and I couldn't break his grip. The gun roared, but the blast went harmlessly off to the side. The shotgun was a pump, and he had to work the slide in order to chamber another round. We wrestled for control, the bell blaring its warning, the water spraying over us. It hurt to breathe. But neither of us would let go of the gun.

I couldn't out-muscle him. Change your tactics, I heard Chappie's voice screaming at me inside my head. Go where he's weak and you're strong.

I brought my leg up and snapped a kick into his balls. He grunted and his grip weakened. Another kick. I managed to pull the shotgun out of his hands, but in the wrenching effort, it slipped from my grasp and dropped into the heap of fallen milk bags. Big Frank staggered, but came back after me. I hit him a quick combination in the gut, but it was like hitting a big bag of cement. Or powdered milk. The water from the sprinklers was mixing with the torn bags forming puddles of white liquid.

Big Frank tried to club me with a clumsy overhand punch, but I moved my head and slipped it. I countered him with another combination to the body, this one aimed more toward his kidneys. He sagged and I got my right arm around his neck and drew it back, trying to choke him. But the big man leaned forward and curled his neck down, breaking my hold. He lashed back and caught me with a forearm smash to my nose. I shoved him away and smashed a sidekick into his ribs. My lungs burned as I involuntarily took a deep breath.

Keep the kicks low, I thought. The floor was too slippery to get fancy. The kick backed him up a couple of feet, then he stopped. Enraged, he hurled himself forward at me. His superior size and strength would give him too big an advantage at close quarters, so I backpedaled, trying to reach the shotgun.

He saw that I was going for it, but he was too late. I picked up the gun, chambered a round, and fired it point blank into his massive chest. The blast stopped his momentum, but didn't kill him right away. Instead, he staggered around holding his chest, his mouth twisted down into a scowl. He danced around in a little semi-circle, then stumbled to his knees, and finally fell forward the rest of the way.

I worked the action, ejecting the spent shell and chambering a new one as I did a slow jog up to the front office area. The smoke was getting dense now, and I knew I had to get out of there. Lipton was in the hallway that connected the offices and the warehouse, cowering against a corner, watching my approach. The sprinklers weren't activated in that section.

"You got them all, Shade," he said. "I'd never have believed it." Then, as I got closer, "They made me do it. Shade, they made me do it."

I let the shotgun drop to the floor and kept walking. He got a real scared look on his face, and I stopped right in front of him.

"Shade, I—"

"Experience," I said.

"What?"

"Experience," I repeated. "Experience, leadership, integrity. Isn't that your campaign slogan?"

He gave a quick, nervous nod.

I sent a hard left into his gut.

"That's for experience," I said. "This is for leadership." A right to his gut. "And this," I smashed in a follow-up left, "is for integrity."

He sagged to the floor, coughing and sputtering, trying to catch his breath in the heavy, putrid haze.

"Where are those computer disks?" I asked.

He shook his head.

"Where are they, god dammit? Or I'll leave you to die in here with the rest of them."

Lipton tried to struggle to his feet, but couldn't quite make it. I pulled him up and dragged him back into Jordan's office. My Beretta was on the desk. I grabbed it and snapped it into the pancake holster. Lipton was pawing through Jordan's desk drawers. The smoke was so thick I could barely see, much less breathe. I heard the shattering of glass, and figured the fire department had arrived.

"Come on," I said, tugging Lipton's arm. "It'll wait." As we stumbled toward the door a fireman ran up to us decked out in his long coat and shiny black helmet.

"You'd better call the toxic waste squad," I said. "And see if you can save that computer room, will you?"

Chapter 42

After being checked by the paramedics, they took us to a nearby hospital emergency room to be treated for smoke inhalation. The Lincoln Estates Police were slightly more successful than I'd been at getting hold of Tremain. He and Stallworth showed up in the ER after about three hours.

"Sorry to get you guys up so late," I said, pulling the plastic oxygen mask away from my face.

"Why'd you do it, Shade?" Tremain asked. "You knew we were on the verge of bringing them down."

"Kinda wish I would've waited," I said, "if it means anything now."

"It doesn't mean a hell of a lot," Stallworth said. "Lipton's clammed up, and we've got a toxic burner over at the factory."

I felt a sudden chill as I thought about the poisons that I'd breathed in as I'd battled Big Frank.

"Lean on Lipton a little," I said. "He's ready to crack."

"Can't," Tremain said. He reached over and pushed away the white curtain surrounding my bed. "His lawyer already called up and told him not to answer any questions."

"Lawyer?" I asked.

"Lawrence C. Peck," Stallworth said. "Ever hear of him?"

"Yeah. Makes sense, too. Lipton told me the DeKooning mob was behind his trucking business."

"That's interesting," said Stallworth. "Got any proof of that?"

"He told me there were some kind of computer records

over at Space Oddities," I said. "That's what we were supposed to be getting when he led me over there."

"The fire's raging out of control," Stallworth said. "It's doubtful that they'll be able to save anything in the building."

"Well, lean on Lipton anyway. I'm sure a couple of pros like you two guys will be able to see that justice is served."

"Listen, Shade," Tremain said, his face reddening. "I don't care for your attitude."

"Yeah? Well, it's the only one I got, so it'll have to do, won't it?"

"Take it easy," Stallworth said, smiling. "Remember, we're all on the same side. But I wouldn't be a smart-ass, if I were you, Shade. They've pulled a couple of bodies out of that fire already, and there's going to be a full investigation."

"Maybe I should see if I can get Lawrence Peck for *my* attorney," I said with a grin. "Anyway, I feel rather faint at the moment. Don't think I can answer any more questions, officers." I slipped the mask back over my nose and mouth.

"We're troopers," Stallworth said, pointing a finger at me in mock anger. "And don't you forget it."

The rest of it limped to a rather dismal, uneven ending. I spent several more days recovering in the hospital. The linings of my lungs had become inflamed from breathing in all that toxic garbage during the fire. This upset my training schedule, and my chance to fight Berger for the championship slipped through my fingers like smoke. Toxic smoke.

While I lay there inhaling pure oxygen, George called and Chappie came to see me. He smiled and said we'd get Berger next time, but looking at the disappointment in his eyes was almost more than I could bear. I'd let him down again. Still, I'd fought the good fight, and I'd won, after a fashion.

Maria and Juanita came to visit me too. They pulled up some chairs and I told them about it. All of it. Juanita seemed satisfied that the men who'd killed Carlos had also died, and Maria . . . She leaned over and lightly kissed my forehead and then my lips.

"I guess I'm not ready to lose you yet," she said, smiling. "Maybe we just need more time to work things out."

"That'd be good," I managed to say, grateful that we'd have another chance to try and get it right.

I used the retainer money that she'd given me to buy the Beater from Doug. The check that I finally got from Midwestern Olympia barely covered the bank loan on the Z-28, but at least by the time I got out I was debt free. The rest of the money went toward renewing my ad in the yellow pages and another cell phone. All I had to do now was drum up some new business.

Two days before Tom Lipton was subpoenaed to appear before a specially convened Grand Jury he disappeared. The prosecution of DeKooning and his associates for the illegal dumping settled into the protracted, legalistic limbo that had the news reporters interviewing a smiling Lawrence Peck in front of the Dirkson Building every other week on the five o'clock news.

I was able to give enough facts to Hoppy for him to complete his environmental piece and publish it in the *Metro*. Just barely. Two weeks later, on a cold morning in late November, we buried him. Rich and I were pallbearers. Maria came with me. As we moved back to our cars I looked over the frost-covered grass of the cemetery and felt a strange sense of closure. For me, and for him.

We'd both done what we'd set out to do. I'd solved the

case, and he'd finished the article. The situation had brought me some unexpected, but much needed publicity. And Hoppy'd summed it beautifully in his ending lines: *"And so the frost finally came last night, dappling the ground with a white dusting, ending the cyclical lives of a myriad of insects and plants, reminding us perhaps of the ephemeral glory of our own limited and finite existence. But we, as individuals, as a society, and as citizens of the world had better heed the warning about this other type of a killing frost that will inevitably descend over all of us, if we don't wake up soon and smell the toxic garbage that is being dumped to illegally seep into the precious underground water beneath our feet."* I remembered how much he'd wanted to finish that article, and make it one that his wife and daughter could be proud of. Somehow I felt that he would have been happy to have that statement as his epitaph.

Maria's hand felt nice inside mine, and, despite the cold, I found myself thinking about the inevitability of spring and looking forward to it. After all, without a few bad times would we really appreciate the good ones?

The employees of Five Star hope you have enjoyed this book. All our books are made to last. Other Five Star books are available at your library, through selected bookstores, or directly from us.

For information about titles, please call:

(800) 223-1244

or visit our Web site at:

www.gale.com/fivestar

To share your comments, please write:

Publisher
Five Star
295 Kennedy Memorial Drive
Waterville, ME 04901